TRAPPED

Sheppard & Sons Investigations, Book 6

Eveline Rose

Sword & Rose

Dedication

This book is dedicated to all the women who are stronger than they think are, and the men who love them.

Also by

<u>**Sheppard & Sons Investigations:**</u>

TAKEN: Jack and Meg's story
BEATEN: Jamie and Emily's story
MISSING: Doug and Beth's story
BETRAYED: AJ and Blake's story
CAGED: Jaden and Catelyn's story
TRAPPED: Ashley & Nathan's story
TBN Christmas Special : The Sheppards
BURNED: Madi & Matt's story

WebPage

Who's Who in SSI

Who's Who at Sheppard & Sons Investigations:

John Sheppard: Founder and CEO – Call sign: Sierra 1

James "Jamie" Sheppard: Founder and CFO – Call sign: Sierra 2

Jackson "Jack" Sheppard: Founder and COO – Call sign: Sierra 3

Andrew "AJ" Janerek: PI/Bodyguard – Call sign: Sierra 4

Doug Sharpe: PI/Bodyguard – Call sign: Sierra 5

Catelyn "Cate/Max" Maxwell: PI/Bodyguard – Call sign: Sierra 6/Bravo 3

Jaden "Jay" Sheppard: PI/Bodyguard – Call sign: Sierra 7/Bravo 2

Nathan Scott Blaszek: PI/Bodyguard – Call sign: Bravo 1

Part-time employees: Samantha "Sammie", Dean, Eric, Hunter.

<u>Who's Who in the SSI series:</u>

Mary Sheppard: Owner of Grannie's Coffee - John's wife - Mama Bear of SSI

Madeleine "Madi" Sheppard: Eldest Sheppard/Jamie's twin - Navy Corpsmen

Beth Wyatt: Mary's best friend - Grannie's Manager - Chase's mom - Doug's fiancée

Meg Sheppard: Executive assistant/HR at SSI - Jack's wife

Emily "Em" Taylor: Jamie's wife

Blake Davenport: AJ's fiancée

Ashley York: Emily's BFF

Nina Novak: College student - Grannie's employee

TRAPPED
Sheppard & Sons Investigations Book 6
by Eveline Rose

Chapter 1

Ashley

If you'd asked me a year ago if I'd come crawling back to Weatherford, TX, the small town I grew up in, my answer would've been a hard no. I'd loved everything about my life in Dallas. My job, my apartment, my active social life.

Two weeks ago, I got fired from my job. For no logical reason.

One week ago, I got evicted. For no logical reason.

Plus, my period was late. I fluctuated from month to month, and sometimes even skipped a month, so I hadn't worried about it until I realized it'd been two months since my last cycle.

At least there was a logical, though improbable, reason for the pregnancy. I always made Finn suit up, but it could still happen. Ninety-nine percent effective means one percent ineffective. And wouldn't it be my dumb luck that I had a one percent result with a guy who had more red flags than a parade in China.

Two weeks before dumping his ass.

Fuck my life.

At least moving back home meant I'd be able to hang out with my best friend more. Emily Taylor, now Sheppard, had married her high school crush—the still super-hot, eldest Sheppard son, Jamie. They went through hell before finding each other. Jamie's first wife was murdered, and Em's ex hit her.

Who would've thought they'd fall in love when Emily's big brother hired Jamie, his best friend, to protect her? Not me, and definitely not her big brother. He legit punched Jamie, but he came around. He even shed a tear during the ceremony, *though he still refuses to admit it.*

The timing of my streak of bad luck couldn't be worse. A month before I got fired, my grandmother, the woman who'd raised me after my parents died when I was a little girl, fell and broke her hip. She'd needed surgery and still needed months of physical therapy. Her insurance covered most of the hospital bills and some of the therapy, but not the in-home help she needed. It was just us, so I had to hire a home nurse until she was strong enough to support herself again.

Gran had argued, but I refused to let her go into debt. I made good money and could afford it.

Well, I could until I lost my job and got evicted.

Afraid of depleting my savings account, I moved back home and took over her care.

When it rains, it fucking pours.

"Look on the bright side, Ashley. You're living rent-free and spending quality time with your grandmother while you look for another job," I said to myself while pulling my dark brown hair into a high ponytail.

Being Monday, I hoped I'd get some responses from the dozens of resumes I'd sent last week.

"Gran, will you be okay for a few hours if I go to Grannie's Coffee Bar?" I asked as I walked into the living room.

"Of course, I've got my knitting, and I may nap in front of the TV for a bit. Will you be back for lunch?"

"Yes."

"Should I make something?"

"No, I will when I come back."

"What will you make?" she asked, her voice thick with skepticism. I wasn't a great cook, and Gran wasn't shy about letting me know.

My skills were above those of a bachelor, but I'd lived alone and eaten out or ordered delivery most days. My skills were rusty. If I put my heart into it, I could follow a recipe and make an amazing meal. I'd just never felt like it. That was changing as I helped Gran with our meals.

"How about turkey burgers with goat cheese and a salad?" I asked. I'd rather have a cheeseburger and fries, but Gran had to watch her cholesterol.

"That sounds good."

I pulled a pound of ground turkey out of the freezer to thaw before leaving.

"Here's your phone." Gran was old school and often forgot to bring her phone with her when she changed rooms. "Call me if you need me."

"I won't need you." Gran was fiercely independent. A trait I both admired and despised. *A trait I inherited.*

"Gran," I said, drawing out the 'a' while putting my hands on my hips.

"Okay, okay, if I need you, I'll call."

I'd swear there were times Gran channeled her inner teenager just to fuck with me. I shook my head, grinned, and kissed her on the cheek before saying goodbye.

Despite feeling like I was running late, I made great time because it never took long to get anywhere in Weatherford. After parking, I rushed through the door to Grannie's, making the bell ring and drawing attention to myself.

Another perk of being back home, I could have Grannie's coffee as often as I could afford it. I breathed in, loving the smell of freshly brewed coffee that permeated the place.

"Sorry I'm late," I said, hugging Emily.

"No worries." She laughed.

"My God, Em, you're literally glowing with happiness." And a nice tan courtesy of her Caribbean cruise honeymoon.

She blushed. "Thanks. Go get a coffee. I'm dying to talk to you."

That sounded like a perfect plan. I soaked in the kitschy mix of cowboy saloon and coffee house decor, loving how it gave Grannie's a unique vibe that welcomed locals and tourists alike.

"Thanks, Mary." Mary was the owner of Grannie's and Emily's new mother-in-law.

It occurred to me after I took the first sip of my vanilla latte that I should switch to decaf. But it was too late. One more coffee couldn't hurt. *Can it?*

No way. Lots of women drank coffee for weeks before finding out they were pregnant, and their kids were just fine. Besides, I wasn't ready to explain why I suddenly wanted decaf when I practically mainlined the regular stuff.

"You're welcome. Are you coming to Craft and Booze tomorrow night?" Mary asked.

"I'll be there."

"Can you make a batch of that sangria you brought to the BBQ?" Beth, Mary's best friend and manager at Grannie's, asked.

"Of course." I laughed. "I'll bring a non-alcoholic version for Meg, too." I'd made a red, white, and blue sangria for the Fourth of July BBQ this year, and everyone loved it. Well, the girls all did. It was a little on the sweet side for the guys. They preferred beer.

Mary's eyes sparkled as she thanked me for looking out for her other daughter-in-law, the one who'd give Mary her first grandchild in December.

I didn't mind making two; it'd be easier to hide the fact that I wasn't drinking. I might not worry about an occasional cup of caffeinated coffee, but until I took a pregnancy test, I needed to be alcohol-free.

Something else that wasn't normal for me, so I had to be careful. And make enough of both that no one would notice the virgin sangria draining as fast as the whorish one.

"You okay?" Emily asked, as I slid into the booth opposite hers.

"Yeah, why?"

"You seem frazzled." She waved her hand in my general direction.

"Yeah, about that. After you tell me your news, I have a confession."

"Do you want to go first?"

"No, I didn't rush in here like a freak for nothing. Spill it."

"I'm pregnant."

I squealed with joy as I jumped up and ran around to hug her again. The look of bliss on Mary's face as she hugged Beth told me she already knew but enjoyed celebrating the good news again.

"Oh, Em, this is so exciting. How are you feeling?" I looked down at her still-flat belly. "When are you due? Is Jamie happy? Are you throwing up a lot?" I fired off questions like a game show host on cocaine.

She laughed and pulled away. "I'm fine. Due in late January. And Jamie's thrilled. He's already rearranging the spare room."

"Guess it's a good thing Jay moved out." Jay, the youngest Sheppard, who'd recently returned from the Marines, oozed raw sexuality with his bad boy attitude, inked up arms, and muscles on top of muscles.

If I hadn't already done the friends with benefits thing with AJ, a private investigator at Sheppard & Sons Investigations—yes, those Sheppards—I might've hooked up with Jay. But I didn't want to earn *that* reputation.

Jay was a lot like AJ, but wilder. Darker.

It was obvious I had a type: strong, inked-up guys who gave off bad-boy vibes. But I didn't want a bad boy. I wanted someone I could settle down with and have a family.

Scott gave off the bad-boy vibe. Which was why I hit on him at the bar in Vegas.

Damn him for living rent-free in my head for the last year. He made it clear he wasn't interested when he ghosted me. Left me standing outside the Eiffel Tower Restaurant instead of meeting me for what should've been our first date. I'd felt like a fool. Worse. Getting stood up sucked. So did walking back to my room in my expensive, new, slinky red dress with my head hung low. I'd ordered room service, changed into an old, comfortable T-shirt, and emptied the mini-bar.

For whatever stupid reason, even after a year, I couldn't stop thinking about him. Scott starred in my fantasies far longer than I cared to admit, no matter how hard I tried to forget him.

"Yeah, though we would've figured something out," Emily said.

I didn't doubt it; they weren't the type to force a family member out of the house.

Not wanting to live with his parents, Jay had crashed with Jamie and Emily while he looked for his own place. Instead, he moved in with his girlfriend Cate, who's now his fiancée, just before Jamie and Emily's wedding.

As much as it disappointed me to see Jay off the market, I knew Cate Maxwell was perfect for him. They butted heads at first, but that changed when they got kidnapped looking for a missing girl. Cate was the calm Jay's storm needed, and he was the chaos her order needed. Besides, I never expected to find my happily ever after with Jay, and not just because I'd slept with AJ.

Jay and I were both chaotic good; we had good hearts, but we liked to do our own thing and challenge authority. We might've had a few mind-blowing nights, but we wouldn't balance each other the way he and Cate did. She soothed his flames; I'd add fuel just to watch them burn brighter.

Thinking of Jay reminded me of Scott, aka Casper the Fucking Ghost, and the night that never happened. I shoved everyone out of my head and focused on Emily.

"Are you getting sick yet?"

Emily deserved all the happiness life could give her after everything Asshat Craig, her abusive ex, put her through. He was the reason we had a blip in our otherwise lifelong best-friends-forever friendship. The memory of the split-heart necklaces we wore in junior high flashed across my mind. Mine said, Best. Hers said, Friends. We'd stopped wearing them in high school because we were more grown up or some other stupid shit, but our friendship never faltered.

The Craig-forced pause didn't count. He didn't want Emily hanging out with me or even talking to me because I was vocal about not trusting him. Isolating her made it easier for him to get away with the abuse. *He'll never hit anyone again.*

Putting him out of my mind, I focused on the present.

The only upside to being pregnant now, if I were, was that I'd have my baby about the same time as Em, and only a little after Meg. Our kids would grow up like siblings.

Only I'd be a struggling single mom, and they'd have the support of their gorgeous, protective, alpha male husbands. Meg was married to Jack, the middle Sheppard son. We met when Emily needed help from SSI a little over a year ago and became fast friends. Fast forward to today, and the three of us were like the three musketeers. We loved laughing late into the night, comparing the men of SSI to the hero in whatever romance we were reading.

Jamie's favorite word when describing our antics was shenanigans.

Meg and Emily were happily married and would be great moms. I couldn't find a good guy to save my life, and doubted my ability to raise a child on my own.

I wanted an alpha male for myself, but didn't think I'd ever find one. I dated around for a reason—I had shit taste in men. Finding a bad boy who was fun for a night or two was easier than finding a good man to be my forever.

When I tried something new, looking for a decent guy who didn't give off bad boy vibes, I ended up with Red Flag Finn. He was nice enough in the beginning, but it turned out he wasn't half the man I thought he was.

"No, but I probably will soon. Meg says it sucks." No doubt. Meg struggled with morning sickness morning, noon, and night.

Emily told me about her amazing honeymoon before changing the subject.

"So, what do you have to confess? Did you find the love of your life?"

I laughed. *Just the opposite.*

"No, after Red Flag Finn, I'm taking a break from dating." I looked at the table and dropped the news without fanfare. "I lost my job."

"What, why?" Em reached across the table and took my hand. "I'm so sorry, Ashley."

"That's just it; there wasn't a reason. My boss called me into his office and told me he had to let me go for budgetary reasons." The timing was suspect, because I'd just broken up with his nephew, the one and only Red Flag Finn. "He gave me a month's severance and sent me on my way. A week later, I got evicted."

"Are you serious? What the hell?"

I shrugged, hiding my emotions behind my coffee cup.

"That's the real reason I came home. I can't get a new apartment without a job, and I can't afford Gran's nurse anymore."

She squeezed my hand. "Let me know what I can do to help."

"Is your company hiring?" My nervous laugh negated my attempt to sound unfazed.

Chapter 2

Nathan

New guy gets the coffee was the Sheppard & Sons Investigations version of hazing. As a former Navy SEAL and black ops civilian operator, I was no stranger to the hazing tradition that came with joining a brotherhood. I just hadn't expected it at a small-town private investigation company. Given the number of military guys and gals in the company, maybe I should've.

"We brew Grannie's here, right?"

"We do." Meg Sheppard, the receptionist and Jack's wife, answered with a smile. "But it's tradition."

I nodded as I pulled up Grannie's location on my phone. "So, I buy a box? Of the same coffee we brew here?" I shook my head. A little friendly hazing was fine, but this seemed silly. *You'd think they'd have me buy beer or lunch or something.*

"Oh no," AJ Janerek, a PI and Jack's best friend, answered, "You need to get individual coffees for everyone who's in the office today."

"Copy that." I counted off in my head. "So, nine, including me. Unless I missed someone?"

"Ten, and a decaf mocha," Meg said, needing decaf because her first child was due in December. "Please?" she added with a big smile.

I smiled back. Meg was easy to like. "Of course." I recounted in my head. "Who'd I miss?"

"Eric and Hunter will be here before you get back." Eric and Hunter were Weatherford cops who worked part-time at SSI. Eric had received a promotion, so this was his last week. Hunter started a month before I had, but we hadn't met yet.

"Right. All black?"

"Yeah, we can doctor them up here," Jack said. I couldn't help but notice his grin was identical to his father's.

When I first interviewed with the team, I had to hold back my laugh when I realized my new bosses would be John, Jamie, and Jack Sheppard. And if that wasn't bad enough, their youngest brother's name was Jay. Towards the end of my second interview, I asked what was up with their names.

I remember John laughing. "Mary and I thought it'd be fun. It didn't take us long to regret it."

"Dude, I can't tell you how many times my teachers called me Jamie or Jack before giving up and calling me Sheppard," Jay added.

"I can imagine," I'd said, even though I couldn't. I was an only child who'd grown up in the system.

I shook off the memory. Buying ten individual coffees seemed silly, but I was a team guy, so I bucked up and said, "I'll be back."

"Wait, can you grab me a blueberry muffin?" Jay asked.

"Sure." Then, despite knowing better, I asked, "Anyone else want anything?"

"I'll text you what everyone wants," Meg offered when the spacious lobby of SSI erupted into chaos. Everyone wanted something. According to my new co-workers, Grannie's sourced the best pastries from a small bakery in town. *I guess I'm about find out.*

Grateful for the chance to escape, I mouthed my thanks before leaving.

During the short drive, I chided myself for being annoyed. As a newbie SEAL, I'd been tasked with bringing a case of beer anytime I fucked up or irritated a senior team member. I wouldn't say it happened a lot, but I helped keep the team supplied until the next green guy joined the team.

Buying beer for the team was a rite of passage, and we always drank it together to build team unity. But buying coffee, the same coffee we brewed, that we'd all drink in our offices, didn't serve the same purpose.

Maybe it annoyed me because I'd been working solo for so long. But being part of a team again was exactly why I'd applied to Sheppard & Sons. They came highly recommended from my former teammate, had a stellar reputation, and saw just enough action to keep my skills honed. *And not feel bored.*

When my teammate and good friend, Kroupa, told me about the small family-run PI/personal protection company with a great reputation, I hadn't hesitated to apply.

When Meg texted to offer me money from the Grannie's Fund, I turned her down with a laugh. *Seriously, how is it hazing if I don't pay for it?*

She probably thought that's why I seemed grumpy, but money wasn't the issue. They had no way of knowing, but I was a wealthy guy. Rich by many standards. Not a billionaire, but wealthy enough to retire.

If I wanted to.

I didn't.

I needed to work, to serve, to keep moving. I'd considered starting a company after leaving Hawken's, the black ops company I'd worked for, but my head wasn't in the right place. The idea still lingered, but I wasn't ready yet.

For now, I was happy working for a company that exuded family values while serving its small-town community and the greater Dallas/Fort Worth area.

I told myself repeatedly that I didn't take the job at SSI so I could stay in Texas. My decision had nothing to do with a certain sexy, sassy brunette I'd met in Vegas who'd told me she lived in Dallas.

I didn't believe myself.

With my experience, I could've worked anywhere in the country. But Ashley'd mentioned she lived in Dallas. So here I was, moving to a small town ninety minutes west of the big city.

Don't be stupid; you'll never find her. Texas was one big-ass state. The second biggest in both population and land area.

You don't know her last name.

It didn't matter. I couldn't get her out of my head. If I tried hard enough and wanted to cross more than one ethical boundary, I could find her. But I wasn't willing to cross those lines. Not anymore.

I gripped the steering wheel as memories of blurring those lines crossed my mind. Being deep undercover required it, and I'd hardened myself to the task for the greater good, but I still carried the guilt.

I'd never killed an innocent, but I'd hurt a few.

I ran my hand through my hair, my thumb feeling the bumpy, rough edge of the scar on my left cheek. A reminder of the life I'd left behind when I quit Hawken's Security Company, a black ops company that hired former spec ops guys, like me, to do a hell of a lot more than provide personal protection. Often off the books, which meant if shit went south, we were on our own.

A chill, that had nothing to do with the A/C blowing in my truck, ran down my spine.

After parking, I took a few minutes to focus on the present and calm my nerves. I released my vice-like grip on the steering wheel and flexed my hands a few times to get the blood flowing again.

Time for the new guy to get the coffee.

I walked into Grannie's, a cute coffee shop owned by my boss's wife, John to be specific. The shop had an eclectic mix of coffee shop and old western saloon decorations like cowboy hats, old-fashioned colored glass bottles and black and white photos. It stood out from the boring chain ones, and I had a feeling I'd like it.

Soft country music filled the space, as did the smell of rich warm coffee. Glancing around, I saw Jamie's wife, Emily, two seconds before I heard it.

A sound I hadn't heard in a year.

A sound I'd dreamed about during my captivity and every day since.

A sound I didn't think I'd ever hear again.

Chapter 3

Ashley

Emily's amazing honeymoon made me jealous. She'd lived like a princess for seven days, being spoiled by her husband and the cruise staff. I was even a little jealous of Jamie's over-the-top protectiveness. I loved how the men of SSI protected the women they loved, but they could be extreme. Often acting ape-brained and needing to be reminded that the women they loved wouldn't break.

Jack was just as bad. I'd swear he'd wrap Meg in bubble wrap and lock her in the house if he could. Some days she loved it; others she'd tear him a new asshole for treating her like she was made of porcelain.

I'd never seen them fight, but Meg claimed they did.

I can only imagine what AJ will be like. He'd found the love of his life earlier in the year, and his protective streak made the other guy's behavior seem tame. The image of a pregnant, bubble-wrapped Blake crossed my mind, making me laugh.

"I don't mind, not really."

Of course she didn't; her last boyfriend was an abusive asshat. Emily deserved a man who loved, cherished and protected her, and Jamie was that man. He was the perfect husband, and he'd be a great dad.

"Think you'll still say that in a few months?"

She shrugged. "Maybe. If he gets as crazy as Jack, I might not like it."

Given how Jamie's first wife had died, he would be just as crazy, if not worse than Jack. Hell, he might even end up more protective than AJ.

"He's going out of his way to give me everything I want."

"Em, you know you can ask him to back off a little. He won't stop loving you."

"I know, but somehow I'm still worried."

Wanting to lighten the mood, I asked, "Do you think he'll pamper you and your bestie with a spa day?"

She laughed. "I think he'd offer to buy the spa if I asked him to."

The image of Jamie giving Emily a pedicure flashed through my mind, causing me to bust out laughing. I was trying to paint the picture for Em, but she stood; concern written all over her face.

"Nathan, are you okay? You look like you've seen a ghost," she asked.

I stood and turned around, eager to see the new guy from SSI.

My eyes just about bugged out of my head as my jaw dropped to the floor.

Holy. Fucking. Shit.

Scott, the guy who ghosted me a year ago in Vegas, was standing in Grannie's.

His eyes were as round as mine as he brought his left hand to his face and turned away so all I could see was the right half of his gorgeous, stupid, lying face as I marched over.

"If it isn't Casper the Fucking Ghost." I stomped my feet and crossed my arms over my chest when I reached him. "What the fuck are you doing here?"

Wait, did Emily just call him Nathan?

What the actual fuck?

"Ashley, what's going on?" Emily asked, walking to stand beside me.

I answered without taking my eyes off Scott. "You remember me telling you about the guy I met in Vegas?" Wanting to make sure Scott knew how pissed I felt, I added, "The dickhead who ghosted me."

Scott still hadn't said anything. He just stood there staring at me, with his face tilted at an odd angle. He hadn't even blinked yet. Was he playing some kind of game, using some stupid mind trick?

"Yeah…" she drew it out.

"This is him." I uncrossed my arms just long enough to point.

"It can't be; his name is Nathan."

But it was. His dirty blond hair was shorter, and his clothing looked more office casual than biker dude, but it was definitely Scott.

"Did you give me a fake name?" I asked, moving so I was in front of his face. "Was the whole thing a fucking joke to you?"

He looked down and kept his face tilted to the left.

"Look at me, you fucking coward!" I yelled. *I'll owe Mary one hell of an apology when this is over.*

"Ashley, please lower your voice." When I nodded, Mary said, "I assure you his name is Nathan, Nathan Blaszek. He's the new guy at SSI."

Mind fucking blown.

Scott, Nathan, Casper the fucking dick-headed ghost, lifted his chin and turned to face me. When he made eye contact, the memory of staring into those gorgeous icy blue eyes while we talked and laughed, and how they looked hooded with desire flashed across my mind.

And scrambled my senses. I wanted to be mad, not turned on. Ignoring the good memories, I focused on the last one and glared at him.

But when I saw what he'd been hiding, the air left my lungs, taking my desire to yell with it as it whooshed out with a whistle.

A big, angry red scar stretched from just outside his left eye to his lower jawbone. What the hell happened?

"Hi, Ashley."

Hi? Anger made my blood boil. Hi? That's all he had to say to me after lying and ghosting me.

"Are you fucking kidding me, Scott?" I whisper-yelled, clenching my fists to channel my anger so I wouldn't yell too loud. "Or is it Nathan now?"

He looked over my head towards the counter before making eye contact with me again. "Can we talk outside?"

Hell yeah we could, because outside I could yell and make a scene without worrying about upsetting the Mama Bear of the extended Sheppard family.

"Fine by me. Lead the way, Casper." I spat the only name I knew fit him for real.

I huffed and puffed as I marched far enough from the door that prying eyes couldn't watch. Emily, Mary, and Beth didn't need to see this.

"What the fuck are you doing here, Scott? Or Nathan. Or whoever the fuck you are."

He didn't flinch as he waited for me to finish. Which pissed me off even more. I was mad enough to incinerate him with my withering glare, but he just stood there like we were sharing pleasantries.

That wasn't entirely true. His body was statue-still, his fists clenched, and his jaw could turn coal to diamond. His chest, on full display in his tight navy blue T-shirt, rose and fell in a slow rhythm as he sucked in air through his nose.

He might have appeared relaxed from a distance, but he was struggling to stay calm.

"It's both. My full name is Nathan Scott Blaszek."

"Should I feel better that you only half-lied?" It was two-thirds of a lie. When he signed the bar bill, I'd noticed his last name was Miller.

"Ashley, I'm sorry." He paused and ran his hand down his face. My anger lessened as I watched his jaw muscles twitch when his fingers traced the scar.

"What happened?" I asked, assuming he'd know I meant his scar.

"It doesn't matter," he answered.

"No, I guess it doesn't." I sighed, knowing I'd now have to see his dumb, gorgeous, lying face all the time. "Why are you here?"

"I work at Sheppard & Sons Investigations," he said, acting like I'd asked a stupid question.

I knew he worked there, but it still wasn't a dumb question. How the hell did an accountant from California become a private investigator in…

Right. *He's not an accountant.* Another lie.

"Why'd you lie to me in Vegas?"

"I had to. I was undercover."

Laying the snark on extra thick, I asked, "How often do accountants go undercover?"

He sighed. "I never told you I was an accountant, Slick. You assumed."

"Don't call me that." He'd given me the nickname Slick when I used a cheesy pickup line at the bar.

I remembered that moment as if it were yesterday. I'd walked up, plopped down on the bar stool next to the man who redefined sex on a stick, and asked, "Did it hurt when you fell from heaven?"

"What was that?" he'd asked, looking so confused it was comical.

I repeated the question, enunciating every syllable of the line I'd heard a thousand times over the years.

"No, Slick, but it hurt when I clawed my way out of hell."

In hindsight, that should've been a warning. Instead, I took it as a challenge.

A year later I regretted that choice almost as much as I regretted dating Finn.

"You didn't correct me." I put my hands on my hips and glared.

"It was easier not to."

"Right, so what do you really do? Why were you in Vegas?"

He had to tilt his head down to stare at me because of his stupid, chiseled, tall body. The frown on his face tugged at his scar.

His expression was enough for me to know he didn't want to tell me. Which was fucking stupid because he worked for my best friend's husband. I'd find out, eventually.

"You know what, Scott, I'm sorry, Nathan," my sarcasm thicker than molasses on a wintry day, "it doesn't matter."

He had the audacity not to budge when I shoved past him.

Too embarrassed and too emotionally scattered, I didn't go back to Grannie's. Instead, I texted my apologies to Emily and Mary from my car, like a coward.

Chapter 4

Nathan

Ashley relaxing was beautiful. Ashley, unleashing a year's worth of pain and frustration, was magnificent. For the second time since walking into Grannie's, all I could do was stare.

The nasty scar was a new addition since I'd last seen her, so I turned to hide the left side of my face as she marched towards me.

The cute T-shirt with a cartoon cat drinking a beer was in stark contrast to the anger rolling off her.

As part of my undercover playboy persona in Vegas, I hung out at the bar and occasionally, I'd pick up women. That's all Ashley was supposed to be—a hookup.

But she crashed into the seat next to me and ended up being so much more than I'd bargained for. Ashley's sassy, no fucks given confidence was a breath of fresh air.

The memory was as clear as if it'd been yesterday.

She walked up to the bar and plopped down on the stool beside me.

"Did it hurt when you fell from heaven?"

Her cheesy pickup line turned out to be the perfect icebreaker, reeling me in with her infectious laugh.

I bought her drinks for the rest of the night, and a basket of chili cheese fries when she got hungry. We talked until the date on my watch flipped over.

When she asked, I eagerly followed to her room. We both expected a night of passionate sex, but we ended up talking. Talking, and making out like teenagers.

Unwilling to risk blowing my cover or putting her in harm's way, I left without exchanging information. My sexless one-night stand was over, and it was time to move on.

It was the best night I'd had in just about forever.

The next night I bent my rule and returned to the same bar, hoping she'd return.

She did. And for the second time, what we thought would be a night of mind-blowing sex turned into a night of talking, drinking, and laughing. When I kissed her, she melted in my arms. When she pulled my hair, I almost lost all control.

But I couldn't. I already knew Ashley was different, and I couldn't love her and leave her like I did with the others. She deserved better than that. She deserved the truth.

Truth I couldn't give her, but I wasn't ready to say goodbye.

Like a moth to her flame, I was hooked. Against my better judgement, I asked, "Can you meet me for lunch tomorrow?"

"I'm done at eleven, so anytime after that works."

We set a time and agreed to meet at a different bar. I'd smiled, thrilled to be having lunch with the most amazing woman I'd ever met. But my smile evaporated as I reminded myself she was meeting Scott. Not Nathan.

The personal details I'd shared were real, but she wouldn't care once she found out I'd lied about my name and job.

Every minute we spent together made it harder to lie, but I couldn't risk her knowing why I was there or what I was doing.

Knowing my op, bringing down the Perpura Cartel, was almost over, I started planning how I'd come clean and what I'd say to get Ashley to give Nathan a chance.

"Thank you for lunch, Angel." She stretched and kissed my cheek. Her fruity shampoo filled my senses, the scent forever tied to Ashley in my mind.

"You're welcome, Slick." I couldn't help but wonder what she'd call me when I confessed I'd lied about my name.

I shouldn't have, but I asked her out to dinner hoping she'd spend her last night in Vegas with me. She accepted. I had my excuse for why I wouldn't be able to talk to her for a few days ready to buy myself enough time to finish my mission.

If I was lucky, we'd finally consummate our relationship.

We agreed to meet outside the Eiffel Tower Restaurant, on the eleventh floor of the Paris Hotel, at seven.

"I'll make your last night in Vegas one you'll never forget," I promised.

"You better." The fire in her eyes told me I wouldn't forget it either.

I never showed.

Images flashed rapid-fire before my eyes.

A table covered with sharp knives.

Count five things you can see, here and now. Brick wall, awning, blue sedan, trash can, people.

The steel shackles on my wrists, my bare feet dangling two inches above the floor.

Count four things you can touch, here and now. Brick wall, wallet, car keys, phone.

The crack Al's whip made seconds before striking my back.

Count three things you can hear, here and now. Traffic, music, people talking.

The scent of blood as leather tore my flesh.

Count two things you can smell, here and now. Coffee, exhaust.

The taste of blood and stale vomit that lingered for days.

Count one thing you can taste, here and now.

Back in the present, I practiced my breathing, knowing coffee would fill that last requirement as soon as I filled the order.

I didn't know how long I'd stood there, clinging to the whitewashed brick wall like a drowning kid to a life preserver.

Too long. Taking another deep breath, I stood straight and flexed my stiff hands.

Fuck. That hadn't gone well.

How could it have? The last person I'd expected to see when I left the office was Ashley. The shock robbed me of all the speeches I'd prepared over the last year, just in case.

Why the hell is she here?

She'd said she lived in Dallas, but Weatherford was a small town ninety minutes west.

What were the chances we'd moved to the same town?

No, that's not it. Ashley couldn't be new in town if she was friends with my boss's wife.

Fuck.

Ashley had every right to be mad. From her perspective, I'd stood her up, ghosted her.

I opened the door, still practicing my combat breathing: in four, hold four, out four, hold four. Repeat as needed, which I suspected I'd need a lot.

"Sorry about that," I said, as I approached the counter under the watchful eyes of three curious women. "We had a bit of a misunderstanding."

Emily glared at me, giving me every reason to believe she knew what happened in Vegas. Mary looked sympathetic. The third woman, who looked familiar but I couldn't place, looked confused.

"It's none of our business," Mary said, before introducing her manager, Beth. Ah, that's why I recognized her—Beth was Doug's fiancée.

Guys in my unit had talked about small-town life, but this was ridiculous. The people here didn't just know each other; they were friends and family.

I'd been at my new job three days and everything was already turning to shit.

Just fucking great.

"Thank you." I didn't need to look at Emily to know she was glaring at me. Not wanting to stay any longer than I needed to, I said, "I need—"

"It's ready to go. Meg messaged me with the order."

Thank God for small favors.

When I tried to pay, Mary said Meg took care of it with the coffee fund, so I put a fifty in the tip jar. I thanked Mary and apologized again for causing a scene.

Driving back to the office, I braced myself for what was coming. There was no way John, Jamie, and Doug wouldn't know what had happened by the time I got back.

Who was I kidding? Everyone would know.

That's what I get for moving to a small town and working for a family business.

As soon as I set the cardboard box of coffee cups and the bag of pastries on Meg's desk, she told me John wanted to see me in his office.

"Jack and Jamie are there, too." She warned me with a sympathetic smile.

"Thanks." I grabbed their coffees, squared my shoulders, and reminded myself that the only easy day was yesterday.

I handed out their coffees as I greeted them. "You wanted to see me, sir." I looked around the room. "Sirs."

"Thanks." John took his coffee. "Mary said you left a rather generous tip." He nodded his approval.

"It didn't feel right letting SSI pay, sir."

"You don't need to call me sir," John said. "Have a seat."

"Everyone contributes to the fund, so the new guy doesn't go broke," Jack said.

"And we get a discount, being family and all," Jamie added, with a grin.

"Good to know." I knew why I was there, so I didn't wait for John to call me out. "I'm sorry about what happened at Grannie's"

"Mary accepted your apology, so we're good," John said.

"That's not why you're here," Jamie said.

"Ashley." I guessed.

"Yes, we don't need to know the details of your history with her," Jamie said.

"But we need to know if it'll be an issue," Jack finished.

I had a feeling they'd heard about Vegas long before now; they just never knew it was me.

I should've moved to a big city where I could disappear in the crowd.

Applying to a small family business had seemed like a good idea. Now I wasn't so sure. SSI was at the opposite end of the spectrum from Hawken's, which was what I wanted.

High-risk civilian black ops was the perfect job for someone who wanted to keep operating but no longer serve in the military. Guys like me, who loved serving but hated the bullshit. But after Vegas, I couldn't do it anymore.

"It won't be a problem," I said. I wasn't sure it was true, but if it was and I had to leave, I'd manage. My skills and experience meant that finding another job would be easy. Or I could say, fuck it and start my own company.

"Good, because Ashley's family," Jamie said.

That close? Thank God my resume was impressive because I'd probably have to look sooner rather than later. *Unless I can convince Ashley to forgive me.*

"Anything you want to share?" John asked.

I forced myself to release the death grip I had on my coffee before I squeezed it too much and made a mess.

"No, sir," I said. Looking John in the eye, I continued, "What happened is between Ashley and me."

"What happens in Vegas, stays in Vegas?" Jack asked. I sensed he wanted to lighten the mood, but it didn't work.

"I wish," I meant to whisper, but from the identical grins on their nodding faces I knew I'd said it too loud.

They wouldn't hear the story from me, but they'd hear about it from their wives. *Hell, they already know, they just don't realize it.* Ashley didn't strike me as the keep-it-to-herself type.

I could only imagine the colorful language she'd used as she cursed my name.

When she calle me Casper the Fucking Dickheaded Ghost, it hadn't sounded spontaneous.

What happened between Ashley and me wasn't the only thing I wanted staying in Vegas.

When I interviewed, I explained the scar by saying I'd gotten into a knife fight. *Not a lie.* I got the expected "I hope the other guy looks worse" remark and gave the appropriate "He's dead" response.

They knew it happened during my last op with Hawken's, but I didn't tell them my cover was blown or that the fight happened during my escape from the Perpura brothers, Tommy and Al, who trafficked weapons—high-value, military-grade weapons of war—to the highest bidder, foreign or domestic.

After two weeks of torture, I stopped fighting and acted like I'd given up. I convinced them I was no longer an escape risk, so when Tommy unhooked me from the ceiling winch, he was alone and unprepared.

The instant he turned his back, I strangled him with the heavy steel chain connecting the shackles on my wrists.

I made quick work of finding the keys to unlock my shackles. Unfortunately, I hadn't finished the job and Tommy regained consciousness, attacking me with a knife.

It was a short, ugly fight—nothing like the long scenes you see in the movies—that ended with my face and his throat being slashed.

Tommy didn't stand up a second time. I stole a random pair of dirty overalls, Tommy's shoes and gun, and a leather jacket I'd found on the back of a chair.

Killing his brother, Al, was easier. I put a nine mil bullet in his chest. With limited ammunition, and even less strength, I wanted to avoid confrontation with the Perpura Brothers' henchmen. I only fired the one shot, killing Al, before sneaking out of the warehouse.

Focusing on the soft chair under me, the carpet under my feet, and the wood under my fingers, I worked my way back to the present.

"You okay?" John asked.

I relaxed my death grip on the arm of the chair. "Fine, thanks." I didn't expect them to believe me; my body was vibrating with tension.

"You don't know us, so I don't expect you to trust us yet," Jamie said. "But if you ever want to talk about it, we're here."

"Thank you, sir."

"It's Jamie."

"Thanks, Jamie. I'm sure you understand there are things I can't talk about." It was the same thing I'd said during my interview. The truth of the statement served my need to avoid talking about it. I could give broad-stroke information, but not the details.

Like why I left Hawken's Security after having my cover blown. Like knowing I could no longer operate at the same level. Like seeing my life flash before my eyes and realizing I wanted more than just thrills and adventure.

I wanted a wife, kids, a dog, and a white picket fence.

Changing the subject, John said, "We have your first assignment. It's a two-day personal protection detail. You'll work it with Jay."

I stood and reached for the file. "Anything specific I need to know?" I asked, already scanning the file.

"It's routine, but we're assigning two for twenty-four-seven coverage," John said.

"When do we leave?"

"In an hour, coordinate with Jay. You have a suit with you?"

"Yes, sir." I corrected myself. "Sorry, it's a habit."

Jack laughed. "We get it." Everyone at SSI had served in the military or in law enforcement.

Jay waved me in before I could knock on the doorframe of the office he shared with his fiancée, Cate. A Marine and former FBI profiler, Cate was an all-around badass.

And someone I'd have to work hard to keep from shrinking my head. I'd already noticed her watching me, trying to figure me out, more than once.

"Morning, Cate, Jay."

"Morning, thanks for the coffee, bro," Jay said. "Best I've ever tasted."

"You've been drinking that coffee your whole life," Cate said.

"No, I haven't. I drank it for a few years before joining the Marines, but I've only been home seven months, Sweetie Pie," Jay corrected her.

"Jaden." There was a warning in her voice.

"Yes, Snookems?"

"How many times—"

"Have you told me not to call you that?"

"Obviously not enough," Cate answered.

"But you don't like being called Sweetums."

Cate turned to me. "Nathan, would you please remove my office mate from the room before I have to kill him?"

"Sure thing." Working with these two would be fun. It was obvious they enjoyed riling each other up and just as obvious they loved each other. "Let's go."

Jay grabbed his gear and laptop, then kissed Cate's temple. "Bye, love." She smiled before saying, "Be careful."

As we walked through the office towards the back door, Meg called out, "Be safe."

"Thanks, Meg." Jay and I answered together.

Chapter 5

Ashley

After making sure my grandmother was asleep, I headed to Meg's place for Craft and Booze night. It'd been the longest Monday in the history of Monday's and I needed my friends. Crafts rarely got finished, but we always had a great time talking. Mary, Beth, Emily, and AJ's fiancée, Blake, were already there.

"My mom can't make it tonight," Emily said as she grabbed one of my bags.

"That's too bad. What about Cate?"

"She'll be here in a few minutes." Because of her schedule, tonight would be the first time Cate could join us.

I set up the two batches of my semi-famous red, white, and blue sangria on the island counter. They both had blueberries, strawberries, and apples, giving the sangria its name. One had lemon vodka and prosecco; the other, lemonade and soda.

The virgin one was now for Meg and Emily. And because I was maybe pregnant, me. For the maybe-baby's health, I had to drink the virgin sangria.

Just because I'm late doesn't mean I'm expecting. A statement I said to myself on repeat.

The internet said stress could disrupt a period, and God knows I'd had more than my fair share of stress lately. I convinced myself that was the reason for my late cycle.

We all filled our plates with sliced meats, hard and soft cheeses, and a carrot or two, and our glasses with our sangria of choice. We sat around Meg's large, rectangle, dark wood kitchen table, which was devoid of the usual decorations to make room for the craft beads we'd be using later.

The table was too big for just her and Jack, even with a baby coming. But after feeling alone for most of her life, Meg embraced her place in the Sheppard family and wanted to host big family gatherings. The table could fit the entire Sheppard clan, which made it perfect for our craft nights.

"Now that we all know Emily is expecting, I say we toast the news," Mary said.

We all clinked our glasses and congratulated Emily.

The club soda in my virgin sangria tickled my nose as I took a healthy swig.

Emily literally fucking glowed with joy. My best friend since, well, forever, was made for motherhood.

Not like me. I was made to party. Not that I didn't want kids; I did. Just not now, and not with Red Flag Finn. He was a spoiled brat, a narcissist, and I didn't doubt he'd do everything in his power to take my baby from me once he found out.

"So,"—Meg dragged out the 'o'—"Tell us how you know Nathan." Her eyes sparkled with mischief.

She already knew, but this is who we were. We supported each other fiercely, loved each other relentlessly, and we teased each other without mercy.

I sipped my virgin drink, wishing it contained liquid courage. "For starters, Casper called himself Scott when I met him in Vegas." Meg and Emily were the only people who'd heard me bitch about getting stood up and ghosted by the gorgeous, hot accountant I'd met during a work trip.

"Casper?" Cate asked.

"Yeah, Casper the Disappearing Ghost." I amended his nickname for the moms in the room. "He stood me up, left me waiting in a new," I almost said fuck me dress and heels, but edited myself again for the moms, "stunning red dress." The pause didn't go unnoticed as my friends smiled and the moms tilted their heads.

Knowing I looked good in red, and had a decent body, I'd bought it that day hoping to knock Scott's socks off. But he never saw it because our first actual date never happened. Because Scott, not Scott, I reminded myself. Our date never happened because Nathan had lied, and not just about his name.

"I'm sorry," Beth said.

"Thanks." I sipped my drink. "Well, it turns out he now works for SSI." How the hell had that happened? "Guess he's not an accountant." I resorted to my default behavior, hiding my pain behind sarcasm and jokes.

No way would I admit how much it hurt when he stood me up. And because it wasn't like me to get attached, it didn't surprise them when I displayed more anger than hurt. Only Emily & Meg understood how much he'd hurt me, not because I told them but because they were smart like that.

But what they didn't know, was that I thought about Scott daily.

Nathan. *His name is Nathan.*

"No, he's a Navy SEAL," Cate said. "Well, he was before he did civilian contract work."

Right. I remembered her mentioning that one of the new guys had a scar, though she left out he was a SEAL, while we were getting ready for Emily's wedding.

In hindsight, I realized it should've been obvious Scott wasn't an accountant. The muscles, the tats, the way he carried himself. But I'd had a few drinks before we met. I wasn't drunk, but I'd had enough that my bullshit meter was off.

So what's your excuse for the second night?

I wanted to believe him. Desperately. He was smoking hot, attentive, and he gave off more than a hint of after-hours bad-boy vibe. Like a hero from a romance novel—a good guy in a suit and tie during the day and a bad boy in leather and chains at night.

And while he wasn't an alpha protector like my friends' husbands, he displayed protective, gentlemanly behavior, and that was enough for me.

"He neglected to mention that," I said, taking a huge sip of my less than satisfying drink. *I could really use some liquor.*

"He was undercover when you met him," Cate said.

"Then he should've left me alone," I barked, giving away my anger. "I'm sorry Cate, you didn't deserve that."

"Forgiven," Cate answered while studying me. She could tell I was rattled, despite my best efforts to hide it. Who was I kidding? My friends didn't need to be FBI profilers to see I wasn't handling the situation well.

Needing the focus off of me, I said, "Moving on, Em, let's talk about your news." I was a little too cheerful as I got up to refresh my drink. Pregnancy wasn't a great subject for me either, but it was easier to deal with than talking about Nathan.

Fuck my life.

The guy I wanted had ghosted me.

The guy I didn't want would be the father of my baby.

If I'm pregnant. I prayed I wasn't. *It has to be the stress.* It just has to be.

Jobless and living with my grandmother wasn't an ideal situation for bringing a child into the world.

How the hell would I survive the next few days? Without alcohol, no less.

I glared at the sangria I wanted as I filled my cup with the sangria I could have.

As if I didn't have enough problems, Nathan blew back into my life like a fucking hurricane. The force of his presence rattled my senses and messed with my emotions.

If things didn't change, I might be stress-induced period-free for the rest of my life.

Fucking Nathan Scott. There was no way I'd admit how hard I'd fallen. Falling for a guy I met in a bar in Vegas wasn't something I did. Being hung up on a guy who ghosted me after two great nights spent talking and one shared lunch—and zero orgasms—didn't just sound ridiculous; it was.

Maybe it'd sound less crazy if my life were a romance novel, but it wasn't.

My life was a clusterfuck, a series of unfortunate events.

"You okay?" Emily asked, making me jump and bringing me back to the present.

"Yeah, I just can't believe Casper works at SSI."

"If it helps you feel any better, he looked shell-shocked when he came back into Grannie's."

It didn't. "He had the balls to go back in?"

"He had to, new guy gets the coffee, remember?"

I nodded. "Right."

"You didn't answer my calls." Emily sounded hurt, making me feel like a terrible friend.

"I'm sorry. I needed some time to process." And I didn't want to take my frustration out on her.

She took the cup out of my hand and pulled me into a hug. "I know. Want me to tell Jamie to fire him?"

"Yes." I laughed. "Maybe." I wiped the tears off my face as I pulled away. I didn't really want them to fire Nathan. "No."

"If you change your mind, we'll get Meg and Mary on our side so Jack and John don't override Jamie."

I agreed, but only because I knew we could hatch all the evil plans we wanted—the guys wouldn't make business decisions based on my hurt feelings.

Casper's job was safe.

My sanity, not so much. My heart, not at all.

"He's in Dallas with Jay until tomorrow night. You won't run into him again until then," Emily said. Hearing that helped me relax a little.

I figured it'd be easy enough to avoid him if I asked Meg to give me a heads up anytime he made a coffee run. And I avoided SSI gatherings like the annual Fourth of July BBQ and the Christmas party.

"Thanks, Em." I refilled my glass again.

Chapter 6

Nathan

Jay and I spoke the same language. Having special forces experience made connecting easy, despite serving in different branches. The brotherhood crossed uniforms.

Until he asked, "So, what's the deal with you and York?"

"Who?"

"Dude, you don't know her last name?"

Fuck, he's talking about Ashley. "No. It never came up." Which wasn't entirely true, I'd intentionally not asked, and she hadn't offered. "She didn't ask for mine either." And I hadn't offered.

How'd we spend so much time together and learn so little?

That wasn't accurate. We talked about everything and nothing. The conversation flowed easily, and we never experienced the awkwardness of a first date. I didn't know her last name, but I'd learned what really mattered; what shaped

Ashley into the amazing woman she was. And despite being undercover, I shared what made me, me.

Because we hooked up in Vegas, we didn't expect more.

Liar. We might have intended for it to be a one-night stand, but we'd both wanted more.

Jay looked at me, shook his head back and forth, and said, "Ashley's last name is York."

Ashley York. If I'd had her full name, I might've looked her up. How many Ashley Yorks lived in Dallas? It didn't matter. The image of her face was etched into my brain, so I could've used social media to find the right one.

Working for a company with government contracts meant there wasn't much I couldn't find out.

If I had their full name.

"So what happened?" he repeated his question.

"Nothing happened."

"I hate to tell you, brother, but the entire office is buzzing about the incident at Grannie's," Jay said, sounding genuinely sympathetic. "You won't be able to avoid talking about it for long."

I'd figured as much. "Copy that."

"Would you rather talk about how you got that scar?"

"Christ, Sheppard, are you always like this?" My fingers tapped on my leg, counting to keep me present.

He laughed. "It's part of my charm."

"Are you sure about that?" I teased, trying to lighten the mood and change the subject.

"Abso-fucking-lutely. Just ask Cate." He glanced my way. "So, about that scar?"

"You know, your brothers weren't half as nosy."

His slight flinch as he tightened his hands on the steering wheel told me I'd hit a nerve.

"You'll see soon enough; I'm nothing like my brothers." His tone held little to no humor.

I nodded. Definitely a sore subject. "Like I said, a knife fight," I answered, wanting to talk about my scar less than I wanted to talk about Ashley. Circumstances had fused the two in my mind forever. I couldn't think about Ashley without flashing back to the warehouse. Or remembering the knife fight that resulted in a facial scar that wasn't easily ignored.

"Okay. I won't push anymore, but I'm here if you want to talk." He wasn't so different from his brothers after all. "I recognize the haunted look in your eyes." He paused, his forearms flexing as his grip on the steering wheel tightened. His voice was gritty when he said, "I've been there."

"Thanks, man. But I'm not ready yet."

"Fair enough."

"Can I ask you a question?" I asked.

"Shoot."

"Did your father say anything about my background check?"

Standard background checks included basic information, like employment and criminal histories. Private investigation agencies ran deeper background checks, though not government or law enforcement deep.

Hawken's ran an extensive check because of the work we did with government agencies. SSI wouldn't have looked that deep, but they may have done extra research.

"Not to me. I'm a son, but not one of 'the sons'", he made air quotes, "so I'm on a need-to-know basis." He shrugged. "I didn't need to know."

I nodded before trying a different tactic. "Brother to brother, what do you know?"

He looked at me, sizing me up, before answering. "I know some shit went south in Vegas during your last op for Hawken's. If they know more, they haven't told me. Obviously, what they learned didn't prevent them from hiring you."

My three interviews had been extensive. The first one was a pre-interview via video chat with John. He didn't push for details, and I didn't offer them. The second was a longer, in-person interview with John, Jamie, and Jack. They asked for more details, and I told them what I could. They seemed to understand I couldn't divulge details about ongoing government operations.

The Perpura brothers were dead, but their cartel was still operating. The FBI was still investigating, but I didn't know if Hawken's had sent someone new in to finish the job.

My final interview with the team felt more like meeting a friend's family than an interview. In hindsight, it made sense. SSI was a family business; they'd make sure I was a good fit professionally and personally.

"Fair enough." During my last interview, I fell back into the easy banter that happens between military brothers and had looked forward to working with a team again.

"So why the SEALs?" he asked, changing the subject. A hint of challenge in his voice.

I laughed. "Why the Raiders?" My challenge matched his.

"Didn't want to serve on a boat."

I laughed. "I hear that a lot."

We spent the next thirty-six hours providing protection for an actress in Dallas. She had her own full-time bodyguard, so our job included crowd control and securing any room she graced with her presence.

We didn't have much time to talk, but I had plenty of time to think.

And a feisty brunette occupied most of my thoughts. Ashley's anger was justified, and she wasn't shy about making sure I knew it. *Casper.* I smiled. She'd used a lot of nicknames for people in Vegas, too. Back then she'd called me Angel because of her silly pickup line. I should've hated it, but her eyes always sparkled when she used it, making me love it.

"What's so funny?" Jay's voice asked over comms.

"Nothing." I lied as I removed the smile from my face.

"Right." I could see him near the entrance, scanning the room.

I had kitchen-door duty. Which meant I couldn't avoid seeing and smelling the amazing food the servers carried. Steak, lobster, and a spicy pasta dish. It was making me hungry, and probably grumpier than usual.

"Just do your job, Grunt." I used the nickname for soldiers in the Marines.

"Aye, aye, Uber." He threw back the nickname the Marines gave the Navy.

I shook my head at the familiar banter. Jay and I would get along just fine. If he didn't pester me about Ashley.

Back at the hotel, my Chicken Alfredo was less than satisfying as I scarfed my dinner before volunteering for the first shift of the night watch.

Standing in a hall for hours on end was boring as fuck, but I'd had worse jobs.

"Can I give you some friendly advice?" Jay asked during the drive back.

"No."

He laughed. "Whatever happened between you and Ashley, apologize. Kiss her ass and make it right."

"I said no." I really didn't want him or anyone else at SSI getting involved.

"I heard you."

"Could've fooled me."

"I know my dad and brothers talked to you. So you know that Ashley and Emily are tight, have been since grade school. And Meg adores her."

"You gonna shut up about this anytime soon?"

"Soonish." He grinned.

I flipped him off.

"Your bosses will be polite, but the girls—they'll kick your ass."

"Should I look for another job?" I tried to sound unconcerned, but he didn't buy it.

"Not yet."

"Noted." I appreciated his brutal honesty, even if I didn't like the message.

"Unfortunately for you, the cat's out of the bag. Ashley told the girls all about the night you stood her up in Vegas."

If only it were that simple.

Ashley had probably called me every name in the book after coming home. Given her penchant for comedic nicknames, I'd bet she'd made up a few too.

"Let me guess, craft and booze night?" She'd laughed until she had tears streaming from her eyes when she'd told me about it.

"Yup." He popped the 'p'. "And there's no way the girls didn't tell their guys as soon as they got home."

"So, who all knows?" I was clueless about who attended craft and booze night. I just remembered Ashley joking about how it started as a book club, but they drank more than they read, so they tried crafts instead.

Remembering the hint of pink in her cheeks as she laughed while telling me they drank more than they crafted made me respond in ways I didn't want Jay to see.

"Hate to be the one to tell you, bro, but everyone. I remember her cursing a guy named Scott." He raised an eyebrow at me.

Everyone. I closed my eyes and recited the SEAL slogan, the only easy day was yesterday, reminding myself I could get through this. "It's my middle name."

He nodded before continuing, "She was so pissed."

"Fuck." I sighed the word as I ran my hand down my face, the jagged scar under my fingers reminding me why I'd stood her up.

Jay noticed my hand lingering. "A wise man once told me that the only emotion that drives that kind of anger is pain."

Feeling a bond despite the newness of our friendship, I opened up a little more. "It wasn't intentional. I was undercover, and shit went south." As a Raider, he'd understand what I meant.

"How far south?"

"Think Cape Horn." An island off the southern tip of South America.

"Damn." The upbeat country song on the radio filled the silence. "That when you fucked up your face?" His tone lightened the mood but not the subject.

"Yeah."

"Does she know?"

No, because I didn't have her contact information. Even if I had, my head was too fucked up to reach out. Why would she talk to me after everything that had happened? After I'd stood her up and hurt her. Add in my physical and emotional scars, and she wouldn't recognize me as the man she met in Vegas.

"No." The situation had too many ugly layers, and Ashley didn't want to hear my side. "She thinks I intentionally ghosted her."

This time, a lopsided grin accompanied his raised eyebrow. "If the only lie you told her was your name, and I assume your profession, you should be okay."

I didn't share his confidence, but circumstances had provided me with a second chance, and I wouldn't waste it.

Seeing her again brought up a lot of shit for me, but it also reminded me of the dreams I had, of the life I wanted. It didn't matter that I'd spent less than forty-eight hours with her; she haunted my dreams. Dreams of marriage and starting a family. Dreams of our three kids who'd have her expressive honey-brown eyes and my sandy blond hair.

Something about Ashley had me wanting to tell her the truth from the moment I met her, but I couldn't risk it. It wasn't just the op; telling her could put her life in danger. But my mission was near completion, so I'd only needed to lie for a few more weeks. Then I could've come clean.

Instead, my cover was blown, and they'd tortured me for information. *And for fun.* The Perpura Brothers were two sick individuals.

Those bastards changed everything.

They ended my career. They ruined my face. They destroyed my chances with Ashley.

I tapped out my countdown, bringing my attention back to the present and Jay.

I had a new career.

I could afford the surgery needed to minimize the scar, something I might do in the future.

Rebuilding my confidence was easier said than done. I'd have to excel at my job and avoid making costly mistakes.

That was what haunted me the most. I'd let my guard down when I needed it the most. I'd missed the signs that something was amiss within the organization, and it almost cost me my life.

If things had been different, my mistakes could've cost Ashley hers.

With the help of a good therapist, and many late nights drinking beer with Kroupa while staring into a fire pit, I'd regained some of my former myself. It was time I reclaimed my life and making myself useful again was at the top of my list.

"It would've been my last undercover op," I said.

"Why was that?"

Even before meeting Ashley, I knew the Perpura op would be my last undercover job with Hawken's.

"I wanted to be me again, no more living under my alias. I'm too old for the demands of deep undercover work, and if I'm being completely honest, I was tired of the bachelor lifestyle."

After the Perpura op, I planned to shift gears and move to the less demanding personal protection branch of the business. But nothing went as planned.

"How much longer did you have when you met Ashley?"

"A day. A week at most."

That mission had cost me everything. My confidence, my outgoing personality, and it almost cost me my life.

During my SEAL days, I was the life of the party; now people called me grumpy or a hermit.

I miss the man I used to be.

Now that I'd found Ashley, I was desperate to find him again.

She was taking up more than her fair share of space in my mind. Ashley York gave me a glimpse of the future I wanted. Just because the Perpura brothers destroyed any chance I had at a romantic relationship with her, didn't mean we couldn't be friends.

And maybe, just maybe, someday we could become more.

I had my work cut out for me. Where things stood, I didn't think I could convince her to talk to me, let alone forgive me. But I had to try.

Suppressing a sigh, I asked, "How deep is my hole?"

"You'll need heavy machinery to dig your way out," he said. "And the patience of a saint. Ashley's intense; I doubt she'll make it easy."

He sounded like he was talking from up-close and personal experience, causing my green-eyed monster to rear its ugly head.

"How well do you know her?" *Great job hiding your jealousy, Blaze.* Jealousy was an emotion I had no right feeling. Ashley wasn't mine. No matter how badly I wanted her, she deserved better than a man haunted by memories and scarred by experience.

"I didn't sleep with her, if that's why your panties are in a bunch. Never dated her either."

My shoulders relaxed. I could see Ashley going for a guy like Jaden Sheppard. After all, she liked me, and Jay and I had a lot in common. We shared the same general build and ink-covered arms. Though his were scar free.

So were mine, when we met.

Hell, we even carried ourselves the same way. No surprise there; spec ops guys never really relaxed. *Even when we do.*

Always alert. We sensed danger before we saw it. A skill that made us good at personal protection jobs.

More memories surfaced.

"The boss wants to see you," one of the Perpura's many goons said.

My instincts told me something was hinky as the hair on the back of my neck stood on end. I dismissed it. We were all on edge because the weapon's exchange hadn't gone as planned and the brothers were scrambling to find a new buyer.

I nodded. "Lead the way." I hoped they'd finally give me the details of the failed sale so I could report back to Hawken's.

Tommy and Al, who should've been behind bars, or dead, were conducting business as usual. I needed to know what had happened.

I felt it the instant I crossed the threshold. The energy felt off. *They know.* My gut screamed, warning me to get out of Dodge. The lock clicking as soon as the door shut behind me removed that option.

Not that I would've run—the Perpura Brothers needed to be taken down, and I wouldn't leave the mission unfinished.

"Come in," Tommy said from his position behind his desk.

Al, his younger brother and the more sadistic of the two, leaned against the wall behind him. His grin was more sneer than smile.

Shoving my hands in my pockets to hide my nerves, I played it cool. "What happened with the deal?"

Tommy held up a hand to silence Al when he growled. "You—"

The butterflies in my gut turned to bees.

"We think there's a mole in our midst," Tommy said, staring me down. Challenging me to give myself up.

The bees turned into angry wasps when four guys surrounded me.

"Do you know who it is?" I asked. By this point, I knew full well they did.

"We do, and so do you." Al's smile turned my blood cold as a hand landed on each shoulder.

Jay chose that moment to grip my shoulder. I turned to fight him off as my name cut through the fog.

"Blaszek, are you okay?"

He pulled over and rolled down the windows.

I sucked in the hot, humid air, taking several deep breaths while doing my countdown ritual to bring me back to the present.

The brothers never mentioned Ashley. She was safe, and that was all that mattered. The Navy taught me how to withstand a lot of abuse, physical and psychological, but I wasn't sure I could watch them hurt her.

When I recovered, I apologized.

"No worries. You good?"

"Yeah, thanks." Prior to seeing Ashley, I hadn't had a flashback in weeks. Since then, I'd had three.

" I hate to be an ass, but will this be a problem?"

"No, seeing Ashey brought up some shit, but I'll deal with it." And I would, because failure wasn't an option.

Chapter 7

Ashley

When I woke up in my childhood room, I had to remind myself where I was. The pale pink and green, colors I loved as a teen, were a harsh reminder I was no longer a self-sufficient adult. It wasn't my choice, but that didn't mean I felt any better about it.

I'd applied to every job advertised between Dallas and Weatherford, and even a few that weren't. Crickets.

It didn't make sense. I had a strong resume, a great portfolio, and my clients loved me. There should've been interest by now.

My phone alarm beeped. The screen reminded me it was Wednesday when I picked it up to silence it.

Wednesday. The day Nathan returns from his job in Dallas.

I washed my face in cold water before joining my grandmother in the kitchen for breakfast. As I came around the corner, I almost tripped over a black cat walking between my legs.

"What the hell?" Gran didn't have a cat.

"Language, dear."

"Sorry, Gran, but this stupid cat just tripped me." I looked around to see where it'd gone. "Give me a sec and I'll shoo him outside."

"There's no need for that." I looked just in time to see the cat's head poke above the table, his green eyes staring at me as he sat on Gran's lap.

"Meow."

"When did you get a cat?"

"Last night. This handsome fella was meowing outside the patio door, so I gave him some tuna." Outwardly, I raised an eyebrow. Inwardly, I thought, what the fuck.

Gran knew better than to feed a stray. *Or so I thought.*

"What?" She shrugged as if it were no big deal. "He was hungry."

She stroked the cat's head as she explained how he'd rubbed up against her leg, begging for attention, before devouring the food.

The cat looked healthy, and he was friendly. "He probably belongs to a neighbor. We need to ask around."

"He doesn't have a collar," she countered. Honey-brown eyes, so much like my own, stared at me, daring me to argue.

I sighed and poured myself a cup of coffee. After adding a generous portion of vanilla creamer, I tried again. "Gran, just because a cat doesn't have a collar doesn't mean he's a stray. We should take him to the vet to see if he's chipped."

"But he likes it here." No argument from me. I could hear the damn cat purring across the small kitchen island.

I tried to use reason. "Gran, his owners probably miss him." A well-fed, friendly cat must have a family who loved him. Gran wouldn't want to deprive them.

"Fine, we can take him to see if he's chipped, but if he's not, I'm keeping him."

"Thank you." I sighed.

"His name is Prince." As if on cue, Prince meowed.

Great. We have a cat. As if I didn't have enough problems.

"Gran, try not to get too attached. He looks healthy, so he probably has a home and a family."

"Nonsense! He adopted us."

Knowing it was a lost cause, I gave up. If the vet found a chip, we'd have to return him to his family. If Prince didn't have a chip, we'd have a cat.

"Emily's coming over after breakfast. We'll take the cat to the vet after she leaves," I said before asking what she wanted for breakfast.

"Just eggs and toast for me."

After breakfast, Prince followed Gran to the living room, where she settled into her favorite comfy chair to read. I could hear her talking to him, asking him what type of toys he wanted.

I prayed he had a chip. Not because I didn't like cats, but I lacked the energy for the added responsibility. And what if he tripped her, like he almost did me this morning? Gran could end up a lot worse off than she already was. I didn't want to think about her needing another surgery or, worse, dying because she fell and hit her head.

Emily didn't help matters by gushing over the damn cat when she greeted my grandmother.

"Your cat is so cute."

"He is, but I doubt we can keep him," I said.

At the same time Gran said, "His name is Prince."

"Why not?"

"Look at him Em, he's probably someone's pet."

"I didn't think of that," Emily said. "Maybe Gran can adopt a different cat if Prince has a home." *Not helping Em.*

I wasn't against Gran having a cat but I wanted to make sure she was safe and could handle caring for it. "Maybe." Maybe I could stay longer than I originally intended to make sure she was steady on her feet, so she'd be less likely to get tripped by a playful cat.

"Let's move to the kitchen so we don't disturb them," Emily said, tearing her eyes away from Prince, who was happily playing with a ball of yarn Gran had rolled on the floor.

"Coffee?" I asked, then immediately apologized.

"It's okay. It'll take time to adjust." Emily put her hand on her belly. *She looks so damn happy.* My hand twitched, wanting to touch my belly, but I refused to draw attention to it. I didn't want to talk about it until I'd taken the test.

"I can make some decaf if you want, or some herbal tea."

"Tea sounds good."

Our conversation started with bad news. Emily's company wasn't hiring, but she suggested I send in my resume anyway. When she asked if I wanted to return to Dallas; I couldn't answer. I loved Dallas, but after Finn, I felt like I wanted a change of pace. *No, I've wanted it longer than that.* I loved the city life, but had been visiting Weatherford more often.

My phone buzzed with a text alert. *Speak of the devil.* Not wanting to read it, I turned my phone screen side down.

"Everything okay?"

"Yeah, just Red Flag Finn. I'll read it later."

Knowing the full story of why I broke up with him, she let it go. "Have you heard from any companies you've applied to?"

"No, I've followed up, but no dice." I sipped my tea. "Which is crazy. My reputation is great. I do good work, and my clients leave rave reviews."

Just like it made no sense for my boss to fire me. Though I reminded myself not to take it personally because my boss said the budget cuts made it necessary. Which was weird; I thought the company was profitable. The nagging feeling that Finn was responsible lingered, but I refused to believe his uncle would be so petty.

My phone buzzed again. I ignored it.

"Mary said she could give you some work, but it's not full time."

"For Grannie's?"

"No, for the Wyatt Foundation. Now that Blake's joined the board as their legal counsel, they're ready to grow the foundation." Blake passed her bar exam earlier in the summer and had the good fortune of landing her dream job before the ink was dry on her certificate.

"I don't mind contract work," I said, knowing it was better than nothing. "Hey, maybe we should start our own company." I said it as a joke, but it wasn't a bad idea. We both had marketing degrees. Emily's skills were branding and website design. My area of expertise was tying in and maintaining social media platforms. We'd make the perfect team.

Having our own company would require a lot of work, but it'd give us flexibility and full control.

"Maybe, but now isn't the right time. Jamie wants me to take time off after the baby's born."

"More than the typical maternity leave?" I looked for signs that she didn't agree, but it was clear she didn't mind Jamie calling the shots.

"Yeah, but I don't think my boss will approve the six months Jamie wants me to take."

"I'm surprised he wants you to take that long, since you work from home." She could set her own hours and work around the baby's needs.

"That's what I said. If my boss won't approve the extended leave, I'll ask to work part-time. I'm sure Jamie will be okay with that."

I didn't doubt it.

"Why didn't Mary ask you to help with the Wyatt Foundation?"

"She did, but I'm not as good at the social media stuff, so I suggested you for the job."

"Em, you didn't have to do that." I didn't want her giving up the opportunity to work with her mother-in-law on a passion project.

"I know. But I'm pregnant and you're out of work, so it makes sense." She sipped her tea. "Say you'll do it, please." She drew out the 'e' while clasping her hands in front of her chest.

"I'd love to." Working for the Wyatt Foundation would be more than just a paycheck; I'd be helping the families of fallen heroes. Plus, finding work was easier if you had a job.

The foundation began three years ago, when John and Mary Sheppard held a fundraiser to help Beth after her husband, a Weatherford cop, died in the line of duty. Poor Beth was seven months pregnant. The small-town community got behind them, and they'd raised so much money they helped Beth and a second widow. Wanting to do more good, they created the Wyatt Foundation and held an annual event near Halloween. They raised a lot of money, and everyone had a good time. *And don't even get me started on how fantasy-inducing it is seeing the SSI guys in chaps!*

An image of Nathan in chaps flashed through my mind.

My phone buzzing again erased the drool-worthy picture from my mind. I imagined shooting daggers out of my eyes straight into my phone at the disruption.

"What if it's not him?"

She had a point, so I turned it over. *Nope, it's him.* I put it back on the table with more force than I intended.

"I'm sorry, Ashley. Want Jamie to tell him to back off?"

"No. He's not worth the energy. Besides, I don't think he's dangerous," I said, trying to convince myself as much as Emily.

I broke up with him because he started showing red flags for abusive behavior: self-centered, blamed me for everything, refused to apologize, jealous fits, and the final straw was when he tried to tell me I couldn't come home to visit my friends.

"Okay, but if you change your mind, call. You know Jamie will help."

I did. I also knew Jamie would tell his newest employee. And with my recent luck, Casper would be the only one available to help.

Hard. Fucking. Pass.

Chapter 8

Nathan

When Jay asked if I wanted to talk about my anxiety attack, I said no. Then he surprised me by explaining why SSI had delayed my interview. He and Cate were investigating a missing person and were held hostage after their cover was blown. He didn't go into detail, but they were tortured.

We have more in common than I realized.

"Because of the drug in my system, I couldn't move. I watched Cate get shot." I wasn't hard to see that Jay still carried guilt.

While I appreciated his openness, I wasn't ready to share yet. Though he'd be the perfect person to talk to if I changed my mind.

Jay's situation happened more recently than mine, and he watched the woman he loved get shot. I couldn't help but wonder, how had he healed so fast?

"Do you still have nightmares?" I asked.

"Yeah, but therapy is helping." He paused. "It also helps that my family understands."

Therapy and family.

One I had. One I didn't.

Never had one. I grew up in the system. Lucky for me, I was smart and strong. One talk with a Navy recruiter, and I'd made my career choice.

"You're lucky."

Jay's eyes glazed over for a second before he said, "I am."

There's a story there.

Growing up, I prayed for a forever family. But it wasn't meant to be.

Joining the military was a no-brainer for me—it gave me the family I'd always wanted. I signed my enlistment papers on my eighteenth birthday. Two years later I entered BUDS, and fifteen months after that I'd earned my Trident. Having that pin punched into my chest was my proudest moment. Only I had no one to share it with.

Except my fellow newly pinned SEALs. Some we'd lost, and some I'd lost touch with after they left the Navy, but there was one person I staying in contact with.

Kroupa wasn't just my teammate; he was a friend.

After we returned to the office, I texted him.

> Hey man, it's been a while. Let's grab a beer.

His reply came a few minutes later.

> Sounds good. How's SSI?

> Good so far. I like being on a team again.

> I won't say I told you so, but...

> Yeah yeah. I gotta run. Give the wife a hug for me.

Kroupa had moved just outside of Dallas, to be near his wife's family after leaving the Navy, and started a dog training business. He specialized in police and search training. I'd stayed with them during my recovery, and he was the reason I was at SSI.

> She'll tell me to say hi, so hi.

I turned off my phone before heading to the SSI training center.

The SSI/Law Enforcement Training Center, also known as SLETC—pronounced as Slet-C—was located at the back end of the SSI property. The construction crews had finished the shoot house construction two weeks ago, and today we'd test it.

"I've set the targets," John said once everyone arrived. "The Sierra team's up first."

Sierra was the original team—Jamie, Jack, AJ, and Doug. John was part of the team, but today he'd run training. The newly formed Bravo team consisted of Jaden, Maxwell, me, and the new guy, Matt, another retired SEAL, who was scheduled to start in two weeks.

Today was a combination of testing the new shoot house and working with our new teams. Despite being our first time working together, I trusted Bravo could clear the house without any issues.

"Bravo One," John said, switching to our call signs.

"Yes, sir," I answered. Initially, it'd surprised me when they named me team lead, but after thinking about it, it made sense; Jaden was our sniper, and Maxwell had less experience, despite being at SSI the longest.

Having led my SEAL team, I felt confident I could lead the SSI team.

"Prep your team," John said.

"Yes, sir."

We walked to the fifty-yard range on the other side of the tall rock and dirt berm to discuss tactics.

"You good?" Jay, Bravo Two, asked. I understood his concern, but I'd been fine since the incident in the car.

"Yes. You have any arguments against covering the door and hall?" It wasn't an exciting job, but as a Marine Raider, he could clear a room without breaking a sweat. I didn't have the same blind faith in Maxwell's skills. I'd need to see her in action and evaluate before trusting her skills.

"I am."

"Good. Bravo Three, you'll go in first after Two breaches the door." After Maxwell nodded, I continued, "I'll follow and Bravo Two will hold the hall."

"Yes, sir," they answered in unison.

We practiced lining up and moving together, miming rifle movements with our hands, while waiting for our turn.

"Bravo Team!" John called over the berm. "You're up."

I fist-bumped Jay and Maxwell before following them to the house.

"How'd it go?" Jay asked as we approached the members of Sierra.

"We killed it," AJ answered with a laugh.

"Funny," Jay said. The rest of us laughed. Cate rolled her eyes.

"Gear up," John ordered.

We holstered our blue training pistols and slung our blue training rifles. The training guns fired non-lethal projectiles and were perfect for close-quarters training with or without human targets. The plastic paintball-like rounds were bullet-shaped and had a colored, water-soluble marking compound. We used them because they were faster and more accurate than paintballs.

They hurt more too. *Pain is a great training aid.*

"Let's go," I said, before putting on my protective face shield.

We lined up outside the door. When John was in position on the catwalk, he gave the order to begin.

I signaled to Maxwell; she signaled Jay. We were ready. After silently counting to three, Jay ripped the door open, and we went to work. Maxwell was better than I expected, and Jay was exactly what I expected from a spec ops guy. It was our first training run of any kind, so it wasn't as smooth as I'd like, but it wasn't shit either.

When we got back to the front, Jay gave his former team shit. "Which one of you idiots shot a hostage?" he asked, taking his mask off.

"What are you talking about?" Jack asked.

"Poor kid had a hole in his head," Jay said, grinning.

"You sure that wasn't you?" AJ asked.

"Wait, I didn't see a kid," Doug said.

"Didn't anyone teach you to identify your target before you fire?" Jay asked.

Before things spiraled out of control, Maxwell reeled Jay in by saying nothing more than his name. "Jaden."

"He's fucking with you." I put their minds at ease.

AJ punched Jay in the arm.

Jay returned the favor.

I just shook my head and watched.

Not what I expected from a small-town family private investigation company. But I liked it.

Back in the office, I showered before scouring the internet for everything I could find on Ashley York. Ignoring the guilt and my conscience calling me a stalker, I scanned her social media accounts and looked into her work history.

I justified my actions by reminding myself that everyone in this day and age did a social media search for the person they were interested in.

Ashley'd be disappointed when she tried to find me. I didn't have a social media presence. I wasn't even listed on the SSI website, since they'd removed everyone from the About Us page after what happened with Jay and Cate.

On the opposite end of the spectrum, Ashley was an open book. Some things I knew from our conversations, like how she'd lost her parents young in a car accident, she was a marketing major in college, and she worked for a marketing firm in Dallas.

In Vegas, she said she'd never been married and didn't have kids.

Thankfully, the search gave me no reason to believe that either of those things had changed. Not that it mattered, despite what Jay said, I didn't expect her to forgive me. She was less than receptive when I explained why I had to lie, and I couldn't, wouldn't, bother her with the details.

Even if it'd make it easier for her to forgive me. She didn't need her innocence shattered with my horrific war stories.

"Back to work." I forced myself to focus on the task at hand.

Ashley spent a lot of time on social media. *Not surprising given her career.* Making it easy to research the last few months of her life.

The most recent posts caught my attention.

She loved her job, *so why is she job hunting*? Going back a little further, there was one post saying she'd broken up with her boyfriend. I scrolled back up and checked the dates. The breakup was six weeks before she moved back home to Weatherford.

The timing set off my alarms. Who was this ex? Was he the reason she lost her job after five years of employment? Did she really move to Weatherford to care for her grandmother, or was there another reason?

A knock on my door interrupted my research.

"Hey Jay."

"We're going out for a beer. You in?"

"Let me guess, new guy buys the beer?" I laughed.

"Nah, but we won't say no if you offer to pick up the first round."

"Sounds good." A chance to escape my racing mind while getting to know my new teammates was exactly what I needed. "Where are we going?"

"The Wing Place. We're heading out now."

"See you there." I packed up my laptop, straightened out my desk and killed the light on my way out. "You joining us, Meg?"

"No, you boys have fun." She kissed Jack and shooed him away from her desk.

The tugging sensation in my gut as I watched them reminded me of what I was missing in my life. Love, support, family.

Jack clapped me on the shoulder and said, "Come on, Blaze. I'll buy you a beer." Half the guys at SSI had started using my SEAL nickname.

Seated between Jack and Jay at the high top, I let Jack buy my first drink. Per Jay's less-than-subtle hint, I offered to pick up the second round.

When our server got tongue-tied while staring at my scar, I turned my face away. It'd been a year, and I still wasn't used to the stares and expressions of disgust or sympathy. Maybe I never would be.

Kroup's wife told me once that I had a tendency to scowl at people who stared too long. She'd gently remind me not to intimidate people whenever it happened. I assumed that's what happened with our server.

"Does that happen a lot?" AJ asked.

"Unfortunately." It'd be a miracle if she got our order right, given how often she asked us to repeat it.

Everyone was there for my final interview, so they knew I didn't like talking about what had happened.

That knowledge didn't stop AJ. "Did it happen in the SEALs?" he asked.

"No." I held the sides of my barstool in an iron grip and counted on the inhale.

"Let it go, Janerek," Jay said. "You know he doesn't like talking about it."

I appreciated his support, but maybe it was time for me to open up. I didn't have to go into detail, but sharing would help me form bonds with my new co-workers and teammates.

"Thanks, Jay, but it's okay." Still clutching the sides of my chair, I shared what I'd told Jay, and his brothers during my second interview. "It happened during an undercover op when shit went south."

My knuckles turned white, and my fingers started to ache, but I held on.

When my skin started itching, I counted five things I could see while methodically counting my breaths. In, two, three, four. Hold, two, three, four. Out…

I didn't make it to the next step before AJ asked, "Let me guess, a year ago in Vegas?" They knew I was the asshole who'd promised Ashley the best night of her life and then ghosted her. All eyes turned to me in anticipation.

No doubt learning I was 'that guy' hurt my reputation at SSI, but maybe knowing I had a good reason would help fix it. *At least with the guys.*

"Yes," I confirmed.

They nodded their understanding. If they expected more, they wouldn't get it.

If I shared more, it'd be with Ashley first, to explain why I'd broken protocol and asked her out when it was so damn risky. And apologize. A lot.

The silence at the table was louder than the chatter of the crowd and the music blasting through the speakers.

"I'm a Cubs fan," Doug ended the silence with a whiplash-inducing subject change, putting everyone back at ease.

I could talk about sports. Sports were a safe topic.

"Are you from Chicago?" I asked.

"Born and raised. Bears fan too," Doug answered.

"What about you? What sports do you like?" Jack asked.

"Football and hockey."

"Don't give us too much all at once." Jay laughed.

"Pot," Jack coughed into his hand.

"What was that?" Jay asked.

I sat back and watched, glad the attention had shifted away from me.

"I seem to recall a certain Jarhead giving nothing but one-word answers for a while."

"Shut up, ground pounder," Jay countered.

"That's rich coming from you, grunt," Jack teased back.

"Technically, Raiders aren't grunts," I said.

Jay held up his fist, and I bumped it with mine. "Yeah," Jay shot back at his brother.

"And the SEAL enters the ring," AJ said.

"The two of us against all of you. Any day," Jay bragged.

"With or without guns?" Doug asked, sizing me up.

Enjoying the banter, I shrugged and asked, "Does it matter?"

"It does. Jamie's as good a shot as Jay, so we've got the distance covered. So it'd come to pistols, and I think we could out shoot you," Doug said.

"Big talk coming from an airman," Jay teased.

"Do you doubt my skills?" Doug asked.

I hadn't seen him handle a gun, but the rest of the team trusted his skills, so I figured he couldn't be too bad a shot.

"What about unarmed?" I asked.

"Jay's batshit crazy on the mat and could easily beat both his brothers at the same time."

"Hey!" the older Sheppards piped up.

"It's true," Jay said, his confidence bordering on arrogance.

AJ and Doug nodded. I tucked away the information, knowing I'd want to remember this conversation when it came time for the monthly sparring session.

"Neither of us," he pointed between himself and AJ, "has beaten Jay on the mat, but we can hold our own. But you're a wild card; no one has seen you fight. Though it's fair to assume you can kick some ass based on your resume."

I laughed. *I can.* "You'll find out soon enough."

"Shall we wager for August?" Jay asked.

"The usual?" Jack asked, flashing a grin.

"Let's make it interesting and double it," Jay said.

"I'm out," Jamie said.

"Me too. Meg will kill me if I lose too much."

"Hey Blaze, did you hear that? They know they'll lose."

"Nice going, dude." AJ smacked Jack in the arm.

"So, Nathan, how about them Cubs?" Doug once again shifted the conversation.

I laughed. "I wouldn't know; I grew up in Colorado." I was a Broncos and Avalanche fan but didn't follow baseball.

It was no surprise the three Sheppard brothers were Cowboy fans. All three played football in high school. Something I couldn't afford to do, and apparently neither could AJ.

"I was a wimpy tech geek, more suited to watching sports than playing," Doug admitted. That may have been true in high school, but Doug was now a well-trained, six-foot-four wall of solid muscle.

When our server delivered our wings, the order was wrong. Not wanting to make her feel more uncomfortable, we ate them. *At least she got the pizza order right.*

The conversation turned to family as we ate. It wasn't surprising. Jamie and Jack were expecting, and the others were engaged.

As the only single guy at the table, I observed more than I spoke.

Deciding it was best not to ask our young server to split the check for us, we split it six ways. I threw in two extra twenties to cover the round of drinks I'd offered to buy.

Dinner was exactly what I'd needed. I connected with the guys and learned that the Sheppards were the only ones who grew up in a loving family.

"Thanks for the invite, Jay. I needed that."

"No problem, man." He clapped my shoulder. "See you tomorrow."

"Bright and early."

Chapter 9

Ashley

I can't believe we have a cat. According to the vet, Prince was in good health and not chipped. He recommended notifying the local animal shelter in case his parents were looking for him, so we did. Well, I did. Gran said it was unnecessary because she believed Prince chose us.

"Gran, we should wait before buying so many toys." Or treats.

"Ashley, Prince needs something to do while I'm resting," Gran all but whined. *God Lord, it's like dealing with a child.*

My hand instinctively went to my belly. Thankfully, Gran was too focused on shopping for Prince to notice that I was panicking because it'd be just my luck that my kid would be just like her. *Like us.*

Time for a new tactic. "Gran," I whispered. "We're on a budget, so let's not go too crazy."

"All right, dear." She patted my arm, her eyes full of sympathy.

We bought more than necessary but not as much as Gran wanted.

After unfolding Gran's walker and helping her out of the car and I carried Prince into the house in his new carrier. He vocalized his displeasure, loudly and without interruption, from the car to the kitchen.

While Gran used the bathroom, I washed Prince's cute new cat bowl. The red and white fish painted on the bottom of the blue ceramic bowl made me smile.

Prince clawed at my legs while I opened the can of food.

"Give me a second, would ya?" I asked, knowing he wouldn't.

He rewarded me with an impatient meow.

"Let me put it down," I huffed at him, hoping he'd let me walk the five steps to his feeding mat without tripping me.

He didn't.

I took two steps before he raced between my feet. Losing my balance and not wanting to step on the little fucker, I grabbed the counter for support. Unfortunately, my face slammed into the corner of an open cabinet door.

Which hurt like hell.

"Fucking cat."

At least I didn't drop his food and make a mess or break his new bowl. After putting his food on the floor, I went to my room to inspect the damage.

I had a scrape on my cheekbone and would likely have a bruise under my eye before dinner.

"Is everything okay?" Gran asked from the hall.

"Yeah, the stupid cat tripped me, and I slammed my face on a cabinet door."

"How bad is it?"

"A scrape and I'll probably have a black eye."

"You know, you really should close those doors," she said, turning towards the kitchen.

"Thanks for the sympathy, Gran," I called out as I followed her.

"It's a scratch; you'll be fine." If I were hurt, she'd be at my side as fast as she could push her walker, helping me.

I would be, but would she be as lucky if the demon cat tripped her?

"That's a good boy," Gran praised the demonic cat like he hadn't just tried to kill me.

My phone buzzed with a text alert.

How'd it go at the vet?

We have a cat. crying emoji

I bet Gran is thrilled.

She is. But he just tried to kill me.

I'm sure that's not true.

He tripped me, and I hit my face on a door.

> I'm sorry.

> Go ahead, laugh. I would.

It was true; I was like that. Not because I didn't care, but because humor helped. As long as no one was seriously injured, which I wasn't.

Emily sent a laugh emoji.

> Any thoughts on the job offer?

> I'll take it. I'll call Mary later.

Working part-time was better than being unemployed. I'd have a paycheck, and employed applicants looked more attractive to potential employers. Working with Blake and Mary was an added bonus.

> Good, I'm glad. I'm still volunteering to revamp the website, so we'll get to work together.

> Cool! Gotta run. Doorbell.

Maybe it's Prince's owners. I felt bad for wanting Prince to have a home, knowing it'd break Gran's heart, but it would be for the best. I'd consider finding her a new cat after I found a job and she was more mobile and stable.

Lost in my thoughts, I didn't check the peephole before opening the door.

And coming face to face with Finn.

"Hey, baby," he said, with an arrogant smirk on his face.

"What the—" I cut myself off before grabbing my keys off the nearby table.

I pushed him away and closed the door behind me. Gran didn't need to see or hear us arguing.

"What the fuck are you doing here?" I hissed.

"Is that anyway to greet your boyfriend?"

What?

"Finn, we broke up. Remember?" I asked.

"Ashley, I let you have your little tantrum. Now it's time to come home."

My little tantrum? Holy shit. Red Flag Finn was delusional!

"I'm not going back to Dallas." I crossed my arms over my chest.

"You have to," he insisted. "I miss you."

I glared instead of answering.

"I didn't think you'd move so far away. I don't like it." He paused. "If you come back, I'll get you your job back."

I'm sure he thought he sounded charming, but to me he sounded nasally and whiny.

"I don't give two flying fucks what you like."

"Don't talk to me like that." He stepped closer.

I should've stepped back and created space, like John taught us in the women's self-defense class; instead, I held my ground so Finn wouldn't know I was afraid.

"You need to leave," I ordered, but my voice wavered.

"I'm not leaving until you agree to come home." He reached out and grabbed my wrist.

When I pulled it away and stepped back, I ran into something hard, unyielding, and growling. *Growling?*

Not something. Someone.

Scott. No, Nathan, I corrected myself. I still wasn't used to his name change.

"Is there a problem here?" Nathan said, stepping beside me.

"Mind your own business, freak." Finn wasn't a small guy, but Nathan dwarfed him. "Baby, tell this jerk to go away."

Nathan looked at me, his eyes narrowing when he noticed the bruise forming under my right eye.

Nathan slowly turned back around to face Finn, squared his shoulders, and glared. It was like he was daring him, inviting him to try something. "You have two seconds to walk away." Nathan stepped between us, blocking my view of Finn. "Before you can't."

The chill running through my body was a mixture of fear and lust.

I was afraid of what Nathan might do to Finn, worried Gran would see it, but my traitorous body thought a growling Nathan defending me was sexy as fuck.

Finn hesitated, but only for the second it took for Nathan to step closer. Then he turned and marched back to his car, mumbling the entire time.

Nathan spun on me. "Did he do that to you?" He pointed at my face.

Still shocked he was here, and dealing with my traitorous, horny body, I just stood there blinking at him as my mind raced.

Not happy with my non-answer, he grabbed my chin and barked. "Who did this to you?"

I probably should've been afraid of him and his giant hand tilting my face up, forcing me to look him in the eye, but I wasn't. When I found my voice, I said, "No one. It's nothing. It was an accident." It wasn't a lie, but the expression on his face made it feel like one. *How dare he act like he cares!*

"If he—"

"The stupid cat tripped me, okay? Not that it's any of your business." I went from grateful and turned on to angry in under two minutes.

He stared at me, his eyes roaming across my face and down my arms.

"What is his name?"

"Does it matter?" I spat back with as much sass as I could muster.

He growled through gritted teeth. "Ashley, if you're in danger, I need to know."

Why? What right did he have showing up on my doorstep and butting into my life after ghosting me?

"I'm not. You can go now. Casper." I waited half a heartbeat before turning and stomping back to the house.

He was staring; I could tell from the prickly feeling covering my skin. Fighting the urge to turn around, I ignored him.

After closing and locking the door, I went to the living room and plopped onto Gran's floral couch. Thank God Prince kept Gran busy, and she hadn't looked outside to see the evidence of the train wreck that was my life. She knew about Finn, of course. But I'd never told her about Nathan.

His real name still feels weird on my tongue.

Ten pounds of black fur jumped into my lap. Green eyes stared at me as tears filled mine. Without thinking, I ran my hand down Prince's silky smooth neck and back.

He reached up, placed one paw on each shoulder, and tucked his head under my chin. *Maybe he's not so bad,* I thought as I hugged him back. His purr calmed me as much as the repetitive motion of petting him.

Chapter 10

Nathan

When I pulled up to Ashley's grandmother's house, all I wanted to do was talk. But she was standing on the front lawn arguing with some asshole.

An asshole who needed a lesson in manners. I volunteered, forming a plan to wipe the smug look off his face as I crossed the street.

Ashley wasn't backing down, but her body language telegraphed her fear.

Neither of them noticed me. Never a good sign. If they were that focused on each other, they'd be easy targets if I'd wanted to harm them.

When he grabbed her wrist, Ashley pulled away. *Fuck stealth.* I closed the remaining distance.

I had to bite back the urge to rip the guy a new asshole. With my hands fisted, I stepped beside her. When I saw the bruise, it took every ounce of control I possessed not to kill the guy.

Demonstrating restraint that'd make a saint proud, I kept my hands to myself while I chased the guy away. *He had to be an ex-boyfriend.*

The idea of this guy touching Ashley didn't help my mood.

When I asked what had happened, she said nothing. When I pressed, she gave me a lame-ass excuse, saying a cat tripped her.

All I wanted to do was wrap her in my arms and hold her until her fear subsided. And protect her from every asshole on the planet.

But I had no more right to touch her than the asshole I'd chased away.

Ashley stomped away from me without answering another question. The fruity scent of her shampoo lingered after she walked away, driving me crazy.

Damn it. I didn't like it, but it wouldn't be hard for me to figure out who he was.

At the top of the list of ways to find out: Jamie. His wife was Ashley's best friend.

I talked myself out of and into asking Jamie several times on my drive back to the office. I landed on asking. If he didn't know or wouldn't tell me, I'd find out for myself.

Before knocking on Jamie's door, I took a few deep breaths to calm myself down. So far, my first week at SSI had been less than stellar, and I didn't need to add suspected stalking to the list of reasons they had to doubt hiring me.

"Come in," Jamie said when I rapped my knuckles on his door frame.

"Thanks. You have a minute?" I asked before pushing the door closed.

"Of course, what's up?"

"I went to see Ashley." His eyes widened, but he said nothing. "She was arguing with a guy on the front lawn. He got physical."

Jamie's curiosity shifted to concern, confirming my suspicions.

"My best guess, her ex, Finn. She dumped him before moving back to Weatherford to take care of her grandmother." He coughed up the information without hesitation.

"Finn have a last name?" I planned on having a talk with her asshole ex and telling him to stay away.

Jamie leaned back and crossed his arms over his chest, never taking his eyes off of me.

"Why?"

"So I can tell him to back off," I admitted.

"Did Ashley ask you to talk to him?"

He knew damn well she hadn't. If she had, I'd know his last name.

I shook my head.

"Let me talk to Ashley. If she wants our help, I'll make sure she gets it."

"I think he hit her."

Now on high alert, Jamie leaned forward. "Did she tell you that?"

"I saw the marks. She claims she tripped over a cat, but I don't believe her."

"Prince," Jamie's shoulders relaxed as he laughed.

"Excuse me?"

"The cat's name is Prince. She told Emily, he tripped her earlier today."

"Just because this Finn guy didn't hit her, doesn't mean he's not a threat." I wasn't ready to let it go.

"I'll look into it. If she needs protection, she'll get it." He rested his arms on his desk and clasped his hands. "Like I've said before, Ashley's family."

I bit my tongue and nodded. "Yes, sir." I saw him shake his head as I turned to leave.

Back in my office, which I'd eventually share with Matt, if I didn't get fired before he started, I sat at my mostly empty desk and opened my laptop. Glancing at Matt's desk while it booted up, I sighed. My desk didn't look much different from his. My SSI logo coffee mug was in a different location, and my laptop was open, but other than that, they were identical.

That'll change soon enough. My desk would eventually be covered with files and pens and such once they'd assigned me more jobs.

I continued my research into Ashley York. If I were lucky, I'd find more information on Finn and pay him a little visit. If I spoke to him off the clock, I wouldn't need permission from any Sheppard. One way or another, Finn would know it'd be in his best interest to leave Ashley alone.

I'd done just enough earlier to learn about her current situation and find her address, which wasn't hard. Ashley had posted on social media that she'd moved in with her grandmother in Weatherford. For a woman who had friends in the PI and protection business, she posted stuff on social media that made it easy to stalk her.

Like I was.

Fuck!

Changing my mind about talking to Finn without her knowledge, I slammed my laptop shut. *I won't be that guy.*

Chapter 11

Ashley

When Em invited me to Wednesday night dinner, I didn't hesitate to accept. Gran ate early, so I had plenty of time to clean before heading out.

"Come in," Jack greeted me at Emily's door. Jack answering wasn't unusual. He'd lived here for almost two years before he and Meg moved into their house. The closeness between the brothers made me wish I had a big brother or sister. Someone I'd known my whole life and could share the best news with and trust with my worst secrets.

Then I remembered what it was like for Em with a protective, interfering big brother and amended my wish to having only sisters. *Who am I kidding?* I was greedy and wanted both. A brother to protect me and a sister to scheme with.

Hearing Emily laugh, I thought, I have Em. She'd been around my whole life and was my sister from another mother.

If I wanted a protective big brother, all I had to do was ask. I'd have my pick from the SSI guys.

"Hey Jack. Where's Meg?" I handed him the twelve-pack of beer I'd brought.

"Thanks. She's in the kitchen with Em. Jamie's manning the grill."

This was why I wanted to stay in Weatherford. Hanging out with Emily and Meg, our group growing to include Blake and Cate, was something I'd missed living in Dallas. I'd been traveling back and forth more frequently, choosing to spend time in Weatherford instead of hanging out in bars.

I wanted to spend more time with my friends, whose friendship meant everything to me. And I liked seeing the guys, too. It'd been a long-standing joke that I wanted a protective, supportive, hot guy for myself. But I didn't think I'd find him.

I'd spent my adult life playing the field and had failed at every real relationship I'd tried. I crashed and burned with Nathan, and apparently Finn would continue to haunt me.

"Ashley!" Meg greeted me with a squeal and a hug. Her small baby bump was noticeable between us. When she pulled away, she asked, "Did Prince really cause that?" As expected, I had a bruise around the minor cut just below my eye. I hadn't bothered with makeup to cover it up.

I laughed. There were no secrets in Weatherford.

Which means they'd probably heard about what happened with Finn.

"Little bugger tripped me, and I smacked my face into a door."

"No one's claimed him?" Em asked.

"No, and I'm kind of hoping they don't. He's growing on me."

There was no need to tell them I'd changed my mind after his furry hug calmed me down.

Jamie carried in a tray full of burgers, interrupting the conversation. "Hey, Ash." He said, knowing full well I no longer went by my high school nickname.

"Hey, James." I used his full name in retaliation.

He laughed. "I'm glad you could make it."

"Thanks. My schedule's more open since moving back home."

"Do you miss the fast pace of city life?" Jack asked.

I didn't. I thought I might, but nope.

"Not really. It was fun, but I miss you guys." Emily was the only one who knew I'd lost my job, which meant Jamie knew too. I was okay with that. *Everyone'll know soon enough anyway.*

"I'm glad you're here, even if it's temporary," Meg said. "When can I meet your grandmother? She sounds like a hoot."

"How about this weekend? I'll host a small cookout." Gran would love that. "Gran can show off her new demon cat, Prince."

"I'm open all day Saturday," Jack chimed in. "Jamie?"

"I'm meeting with a potential client in the morning, but I'll be done by noon," Jamie answered.

"Saturday afternoon it is." I clapped my hands. "I'll invite AJ and Blake, too."

AJ and I were still friends, and despite getting off to a rocky start, Blake and I were building our friendship one Craft and Booze night at a time. Blake was smart, sweet, and generous. It was impossible not to like the girl who made AJ embarrassingly happy. And she was shockingly humble for someone worth many millions.

"Should I invite Jay and Cate?" I asked. I wasn't exactly friends with either of them, but we were on friendly terms. And prior to his relationship with Cate, Jay had been fun to flirt with.

"They're working a three-day protection detail this weekend," Meg said.

"And AJ?" I asked, since she knew everyone's schedule.

"He doesn't have anything scheduled yet," she said.

"Cool. I'll message him and Blake later and invite them."

Conversation flowed as we ate, the guys drinking beer, while the girls drank water.

"No beer, Ashley?"

"No, I'm abstaining when I'm with my girls." I raised my glass. Solidarity provided the perfect excuse.

"Aww, thanks," Meg and Em said together.

After dinner, Jamie and Jack cleared the table while Emily brought out dessert.

"That looks good," I said. The glass lid showed off a tall cake, the layers visible where a piece was missing.

"Thanks, it's my first time making it, so I hope it's good," she said shyly. Poor girl still got nervous about disappointing people.

"It's delicious," Jamie said, while giving her a hug from behind.

"You have to say that."

"She has a point. Only an idiot would tell his pregnant wife her cake tasted bad."

Jamie scowled. I gave him my biggest, toothiest smile.

"Emily, if I didn't like it, I wouldn't have snuck a second piece," Jamie said before giving her a peck on the cheek.

I might not know what a healthy relationship felt like, but I knew what it looked like. Two perfect examples sat beside me. Not that they didn't argue. Like all couples, they had issues, but they worked through them.

"So what's in it?" Jack asked, staring at the layers while practically drooling.

"The bottom is a chocolate ganache-covered brownie. The middle layer is vanilla pudding. The top layer is chocolate cake covered in chocolate frosting." Emily's description made my mouth water and my ass expand.

Jamie cut and served slices of Emily's masterpiece. Conversation paused while we all dug in; the only sounds were our happy murmurings around mouthfuls.

"Ashley." Something about the change in Jamie's tone made the hair on my arms stand up. "Nathan said Finn paid you a visit earlier today." His words were casual, but his tone was not.

Because of course Casper said something.

"Yeah, it's no big deal. He wanted to get back together. I told him to go away."

Jamie nodded. Jack listened.

"So he didn't grab you?" Jamie asked.

"Fucking Casper." I wished I could drink. With each passing day, I wanted one night where I could drown my sorrows and have an unhealthy but liberating drunken crying session.

"Don't be mad at him. He's worried about you."

"It's none of his damn business," I said more forcefully than I intended. "I'm sorry. I just wish he'd leave me alone."

"Which one?"

"Both." I sighed. "But mostly Finn." I suspected Nathan would leave me alone if I told him to.

"We can ask him to keep his distance," Jack said.

"No, thanks. I can fight my own battles." I would've kicked him in the balls if Nathan hadn't shown up. Besides, I doubted he'd come back after Nathan embarrassed him. "Sorry for being so bitchy."

It was bad enough my friends were now involved with the disaster that was my hookup with Nathan; I didn't need SSI getting involved with my narcissistic ex-boyfriend too.

"You know we're here to help, no matter what you need," Jack said.

Jamie grabbed Em's hand. "And you know how quickly things can escalate, so please don't hesitate to ask for help if Finn contacts you again."

"I won't. Finn's a douchebag, and a coward."

Wanting to change the subject, I asked Em and Meg about their pregnancies. Not only would it change the subject, but I'd hear what the future might hold for me.

I noticed Jamie and Jack exchange a look. I'd changed the subject, but I could tell they weren't convinced I wasn't hiding something.

Stupid PIs and their ability to see through my lies and false bravado. They couldn't guess my secret—even they weren't that good—but they sensed I was hiding something.

Ignoring them, I focused on Meg and Em, and listened to all the ways my body would change.

If I'm carrying Douchebag's baby.

I calculated my due date based on our last night together. At the latest, I'd be due in March.

Thinking back, it surprised me I'd even let that last night happen. I blamed the shots I'd been doing all night for the stupid decision to sleep with him when I wasn't into him anymore.

It should be illegal to get pregnant accidentally during drunken, boring sex. I'd blame his performance on the shots he'd had, but he was never that good in bed.

"Our babies will be cousins, and so close in age they'll practically be twins."

Meg was due in mid-December, Emily in late February. If I'm pregnant, my kid would be a cousin to theirs in all but name.

I didn't need the Sheppard name to be a part of the family.

"Three months is hardly close enough to be considered twins," Jack said.

"Well, first babies are usually late and twins are often early, so we'll give birth closer than three months apart."

"Wait. What?" My head whipped to face Emily.

Her eyes widened before she looked at Jamie and apologized.

"It's okay. I know you're excited," he said.

"You're having twins? Why didn't you tell me?" Meg asked.

"Yeah, why didn't you tell us?" I added myself to the question.

"Glad it's you," Jack said, clapping Jamie on the shoulder.

Twins ran in Mary's side of the family. If I remembered correctly, her oldest brother had twins.

Lounging in the living room after dinner, I worked up the courage to tell Meg and Jack I'd lost my job.

"That's why I moved back. I'm having trouble finding a job and didn't want to deplete my savings account paying for Gran's nurse." I left out the eviction part, thinking it didn't matter.

"I'm sorry." Meg got up and gave me a hug. "Is there anything we can do to help?"

This is why I loved her. She'd been through hell, and instead of becoming cold and bitter, Meg had a heart of gold and always wanted to help others.

"Only if you know someone looking for a social media marketing expert."

"I thought you took the job at the Wyatt Foundation," Jamie said.

"I did, but it's only part-time. I need a full-time job. You know, benefits, paid vacation, all that jazz." I splayed my fingers and waved my hands around.

"Right."

"I can't believe you're having so much trouble finding a job," Emily said. *Neither can I.*

"Ho-ly shit." I half whispered, remembering something Finn said: if you come back, I can get you your job back. I'd questioned if he was the reason I lost it? But I never would've expected my boss to stoop so low as to fire me because I broke up with his nephew.

I wasn't even mean about it. Though maybe I should've been, since Finn clearly didn't get the message.

"Ashley?" Emily asked.

I shook my head. "Right, sorry. I just remembered something Red Flag Finn said about getting me my job back, and now I'm wondering if he's the reason I lost it."

I explained the situation and told them what he'd said.

"Do you want us to check?"

"No, thanks. It's not in my budget at the moment." I hated having to say those words.

"Don't be stupid. They won't charge you." Emily turned to Jamie. "Will you?"

"Of course not. Research is easy to do off the clock," Jamie answered.

"I'll help too," Jack said.

"You don't need—"

Meg cut me off. "It's not worth the effort. You know how they are." She laughed as she patted Jack's arm.

I did. They were the protective big brothers I'd never had but always wanted.

Chapter 12

Nathan

It took time, but I found Finn's last name and a lot more. Sadly, there was nothing I could use to justify threatening his stupid ass. He had money, but unlike me, he hadn't earned his. Finn worked for his parents, but his job title hadn't existed before he joined the company. He'd had minor run-ins with the law but had never been arrested. I didn't find any evidence suggesting other women had filed harassment complaints or orders of protection against him. His social media pages were full of selfies and humblebrags.

"Another spoiled rich kid," I said to my empty office.

Knowing that made me like him even less.

Guys like him always thought it was fun to torment the poor foster kids who didn't have anyone to help them. I did what I could to protect the smaller, weaker kids, but I didn't gain my height or strength until later and often got my ass kicked.

I'm not a poor, weak orphan anymore. And I'd happily teach the fucker a lesson.

Finn Bentley was an arrogant piece of shit, but not a criminal. But one thing gave me pause. He mentioned Ashley a lot, but not the breakup. Whereas Ashley either hadn't mentioned him at all, or she'd deleted any posts he was in after breaking up with him.

My computer skills were good, but not good enough to retrieve deleted information, so I'd never know for sure, but I suspected she'd deleted them. A quick scan of her friend's list, and his absence from it, supported that suspicion.

What I learned was concerning enough that I wanted to keep a watchful eye on her ex. If he returned to Weatherford and so much as stood too close to Ashley, he'd deal with me.

I slammed my laptop shut. Needing to work off the energy burning me up, I went home, changed, and headed to the hotel gym. Some heavy lifting and a long run should calm me down.

The upscale hotel was temporary while I searched for a house. I didn't need a big one, but I wanted a few acres of land with a barn. I didn't know anything about farming but figured I could learn. I wanted animals—chickens, cows, and maybe a horse. *Maybe I'll plant a small garden.* It'd give me something to focus on during my downtime.

The heat and humidity of August meant I was dripping in sweat before I finished my warmup jog. I didn't mind. I wanted to exhaust myself and melt all thoughts of Ashley from my mind.

I should have known it wouldn't work. The entire run consisted of thoughts of the life we could have together. I pictured us holding hands while we watched the cows frolic. Having a picnic and watching the sunset in our backyard. Picking vegetables together, then cooking dinner we'd eat on our back porch.

I ran my hand down my face. It'd take a hell of a lot more than a few heavy weights and running until my legs shook to erase her from my mind.

Before hopping in the shower, I ordered dinner. My phone rang as I dried off. *How long was I in the shower?* No way had the thirty-five to forty minutes the delivery app said it'd take passed.

The caller ID displayed Jamie Sheppard, so I answered. "Blaszek."

"Hey, you got a minute?"

"Yeah, what's up?" I rubbed the towel over my hair.

"What'd you find when you researched Finn?"

I hit the speaker button on my phone and put it on the bedside table. Laughing, I asked, "Not asking if?"

"Nah, man, I wouldn't have listened either." He chuckled. "As long as you didn't break any rules, we're good."

He understood. *Good to know.* I wrapped the towel around my hips.

"Not much. Based on his social media, he thinks he and Ashley are still a thing."

"Jack said the same thing. I'm putting you on speaker." After a brief pause, he said, "Go ahead."

"He's clean, not squeaky, but clean enough not to raise any red flags."

Jack's laugh caught me off guard.

"What's so funny?"

"Sorry, man, but Ashley literally calls him Red Flag Finn."

"Why?" My question was more of a barked order. Why the hell hadn't they done something before he laid hands on her?

"Damn, dude, you need to calm down. Especially if you want to fix things with Ashley," Jack said.

Great, another Sheppard butting into my private life and telling me what I didn't want to hear.

"There's nothing to fix with Ashley." This time my tone was less aggressive, though no one would call it polite or friendly.

"Okay," Jack said, drawing out the 'o' and clearly not buying what I was selling.

Jamie brought us back to the subject that mattered. "Apparently she broke up with him because he was exhibiting controlling behavior, and, I quote, 'he's a selfish douchebag'."

"Why didn't you look into him earlier?" I growled. If I hadn't shown up today, he could have hurt her. I clenched and unclenched my fists as I thought about pounding the shit out of Finn. His social media posts gave me pause but wouldn't have concerned me without hearing what they'd just told me. But add them together, and Finn could be more dangerous than I thought.

"Because we just found out. That's why we're looking now," Jamie said.

"How'd you find out?" My frustration was obvious from my tone. It didn't matter that I had no right to worry; knowing she might be in danger was killing me.

"Dude, seriously, you need to get a grip," Jack warned.

I ran my hand through my hair, then down my face. My fingers brushing against my scar reminded me how quickly a situation could turn to shit. I had to remind myself the Sheppard's weren't just my bosses; they considered Ashley family and would do everything in their power to help her.

If they'd known, or even thought, he was a threat to her safety, they would've done something.

"I'm sorry. I'm worried she's in danger and doesn't realize it."

"So are we." There was a pause. "It's late, and I'm done listening to you growl. Email us what you found, and we'll discuss it in the morning," Jamie said.

"Right. Sorry. You'll have the email within thirty."

"Thanks. Get some rest," Jamie said.

Jack said goodbye before adding, "And Blaszek, let's leave the caveman attitude at home, yeah?"

"Copy that." They didn't deserve my attitude.

I disconnected the call and opened my laptop. I hadn't finished entering their email addresses when my phone alerted me that my dinner was here.

I chomped into my burger before typing out the email. By the time I finished, my burger was lukewarm and my fries were soggy. Shrugging, I took a bite. *I've eaten worse.*

Chapter 13

Ashley

"Gran I—" A thud from the kitchen interrupted me. "What the hell?"

I raced to the kitchen to see Prince sitting on the counter, licking a paw. On the floor in front of him was my bottle of vanilla creamer, creating a puddle as it spilled out of a crack in the plastic bottle.

"Stupid cat." I grabbed the roll of paper towels and got down on my hands and knees to clean the mess off the brown marbled floor tiles.

I spent extra time to make sure it was clean and dry so Gran wouldn't slip.

After cleaning the cat's mess and finishing my cold breakfast, I left to meet with John, Mary, Blake, and Emily about the Wyatt Foundation.

"Bye Gran. Don't let that cat destroy the house while I'm gone." I half-joked.

"He'd never. He's a good boy." She scratched his head between his ears. "Aren't you?"

Gran and I had drastically different opinions of what defined a good boy. But I wouldn't win any arguments with her, so I left.

During the short drive, I considered the challenges of working as a contractor. Redesigning the foundation's social media sites and making them work seamlessly with the new website would be easy. It was the business part of contracting that'd be hard.

I was grateful for the opportunity to help the foundation grow and eventually help a lot more people, and it'd be fun working with Emily.

I was already thinking of myself as part of the team. *I'd do the work for free if I wasn't struggling.*

I turned onto the main street where Grannie's was located, and the hair on the back of my neck stood up. *I'm being watched.* Only that made zero sense; I was driving. Unless. I glanced in the rearview mirror. Was that the same black car from Gran's street? Were they following me? I should've paid closer attention when I pulled out of the driveway, but then again, why would I? It wasn't like I expected someone to follow me.

I grabbed my phone out of my purse, ready to call 9-1-1. It's probably a coincidence. *No need to overreact.*

"John always says to trust your instincts," I said to no one.

When I pulled into the parking lot across the street from Grannie's, the car kept going.

If they were following me, they would have pulled in too. *Right?*

I convinced myself it was nothing. Using the mirror on my visor, I touched up my lip gloss to buy myself a few seconds and calm my nerves. If I walked into Grannie's nervous, John would notice. He was a former county cop and detective; I'd never be able to fool him. And like his sons, he'd want to help. Technically, they were like him; he'd raised them to be kind, generous, and protective men.

People watching a tennis match turned their heads less than I did as I crossed the street to Grannie's. I felt like an overreacting idiot. Plastering a smile on my face, I opened the door, setting off the bell.

"Morning, Ashley," Mary greeted me.

After a round of hugs, we settled down.

"Are you okay?" Mary asked. I saw John's eyebrow raise before I shifted my focus to Mary.

"Yeah, why?"

"You're fidgeting."

Crap.

"Just excited to join the team," I lied, avoiding eye contact with John.

It occurred to me he'd probably heard all about his new employee and me making a scene here a few days earlier. I didn't think he'd bring it up, but that didn't mean I wasn't nervous he might.

She nodded. "We're happy you're here. Though I'm sorry you lost your job."

"Thanks, I'm sure I'll find something soon." The confidence in my voice shocked me.

"You and Emily should open your own business," Blake suggested.

"Maybe someday." I smiled at Emily.

Blake didn't know we'd just had this conversation, and that the idea was on hold because of Emily's pregnancy.

A problem I might have, too. Though Emily didn't think of her impending motherhood as a problem.

Beth set an iced vanilla latte in front of me. Beth Wyatt was the first recipient of The Wyatt Foundation funds, before it was a foundation. When John and Mary decided to create a foundation, they named it in honor of Beth's late husband, a cop who worked with John and died in the line of duty. Beth was on the board of directors but wouldn't be joining us today.

"Thanks, Beth." If I sipped slowly enough, I might not finish it.

She smiled. "Thanks for helping."

"It's an honor."

"Let's get started," John said.

John and Mary explained what they hoped to achieve and what my role would be in helping them. The foundation was originally just for local recipients in Parker County, but it'd grown so much they wanted to include the adjacent counties this year.

"We're not expanding much this year, but we're adding two scholarships, thanks to Blake." Blake blushed and looked down. She'd donated fifty thousand dollars to fund the scholarships for kids who needed help with college tuition.

"We'd like to include all of Texas next year or the year after, and add more scholarships if we can," John added.

It was ambitious, but given the foundation's growth in three years, I thought the goal was attainable.

Emily'd redesign the website, and I'd update and run their social media accounts. Hearing them say they wanted me to maintain it was a relief; it meant a steady paycheck, even if it was small.

"How many hours a week do you think you'll need?" Mary asked.

She had a Facebook page for Grannie's, but rarely posted. As a local and tourist favorite, customers posted more than she did. SSI had a website, recently updated by Emily, but no social media presence. Which meant that neither John nor Mary understood what it took to grow a business via social media.

Which is why I'm here.

"It depends on how many media sites and what kind of engagement you want, and how fast you want to grow." Steady, focused engagement would grow the foundation faster, but it'd still take time.

Mary looked at John, then at Emily. "We have no idea."

"Why don't you draw up a proposal with the different levels of service, and your rates, and we'll go from there," John suggested.

"When do you want the proposal?" I asked.

Ideas flooded my mind as I thought of different ways I could engage the audience with regular posts, features, livestreams, and recipient followup interviews.

Creating content was easy. It was the business aspect that I'd struggle with. My boss always did that part. *Look on the bright side; it's good experience for when we start our company.*

"If I may?" Blake asked.

"Of course," Mary answered.

"Ashley, can you include market research on which sites would best serve a nonprofit as well?" Blake asked. Fresh out of law school, Blake understood social media better than the Sheppard parents.

"Of course. Do you know your target audience? Having the demographics of your biggest donors would help too."

"I'll send it by the end of the day," Blake answered as she jotted down notes on her yellow legal pad. Blake hadn't been with the foundation long, having only passed the bar a few weeks ago, but it was clear she'd done her homework and was in her element.

"I don't have any more questions," I said as we wrapped up. "When would you like the proposal?" I asked again, because we'd moved off topic before anyone had answered.

"How about a week from today? We'll meet here next Thursday," Mary said. "Does that work for you, John?"

He pulled up the calendar on his phone. "I'm free before eleven."

"Will nine work?" I asked, hoping they wouldn't want to meet earlier. I hated not having a job, but loved sleeping in.

After we agreed, I hugged the girls goodbye.

Mary held me a little tighter than usual and whispered, "I'm here if you want to talk." Of course, she'd noticed I wasn't myself.

"Thank you. I'm fine. Really." I lied.

When I walked out the door that I saw the black car. No, a black car. *You're being paranoid.* There were millions of black cars, so the chances of it being the same one were slim to none.

My nervous system didn't believe me, but a quick look around and I saw four other black cars. I couldn't have picked one from the others in a police lineup.

Forcing myself to walk casually, I made it to my car, tossed my bag onto the passenger seat, and slammed the door behind me. I heard John's voice in my head "Always lock your doors."

I hit the lock button before starting the engine. To avoid the street where I saw the car, I used the exit on the opposite side of the lot.

Not caring if I seemed paranoid, I checked the rearview mirror to make sure no one followed me.

Prince greeted me at the door. "Hey shithead, where's Gran?" I asked as I leaned down to scratch his head. "Please tell me you didn't destroy anything else today."

He swished his tail and trotted down the hall.

"In the kitchen," Gran answered. "You got flowers."

"Who sent them?" I asked, half hoping they were from Nathan.

"There's no note." Bummer, I thought as I entered the kitchen.

What the fuck! Someone sent me black roses in a crystal vase.

Fucking Red Flag Finn. Who else would send me black roses?

I should call Jamie. The roses themselves weren't a big deal, but I wanted an official record if things escalated.

Meg answered on the second ring. "Sheppard and Sons Invest—"

"Hey Meg, it's Ashley."

"Is everything okay?"

"Yes, no. I don't know." I sighed. "Is Jamie available?"

"He's in a meeting."

"What about Jack or AJ?" Really, anyone not named Nathan would do.

"I'll put you through to Jack."

Soft music filled the line while I waited.

"Hey Ashley, what's wrong?"

"Someone sent me black flowers, without a note."

"You think they're from Finn?"

"Probably. Who else would send them?"

"Who delivered them?"

"I don't know. They came while I was at Grannie's. Hold on." I held the phone away from my ear before asking, "Gran, did you talk to the delivery person?"

"No, they knocked on the door, but were gone before I answered. The vase was sitting on the top step."

"Jack?"

"Yeah. I heard. I'll be right over," Jack said.

"I don't think that's necessary."

"I'll see you in a few minutes. Don't touch the vase or the flowers."

Too late. I'd already touched both, so had Gran.

"Do you think they're poisoned?"

Jack chuckled. "You watch too many crime shows, Ashley. I'm hoping we can lift prints."

"Right, right." Probably not poisoned.

"I'll be right there." He hung up.

"If we can't touch them, you can't eat them," I said, pulling Prince off the counter before he could chew on the petals or knock the vase on the floor.

Nathan

Jack and Jamie called me into a meeting after lunch. When I wrapped my knuckles on his door frame, Jaime said, "Come in and close the door."

Jack added, "Have a seat."

This can't be good. I sat and balanced my laptop on my thighs.

"What's up?"

"Ashley called earlier," Jack said. My back stiffened as I leaned forward. I pressed my feet into the floor and held my laptop with a death grip to minimize my reaction.

"She got an unexpected delivery." Jack showed me the pictures he'd taken of the black roses. "I bagged everything. Dad's dusting the vase for prints now."

"Note?" I failed to sound calm.

"None. She wasn't home, and the delivery person was gone by the time her grandmother answered the door."

If it was fucking Finn… Instead of finishing my thought, I asked, "Neighbors see anything?"

"No, and before you ask, I talked to them all."

I nodded.

"What can I do?"

"You've met Finn. We haven't. What's your impression?"

Ashley had dated Finn for several months but had never introduced him to her friends. *Interesting.*

My impression was that Finn was a spoiled, narcissistic brat who needed someone to break his nose, but I couldn't say that.

"He's arrogant and used to getting what he wants. Acted like a tough guy when it was just Ashley but tucked his tail and ran when I challenged him." I left out my less-than-subtle threats.

"Does he strike you as the type to send anonymous black roses?"

"Maybe." Sending anonymous gifts was the behavior of a coward. A way to harass her without repercussions. *Was it dumb luck or by design that they delivered the flowers while Ashley was out?* "I don't know him, but from what I've seen, I wouldn't rule it out."

"Anything in your interaction lead you to believe he'd stalk her?" Jamie asked.

I held eye contact while I considered it. Given what I knew, I had to say yes. Finn struck me as a guy who'd think stalking and harassment were acceptable behavior to get what he wanted. And he wanted Ashley.

Wanting to sound professional, detached, I chose my words carefully. "He wants her back, and I think he'd do just about anything to get what he wants."

"I was afraid you'd say that," Jamie said. "Ashley won't like it, but we should have someone covering the house just in case."

"I can take—"

"I'll do it." I cut Jack off.

"Why aren't I surprised?" Jamie asked. Jack just grinned.

"What? You both have pregnant wives at home, so it only makes sense for me to be the one." My defense fell on deaf ears.

"Sure. You keep telling yourself that. But since we're doing this off the books, it has to be Jack or me."

I failed to hold back the growl in my throat. "Then don't bill my hours," I said, giving them more evidence that I was doing this because of my feelings for Ashley. "My schedule's open, so if you're good with it, I'll leave now."

They shared a look before Jack nodded and Jamie said, "You can go."

"Since we're doing this, you should know her call sign. It's Flirty," Jack said.

"Excuse me?" I barked. "Why does Ashley have a call sign? Has someone threatened her before?" Who did I have to strangle? And who the hell decided on Flirty?

"No. She wanted one when we protected Emily, whose call sign was Snow White. We argued over which dwarf suited her, but she had the last laugh and named herself. I see no reason to change it," Jamie explained.

Knowing she named herself didn't make me feel any better, but knowing she'd never needed their services did.

"Flirty it is." It wasn't my job to like it.

"Before Meg started at SSI, we used boring call signs for clients, if we used them at all. Meg thought using princes-themed names would help lift their spirits while we helped them," Jack answered a question I hadn't asked.

I couldn't argue with her logic.

"Blake hated it." Jack laughed. "She thought it was dehumanizing to use call signs. But everyone else seems to like it."

I nodded, hoping story time was over. "I'll call when I get there."

As I walked out, I heard Jack say, "He's got it bad."

And Jamie's reply. "Let's just hope it's not a problem."

It won't be. I won't let it.

But Jack was right. Despite trying to ignore and deny my feelings, there was no point in lying. I had it bad for Ashley. Maybe I could've ignored my feelings, but the idea of her being in danger made me act like a fucking caveman.

Not that it mattered. She'd never forgive me for standing her up. For hurting her.

I ran my hand down my face, the scar a reminder of all I'd endured. Holding the panic at bay, I grabbed my gear from my office and took off.

Forgiven or not, I can protect her.

And if Finn made the mistake of threatening her again, I'd make sure he lived to regret it. I parked far enough from the house that Ashley couldn't see me, unless she walked outside, but close enough that I could easily close the distance if needed.

Meg and Jack stopped by to drop off a burger and fries, plus a few bottles of water, for dinner. My stomach appreciated the food, and my bladder appreciated the bathroom break.

"I'll be back to relieve you at ten so you can get some rest," Jack said after I gave him my update.

When I opened my mouth to argue, he held up a hand. "Don't."

Knowing he'd never let anything happen, and that I'd be no good to Ashley without at least a few hours of sleep, I nodded. "Thanks for the grub."

"You're welcome." He laughed. "Thanks for not arguing."

Falling asleep wasn't easy, but around midnight, I finally did. Not long after that, the memory-induced nightmares started.

Nightmares that were more memory than dream.

"How'd you find out?" I asked. Tommy and Al were taking turns punching me while I was chained to a chair.

"We spotted the feds at the meetup," Al answered, punching me in the ribs. "So we called it off." Another punch.

"But we didn't leave," Tommy said before punching me in the gut. "We held back and watched the buyer. And wouldn't you know it? He was talking to the feds." He backhanded my face, the hit splitting my lip and his rings slicing my cheek.

My blood stained the cuffs of his pale blue, long-sleeved shirt.

"What's that got to do with me?" I played dumb.

More punches directed at my face and head had me seeing stars.

"We're not done with our story," Al said, punching me in the sternum hard enough to knock the wind out of me. "We waited until the buyer was alone, and we grabbed him."

"He sang like a canary, gave you up to save his hand." Tommy laughed as he landed another punch to my face. The swelling around my eyes made me squint; the blood seeping in tinted everything red.

Al's villainous laugh might've been comical if it hadn't made me sick to my stomach. "I kept my word. He died with both his hands."

The meeting was part of the joint operation between Hawken's and the FBI, but I didn't know who they sent to pose as a buyer. I still didn't know, and it didn't matter. What mattered was getting out alive and taking these two bastards down.

Tommy stepped back and admired their handiwork. "He wasn't as strong as you."

"But you'll break, Nathan. Everyone does," Al said with a sneer, using my first name.

If the buyer had ratted me out, why the games? Why not just kill me?

Fearing the answer didn't stop me from asking, "Didn't the buyer already 'sing like a canary' and tell you everything you wanted to know?"

"He would have, but Tommy was so pissed off when he found out you're the fucking mole he got carried away and killed him after he coughed up your real name," Al said, giving his brother a scathing look. "So now we're asking you. Let's start with a simple question: Who do you work for?"

I wasn't sure who scared me more—Tommy and his volatile temper or Al and his calm sadistic smile.

"Go to hell." My pink spit added more color to Tommy's shirt.

The scene changed in my dream.

I was hanging by my wrists from a meat hook in the ceiling. The metal shackles dug into my flesh, the rough edges shredding my skin anytime I moved. Tommy doused me with water before using an industrial-sized power generator to shock me.

The pain in the dream forced me awake with a jerk. I bolted out of bed and onto my feet, reaching out to protect myself before realizing I was alone in my room. My hand came away wet when I ran it through my hair; sweat covered my body.

The face of my watch lit up when I tapped it. Three-thirty.

I wouldn't be able to fall back asleep, so I drank a glass of water and headed for the bathroom.

The hot shower felt good as it washed away the images of my lingering nightmare. Needing something to do, I cleaned my pistol. The ritual always calmed my mind.

Knowing I needed sleep, I opened the sleep app on my phone and turned on some white noise.

Chapter 15

Ashley

During breakfast Friday morning, Gran droned on about how nice Jack was and how I needed to find a hot—she said handsome, but who says that anymore?—protective man like him. I agreed. I wanted a man like Jack, but didn't think it'd happen. There weren't many single men like Jack left in the world.

It didn't help that I wanted a man like Jack, but chased men like Nathan. I wanted the gentleman but craved the bad boy.

Finn was neither. I meant for him to be nothing more than a short fling, but our fling turned into dating. He wasn't exactly a gentleman, but he was nice.

Typical of the guys I'd dated, his nice demeanor faded after we agreed to be monogamous. And Finn definitely wasn't the bad-boy type. It turned out he was a spoiled, self-centered egomaniac.

The sex wasn't even that good. It didn't suck, but I'd had much better. *Do not think about AJ.* To kill those thoughts, I pictured Nathan. The guy who'd looked like a bad boy and acted like a gentleman. Then disappeared like Casper the Fucking Ghost. Knowing he was working undercover didn't make it better. He should've walked away when I hit on him, not lied to me and led me on. That's what hurt the most.

I could forgive him for something bad happening, causing him to stand me up. But the lying, the games, the pain. I couldn't forgive that so easily.

Needing to work on my proposal, I said. "Why don't you two go watch TV or knit while I work?"

"Okay dear. Come on, Prince, let's give Ashley her space."

Prince meow-yelled at me before following my grandmother to her favorite chair.

I tried working, but couldn't concentrate. My period was late enough to elevate my concern from nervous to worried, and now that I'd accepted the possibility I couldn't stop thinking about it, making it damn near impossible to work on my proposal.

"Gran, I'm going shopping after I meet with Emily. Do you need anything?"

"How about some tuna?" she asked, sounding innocent but looking anything but as she rubbed Prince between his cute, fuzzy black ears.

"Prince has plenty of food. You don't want him to get fat, do you?"

She didn't answer, but he did. I interpreted his long, loud meow to mean he wanted tuna.

"It's okay. She didn't mean it. You're perfect just the way you are." Apparently, Gran thought his meow was because he felt insulted.

I shook my head and laughed. Gran bonded with that cat faster than crazy glue dries on a finger.

Was she really that lonely? Guilt washed over me. *I should've visited more.*

When I left to meet Emily, I glanced in the rearview mirror far more often than necessary. I didn't notice anyone following me, but that didn't stop me from looking around before getting out of my car.

Nothing stood out. *Thank God.* I had enough on my plate and didn't need to add Finn stalking me to it. My sigh was too loud, even in the busy parking lot.

Settled in at Grannie's, Emily showed me her website designs for the Wyatt Foundation. Ideas started flowing about how I could tie the social media accounts to the new site. Together, we'd create the perfect brand for the foundation.

"Did you redesign the logo?" I asked.

"I did. Do you like it?"

I ignored my phone vibrating in my back pocket.

"It's great. It fits the future vision of the foundation," I answered. Emily was great at her job and always went above and beyond for her clients. Sometimes, to the detriment of her health. Like when she'd get so focused on a project she'd forget to eat. No wonder Jamie wanted her to take extra time off.

"Once they approve it, can you send me the graphics?"

"Of course."

I told her my ideas for the socials, and she loved them. They still needed refining, but I was off to a good start. My goal was to finish the proposal early and have Emily critique it for me, so I could put my best foot forward. I didn't want to abuse my friendship with the board members by turning in less than perfect work.

"Em, can I tell you something that you can't tell anyone?" She'd tell Jamie, but he'd keep the secret.

"Of course, is everything okay?" she asked. Her concern was palpable as it took up space between us.

"I'm two months late."

"For what?" Her eyes widened in shock as it clicked. "Oh!"

"Yeah."

"Have you taken a test?"

"No, I'm buying one on the way home."

"Finn?"

"Unfortunately. And before you ask, yes, we used protection."

"Does he know?"

"Hell no. I'm not giving him a reason to come back here."

"You'll have to tell him." She sounded as unhappy about it as I felt.

"I know, and I will. But not until I know for sure." There was no point in telling him until I had taken the test. If it were positive, I'd verify the results with a doctor. Then I'd tell him.

"Are you okay?" I knew she meant with the idea of being pregnant.

"Do I have a choice?" I did. There were ways to change the outcome, but I couldn't bring myself to consider them.

Emily hugged me for a good long time, letting her love and support flow into me. I allowed myself a moment to feel the fear and let the tears fall.

"Thank you." No matter what, she'd have my back. She kissed my cheek when she pulled away.

"I love you, Ash, and I'll be here for whatever you need."

"Love you too, Em. And thanks. God knows I'll need help if I get a positive." I'd need a shoulder to cry on, but no point dwelling on that yet.

Having told Emily, I was eager to take a pregnancy test. So eager that I walked back to my car without worrying about being followed.

Before I buckled my seatbelt, my phone vibrating again reminded me to check my messages. They weren't that different from the last string he'd sent.

> Hey baby. I miss you.

> I know you miss me too, so why aren't you answering me?

> Don't you want your old job back? I know you're still unemployed.

> When did you get a cat? You know I'm allergic.

What the fuck. How does he know about Prince? I made a mental note to tell Jamie and Jack about Finn's messages. *After I take my pregnancy test.*

I peed on the stupid stick, washed my hands and set a timer on my phone. Then I hid the stick in case Gran needed the bathroom before my timer went off. I couldn't wait in the bathroom with nothing to do but stare at the stupid tiny display window.

I wore a path in the beige carpet in the bedroom I grew up in, biting at my thumbnail as I waited. Because I was working so hard on not thinking about the test, my alarm scared me when it went off.

Practically running, I went to the bathroom and locked the door. I stood there with my hand on the cabinet handle, staring in the mirror. I needed to know, but I didn't want to know. Which wasn't entirely true. If I weren't, I wanted to know.

Praying for a dash, not a plus sign, I opened the door and grabbed the stick.

[+]

Fuck. *I'm pregnant.*

Fuck! Tears rolled down my cheeks as I sank to the cold linoleum floor.

This has to be a nightmare. I pinched myself, hoping I'd wake up in Dallas and my old life. What did I do to deserve this?

I wasn't perfect, but I was a good person. How had I earned such bad karma?

Then, the other set of questions started.

How would I pay for all this? Where would I live? I was single, unemployed, had no insurance, and currently lived with my grandmother. What kind of mother would I be?

A bad one.

After throwing myself a pity party, I picked myself up off the floor, wrapped the test stick in tissue and threw it away. Just to be extra safe, I tied off the trash bag and replaced it with a new one. *No point in taking chances.* Gran deserved to be told, not to find out be finding a dirty test stick.

But not yet. I'd tell Gran when I was ready.

I washed my face in cold water to help reduce the red puffiness.

I barely remembered making dinner, but I must have because we ate. Somehow, I got through dinner without my grandmother picking up on my stress. Nah, Gran knew me too well; she chose not to say anything, trusting that I'd talk to her when I was ready.

After cleaning up, I messaged Emily.

Can I come over?

Of course. Want dinner?

No, I ate with Gran. Thanks.

Emily took one look at me when she answered the door and understood. Pulling me into a hug, she said, "I'm so sorry, Ashley. I know this isn't what you want." One hand rubbed my back while the other held me tight, providing the comfort I needed.

"I want it, just not with Finn, and not when I'm unemployed, single, and living with my grandmother." My laugh sounded manic.

"You have the Wyatt job."

"You know what I mean. Contract work is fine, but it won't pay for an apartment or doctor's visits." Or the expenses of raising a child. I groaned at the thought.

"Come sit. Jamie's making us tea."

"Did you tell him?"

"No, I figured this was a secret he'd be okay with me keeping."

I hugged her. "Thanks. Now that I know for sure, I guess you can tell him."

"At least we'll have our babies together." Emily tried to add a positive perspective.

"That's the only positive part. Our kids will grow up like brothers."

"Your what?" Jamie asked, shock evident in his voice.

My eyes rounded. So did Emily's. "I, um, turns out I'm pregnant too," I stuttered.

"Is this a congrats or an I'm sorry kind of announcement?" Typical Jamie, wanting to give me what I needed, despite looking lost and confused.

Definitely a sympathy announcement. "I didn't plan it, and it's Finn's." Just the thought of having his baby made my stomach turn.

"How about I give you a supportive hug and not say anything?" Jamie asked.

I stood and let him hug me.

"We'll do whatever we can to help," he whispered before breaking the hug.

"Thanks."

"Did you tell Gran?" Emily asked.

"Don't make me think about it." She wasn't a prude or overly judgmental, but she'd worry about me.

"You'll tell her when you're ready," Emily said.

"Is there anything I can do right now to help?" Jamie asked.

When I shook my head no, he left us alone.

"He won't tell anyone," Emily said, wrapping her arm around my shoulders.

"I know. This is just... It's too much."

For the second time, I broke down and cried.

When I was all cried out, I used half a box of tissues to clean tears and snot off my face.

Thankfully, the lemon tea tasted almost as good cold as it would have hot. I didn't have the energy to warm it up, and with my luck my trembling hands would spill it when I tried to take a sip, and I'd get burned.

"Thanks." A million problems occupied my mind, but I was too exhausted to sort through the clutter.

"Of course," she said. "How far along are you? Has morning sickness started yet?"

"About six weeks, maybe. And no, thank God." Emily's morning sickness wasn't too bad, but poor Meg had it morning, noon, and night. Jack was beyond sweet, taking care of her and making sure she had what she needed. Jamie would take care of Emily the same way, if she needed it.

Who'll take care of me?

Certainly not Finn. I'd have to do this alone. My hand instinctively went to my belly, ready to protect the new life growing inside me.

Chapter 16

Nathan

Unable to sleep, I relieved Jack early Saturday morning. I'd just finished a protein bar when Jamie called to tell me I'd have the afternoon off because he, Jack, and AJ would be at Ashley's. Along with their girls, as they liked to call their significant others. Certain he'd chosen video chat to watch my reactions, I put extra effort into maintaining a neutral expression.

Jamie volunteered the reason when I didn't ask; Ashley was hosting a small gathering. I wasn't invited. Was that why she'd visited them, to plan the party?

No, she'd looked upset when she left. Enough so that she didn't see me when she walked to the car or notice me following her.

"Is Ashley okay?" I asked. "She looked upset driving to your house last night." Ashley had spent several hours at Jamie's. Which I only knew because I'd parked outside until she left.

He raised an eyebrow.

"What, did you think I'd let her drive around without protection?"

"No, but your assignment is to watch the house."

"My priority is Ashley." My tone was rough; my expression, rougher. My actions weren't earning me any brownie points.

"Good," he said, with a nod. *Or maybe they are.* "Ashley came to visit Emily. I wasn't privy to their conversation."

"Did she seem upset when she arrived?" I asked, hoping he'd share at least a little, knowing I wanted to keep her safe.

Jamie leaned forward, rested his elbows on his desk, and clasped his hands together. "Nathan, Ashley's a friend, and I won't betray her trust."

I nodded. I appreciated his loyalty but was frustrated by the lack of information.

"We have a quick job for you this afternoon."

Hating the idea of leaving Ashley, I ground my back teeth together before asking for the details. The job was an easy security detail, assisting another company, which was low on manpower. I'd be filling in for Eric, who got called into work. Like the other part-time employees at the company, he was a local cop. He'd recently been promoted, and this was his last week at SSI.

"I need to know you can stay focused."

That hurt. I was a US Navy SEAL; getting the job done, no matter what, was part of who I was. Losing focus wasn't an option. Quitting wasn't an option. Failing wasn't an option.

Except I'd lost focus in Vegas and failed. No, even if I hadn't met Ashley, my fate was sealed when the undercover agent ratted me out.

Squaring my shoulders, I answered the only way I could. "Yes, sir."

"Good. I'll text the details."

"Call me when you leave Ashley's," I ordered. Then I added "please" so I wouldn't sound like a total jerk.

I'm really not a bad guy. A little rough around the edges maybe, but I wasn't usually an asshole.

He shook his head. "Only because you said please." Jamie paused, his hazel eyes honing in on mine.

I forced my tone to be less confrontational when I asked, "What?"

"Figure your shit out. It's obvious you care about Ashley, but we won't tolerate your attitude."

I had a feeling the only reason they hadn't fired me was because my attitude stemmed from my feelings for Ashley.

"Yes, sir."

So much for my fresh start.

Get your head on straight, Blaze

Blaze was the man I'd worked my ass off to be. The man I wanted to be again. The man I'd lost touch with in Vegas.

The man I can be again.

My job was to guard the entrance to a swanky party and make sure no one without proper identification entered the venue. The hardest part was ignoring the picture-perfect people in their expensive three-piece suits and floor-length gowns, staring at my scar and whispering behind their hands.

I wondered if I'd ever get used to that reaction. The four-hour detail was uneventful; always a good outcome in our line of work.

Not bothering to wait for Jamie's call, I parked outside Ashley's. Something about the flower situation felt hinky, but I couldn't put my finger on it. Finn struck me as the type to harass someone because he felt entitled to their attention, but playing games didn't seem like his style.

I figured him to be the type of guy who'd want credit for his deeds.

Unless the black roses were a message only Ashley would understand.

No, she would've told Jack, and we'd all feel more confident in our assumption that Finn had sent them.

Was Finn unhinged enough to hire someone to terrorize her? Was his plan to scare her, then swoop in and play the hero?

Not knowing his motive made me nervous. Because I trusted my gut, I refused to ignore it. Consequences be damned.

Her ex could escalate without warning, and while I trusted the Sheppards to protect Ashley, I still needed to be here. How much trouble could I get into? I was off the clock. Besides, it couldn't hurt to have an extra layer of protection.

Good thing too, I thought, staring at the black sedan with dark tinted windows parked down the street. The tint on the windows prevented me from seeing any identifying features.

Except for the license plate, which I wrote down and sent to Doug, asking him to look it up when he had a chance.

When I rolled down my window, I heard laughter from the backyard, just before a chorus of voices yelled, "Gran!" followed by more laughter.

Once again, an emotion that felt a lot like jealousy flowed through my system.

Knowing it was a bad idea to call attention to my presence, but wanting to warn the guys, I texted Jamie, Jack, and AJ.

They must've held a mini-meeting because it took forever for me to get a response. A response in the form of Jack walking to my truck two minutes after the suspicious sedan drove off.

Jack put his hand on the roof and casually glanced around. "Where is it?"

I nodded my head in the direction the car had been. "It's gone."

"Any reason to suspect it's a foe, not a friend?"

"My gut." He smiled but didn't say anything. "The same car was here when Finn was. The dark tinted windows made it stand out."

He nodded. "You get the license plate?"

Holding back my wiseass remark about knowing how to do my job, I said, "Yes."

"Any chance you're going back to the office to run it?"

"No. I sent it to Doug." I hated knowing I might not hear back until morning, but I couldn't justify pulling him away from his family.

"You know you don't need to stay, right?"

"I know." How could I explain my need to Jack when I couldn't explain it to myself?

Liar. You know why; you just won't let yourself accept it because you know you can't act on it.

He looked around again. "If you insist on staying, you might as well join us."

"That's not a good idea. Ashley doesn't know I'm here."

He raised an eyebrow, the same expression I'd seen on Jamie's face.

"She knows."

Of course, they'd told her. "Right. It doesn't change the fact that she doesn't want me here."

"But you're not leaving?"

"No, I'll cover the front. Go, have fun."

He shook his head, clearly confused by my actions. Or maybe not. Given his fierce protectiveness of Meg, he'd understand my desire to protect Ashley.

Just because she didn't trust me didn't negate my feelings. Keeping Ashley safe, even if she wouldn't acknowledge the threat, was the least I could do.

"Suit yourself. You know where we are if you change your mind."

Jack wasn't gone more than a few minutes before Ashley walked out the front door and marched over to my truck.

"What the fuck, Casper. You just going to sit here staring at the house like a fucking creeper?" The sexy flush on her cheeks had me thinking with the wrong head.

"I'm not staring." *Lame response, Blaze.*

She rolled her eyes so hard her lashes created a breeze.

"Look, I don't want you here, but Jack said you won't leave."

Once again, I appreciated their loyalty to Ashley but hated that it was at the expense of their loyalty to me.

Who am I kidding? They have no loyalty to me. I'm an employee. And a pain-in-the-ass one at that.

"I'm here to make sure you're safe." In addition to the three armed, trained professionals in her backyard.

"Like you care." She huffed as she crossed her arms over her perfect sun-kissed chest.

For two heartbeats, the world ceased to exist as we stared at each other. Pain and frustration were evident in her eyes. Desire and determination in mine. At least that's what I felt.

I wanted to tell her I cared, that I couldn't stop thinking about her. But I didn't know how to do it without creating a bigger mess.

I couldn't, at least not here.

Wanting to give her the staring contest win, I looked down.

Long seconds passed as I sensed her staring at me. When I finally looked back up, I caught her staring at my scar and confirmed my suspicions.

Sympathy had replaced the pain and frustration in her eyes.

Fuck that. I didn't want or need her sympathy. Before I could say anything, someone called Ashley's name.

An older woman using a walker for support walked out the door.

"I'll be right there, Gran," Ashley called over her shoulder.

Her grandmother kept right on walking.

"Gran, you can wait—"

Her grandmother cut her off. "Nonsense. I'll be right there."

Ashley sighed. "Just go. Please," she begged before walking away.

Her pained, pleading voice almost destroyed me, but I didn't have time to act.

"Ashley Nicole York, you walk right back over there and introduce me to the young man everyone's talking about."

Great.

As Gran, as Ashley called her, walked towards my truck, I couldn't help but notice how much she and Ashley looked alike. It was like getting a glimpse of the future. A future I'd never see.

I'd crossed too many lines; my time here was limited. *Sorry Kroupa.* His reference wouldn't mean shit at SSI after I crashed and burned. He'd given me a glowing recommendation, and I wasn't living up to it.

But I could. I just needed to stop fucking up and clear things up with Ashley. I'd have to settle for polite acquaintanceship, or maybe friendship, if I wanted to stay in Weatherford.

I'd have to decide whether staying here would be worth the pain of seeing Ashley knowing I could never have her.

I looked in the mirror and adjusted my ball cap before stepping out of my truck. There was only one way to meet the elder York—with respect. Respect I couldn't give sitting behind the wheel.

"My, my, aren't you a tall one?" Gran said as she stopped in front of me.

I chuckled as I removed my cap. "I'm Nathan. It's nice to meet you, ma'am."

"Oh, don't give me any of that ma'am crap."

"Yes, ma'am, Mrs…" Was she a York too?

"Violet York. Ashley's daddy was my son."

I remembered Ashley telling me her parents had died when she was young, and how her grandmother raised her.

"It's nice to meet you, Mrs. York," I said, holding out my hand.

She shook it. "Everyone calls me Gran."

I nodded. No way in hell would I incur the wrath of Ashley by calling her grandmother, Gran. Looking over Gran's shoulder, Ashley's scowl confirmed I'd made the right call.

"Come join us. We have beer and plenty of food," Gran offered.

"Thank you, but I'm work—"

She cut me off. "Working? Here? Why?" She might be using a walker, but her mind was sharp. Her stare felt like she was trying to penetrate my mind with her eyes.

Shit. I'd dealt with a lot of unexpected situations in my life, many of them dangerous, but none had felt as dangerous as this conversation.

"He needed to report in after finishing a job, right, Nathan?"

"Right." I nodded, grateful for Ashley's quick thinking because I felt like a deer in the headlights under her grandmother's watchful eyes.

Terrorists with rifles in the Middle East, no problem.

Little old lady using a walker in Weatherford, scared stupid.

"Well, you can just march your handsome self to the backyard and report to the boys in person." It was easy to see where Ashley got her feisty attitude.

I couldn't very well say no to Mrs. York, but accepting meant pissing off Ashley. It was a lose-lose situation for me.

Fuck my life. I erred on the side of not pissing off Ashley's grandmother.

"Yes, ma'am, Mrs. York," I corrected myself.

All sass disappeared once I agreed. "Ashley, be a dear and go inside and fetch me more iced tea."

If she'd had the ability, Ashley would have shot daggers out of her eyes and shredded me to pieces. "Yes, Gran," she said before walking away.

"Now, Nathan, be a gentleman and help an old lady cross the street."

Wanting to keep all my body parts, I didn't remind her that she hadn't needed my help the first time she'd crossed.

"Look, everyone," Mrs. York announced as we walked through the gate to the backyard. "Nathan decided to join us." She said it as if I'd had a choice.

Surprised faces turned to see me holding the fence gate for Ashley's grandmother. I took my time making sure it latched as I closed it.

"Glad you could join us, Blaszek," Jack said, a shit-eating grin on his face.

AJ raised his beer. "Welcome to the party."

Jamie handed me an open, cold bottle of beer. "Sorry, she overheard me telling Ashley."

"Don't worry about it." I couldn't blame him for telling Ashley, or for her grandmother overhearing. I tapped my bottle against his. "Thanks."

"She's a force to be reckoned with," Jamie said.

That she was. Watching Ashley's grandmother in action was like getting a glimpse of the future Ashley. A future I was disappointed I wouldn't get to witness.

"If you're hungry, we have burgers, hot dogs, Meg's bacon mac and cheese, salad, and snacks."

Too unsettled to eat, I passed.

As we sat around the backyard talking, I kept to myself. Observing the people I worked with, and their families, as the conversation flowed. I envied the easygoing relationship they shared. Even Blake, the newest member of the group, seemed to fit in.

Not like me. They didn't exclude me from the conversation, but that didn't mean I felt like part of the group.

My eyes refused to stray from Ashley for longer than a few minutes. Even as I listened to the others, I found myself turning back to watch her.

A neon sign flashing over my head would have been more subtle.

There was sadness in her eyes, easily overlooked as she played the perfect hostess. She joked and laughed at the right times and added her own sassy or sarcastic comments often enough that no one seemed to notice.

Except me.

But I couldn't say anything. *I'm part of the problem.* I still had a lingering feeling there was more to her sadness, but if I brought it up, it'd cause a scene, piss her off, and ruin the evening.

Chapter 17

Ashley

If not for Gran, the day would've been the perfect distraction I needed. But the instant she laid eyes on Nathan, she fell for him.

Him and his gravelly 'yes, ma'am'. The fact that his voice sent tingles straight to my core pissed me off almost as much as him sitting in his big black truck staring at my house.

The only thing I wasn't mad at him for was accepting Gran's invitation. He never stood a chance; Gran always got what she wanted.

He sat with us but didn't talk except to answer questions.

He accepted a beer but barely drank it.

He stared at me as if he were trying to read my mind or see into my soul.

"So, Nathan," I said after catching him staring again. "What'd you do before joining SSI? Let me guess." I tapped my finger on my chin as if I were thinking. "Oh, I know, I bet you were an accountant."

Irritation flashed across Nathan's eyes, his lips pressing into a thin line, as I finished.

"I was a Navy SEAL." His answer was a convenient half-truth, because of course it was. Something I knew, because Maxwell told me that both the new guys starting at SSI this summer were former Navy SEALs.

"Is there a Navy base in Vegas?" I asked, all innocence. Everyone except Gran, who was enthralled with Nathan, looked uncomfortable.

"No."

It was my turn to squint my eyes at him. "How long have you been out of the Navy?"

"Ashley." There was a warning in Jamie's tone.

"What?" I batted my eyelashes, laying my innocence on thick. Not that it fooled anyone. Everyone except Gran knew he was the guy who ghosted me in Vegas. "I'm just curious about your new guy."

AJ turned to Nathan. "So you're Casper," he said, like he'd just put two and two together.

Blake smacked AJ on the arm. Gran tilted her head in confusion.

Nathan's eyes rounded and his mouth opened before he snapped his lips closed and clenched his teeth.

The rest of my friends hid their laughs behind their hands.

AJ looked at me, saw my shut-the-fuck-up look and said, "My bad, I must have confused you with someone else."

"Hard to confuse this ugly mug with anyone else." Defeat, or maybe sadness, crossed Nathan's eyes. He looked at me and answered, "I've been out two years."

He held my gaze, challenging me to keep playing the game. So far, he'd answered my questions, but how far could I go? How far did I want to go?

Gran watched the back and forth with a wicked grin on her face. *Not very far.* I didn't want Gran finding out about Vegas.

"Dear, you're not ugly." Gran leaned over and patted his thigh.

A thigh she could have bounced a quarter off. A thigh I'd dreamt about more than once. *NOPE.* Not going there.

"You're just a little rough around the edges," Gran added, with a loving smile.

Nathan's Adam's apple bobbed up and down as he swallowed. He blinked a few times before saying, "Thank you."

Did he really think he was ugly? Sure, he had a gnarly scar on the left side of his face, but it didn't detract from his good looks. It did, however, add to his mystery and bad-boy sex appeal.

His scar wasn't the only new thing since Vegas. The version of Nathan I met, when he called himself Scott, oozed confidence. The man sitting here tonight didn't.

Nathan met my eyes, turning his head just enough so the scar I'd been staring at was no longer visible. I tried to imagine how I'd feel if my face were scarred. Awful. Hideous. Unlovable. But I could hide it with makeup.

"Any more questions, Ms. York?" He asked, his tone formal, flat, cold. Like he didn't give two fucks about me or the pain he'd caused.

Way to kill my sympathy, asshole.

"No, Scott, none." His eyes rounded again at the use of his fake name.

I cursed myself when Gran asked, "I thought your name was Nathan?"

"Scott is my middle name."

And the only name he'd given me in Vegas. Nathan told me he was undercover, but he shouldn't have lied to me. If lying was his only option, he should've left me alone.

"Oh. What's your last name, dear?" Gran asked.

His eyes never left mine, as if he thought maybe I'd forgotten it. "Blaszek, Nathan Scott Blaszek."

"That's a good strong name, don't you think, Ashley?" she asked, all smiles.

"I don't know; it sounds fishy to me," I answered.

"Pay her no mind, Nathan; judging from the way she's looking at you, she thinks it's a fine name."

Laughter erupted as I yelled, "GRAN!"

Gran had diffused the situation, but Nathan wasn't laughing. Neither was I.

"Thank you for an interesting evening, but I should go." Nathan stood and reached down to shake Gran's hand.

She stood, with his help, and hugged him. The shock on his face was priceless. Almost worth the humiliation I'd just suffered. *Almost.*

"I hope to see you again soon," Gran said. "Ashley, be a good hostess and walk our guest out."

She was bound and determined to put Nathan and me together. I didn't want to, but I couldn't say no. "Okay." I stood and went out of my way to avoid looking at my friends, knowing I couldn't handle seeing their amused expressions.

They'd never seen this side of me. The good girl who followed orders and doted on her grandmother.

I'll hear about this sixfold as soon as Gran goes to bed.

I escorted our guest to his truck. As soon as we exited the gate, he scanned left and right, like he were searching for someone. No, I recognized the act. He wasn't searching for someone; he was checking for threats.

"What are you doing?" I hid my fear by feigning annoyance. His overbearing reaction seemed a bit much for a vase full of flowers.

"What?" he asked, looking down at me.

"Never mind." I sighed. "Just go."

He stopped on the sidewalk, turned to me, and said, "Ashley, I've already apologized for lying. I didn't like doing it, but I had to."

"No one has to lie. And you certainly didn't need to play games with me." I crossed my arms over my chest and tilted my head back to glare at him.

Emotions swirled behind his eyes; the predominant one was sadness.

"Why'd you tell me you were an accountant?"

"I didn't." I didn't need to call him out; my expression did it for me. "Ashley, I never told you I was an accountant. You assumed, and I didn't correct you."

I stepped closer and poked his solid chest. "Not correcting me is the same as lying."

"Fine. I lied." His voice was low but forceful. "But what was I supposed to say? I know I told you my name is Scott, but it's only an alias while I work with the FBI to take down weapon-smuggling terrorists?" He slammed his mouth shut. He glanced around again, this time seeming more nervous than watchful.

FBI? Weapon smuggling terrorists?

A million and one thoughts rapid-fired through my mind, the intensity causing me to sway on my feet.

When I didn't answer, because I couldn't get my mind to stop spinning, Nathan reached out to steady me.

"I planned on coming clean, as much as I safely could, at dinner, but," his eyes lost focus for a second. He swallowed hard before finishing, "Things happened, and I couldn't make it."

When I'd hit on the sexy, mysterious guy at the bar, all I wanted was a one-night stand. But the instant our gazes connected, I'd felt a connection. When we talked, there was no awkwardness; it felt like old friends reconnecting. When the bar music interfered with our conversation, we went back to my room. Surprisingly, we didn't sleep together, though we made out like horny teenagers before he got a call and had to leave.

I was more than a little disappointed my one-night stand ended without the orgasms I'd anticipated. I won't admit to wearing out the batteries in my adult toys that night thinking about Scott.

"What happened, Nathan?" I asked, my voice soft and calm as my eyes drifted to his scar.

He didn't miss the movement. "Cliff note version, my cover was blown, and this happened." He pointed at his face before running his hand through his hair.

Was I the reason his cover was blown?

Wanting to see him again, I'd gone back to the bar hoping he'd be there, but not expecting it. I remember stopping and staring at his back when I saw him on the same bar stool. It felt like fate. When he admitted he was glad I'd come back, I thought I was staring in a fucking romance novel. When he asked me out to dinner, I half expected our story to end with a happily ever after.

Only my Prince Charming ghosted me.

Not because he wanted to, but because he had to.

"Was it because of me?" My words were barely audible as guilt weighed me down.

He reached out and took my hand. Nathan didn't speak until I made eye contact again. "No. It wasn't because of you."

My ability to speak had taken a vacation, so I nodded instead. Then I stared at my hands, still in his. He squeezed them, but I still couldn't meet his eyes, so I lowered my head and stared at the ground between our feet.

"Ashley, look at me," Nathan ordered.

Obeying wasn't an option. I shifted my focus from the ground to his black boots, to his muscular legs and what I assumed were six-pack abs, and then finally to his eyes.

"It wasn't your fault." His voice was thick with emotion.

I freed a hand from his and reached for his face. He flinched but didn't back away.

"This is why you stood me up?"

The scar felt rough under my fingertips. Nathan closed his eyes before saying, "Yes."

With a sigh, he leaned into my touch.

"I'm so sorry." My apology was inadequate. I'd been a total bitch, never giving him a chance to explain. And he took it, never once calling me out for it.

"Why didn't you tell me?"

"I…" He looked around, nodded towards the gate, directing my attention to Gran. "Not like this. Can we meet tomorrow?"

I nodded. "How about breakfast at Grannie's?" I suggested, wanting to avoid any meal or restaurant that served alcohol. Nathan frowned but nodded.

"Eight?"

I'd get to bed late after cleaning up, and I wanted to have breakfast with Gran. "No need to be crazy. Let's meet at nine."

"Nine."

"And Nathan."

"Yes?"

"No more secrets." I said. Knowing I was keeping a pretty big one myself, guilt settled in my gut. But I hadn't confirmed the results, so I felt justified.

"No more secrets," he agreed.

Gran was all smiles when I returned to the backyard. "You found yourself a good one. Nathan is so much better than schmuck-face Finn."

Laughter filled the space.

"You weren't kidding," Jamie said to Emily.

"Nope, I told you she gets it from her grandmother."

"Damn straight she does. I taught her everything she knows." Gran glowed with pride. "Now you kids have fun and don't do anything I wouldn't do." She laughed and said her goodbyes.

I laughed too; it wasn't much of a restriction. In her heyday, there wasn't much Gran wouldn't do.

I settled back onto Gran's comfortable patio couch and pretended the awkward silence wasn't happening.

Emily and Meg stood up and rushed over to plop down next to me.

"Come on, we're dying to know what happened," Meg said.

"Did you talk? Did he tell you why he stood you up?" Emily asked.

I turned my head between them as they fired off more questions.

"Do you like him?" Meg asked.

"Will you give him another chance?" Emily asked.

"Give her a chance to answer," Jack interjected.

Emily and Meg looked at him and stuck out their tongues, making everyone laugh.

"We talked. I know something bad happened." I paused. "We're meeting for coffee tomorrow." My answers fell short of their expectations, but there was nothing more to tell. Hell, Jamie and Jack probably knew more than I did.

When it came time to say goodbye, AJ pulled me aside.

"You don't seem like yourself. Are you doing okay?"

Of course he noticed. Everyone else probably had too, but AJ had zero qualms about asking bluntly.

"Yeah, just shocked by Nathan's sudden appearance after a year."

He squinted, staring deep into my eyes. "Is that all? You seemed off before he arrived."

Direct, caring, and still gorgeous. AJ hadn't changed much since we'd hooked up. Except now, he was madly, sickeningly in love with Blake.

We were great together, but weren't meant to be more than friends with benefits. Blake was perfect for him. She soothed the demons of his past, and I loved her for it.

"I'm good, big guy, thanks for checking." I hugged him goodbye.

Before he released me, he said, "Call if you need anything. Okay?"

I fought back the tears threatening to spill over. I blamed the hormones but couldn't tell him that. AJ went from lover to protective big brother when he met Blake, and much to my surprise, I didn't mind.

Chapter 18

Nathan

I didn't recognize anyone behind the counter when I walked into Grannie's Sunday morning. Which was a good thing. I wasn't ready to face Mary or Beth after my last visit. Hopefully, today would be more civil, so I wouldn't owe Mary yet another apology. *Maybe I should've suggested somewhere else.*

It was too late. Ashley would be here any minute. Besides, I wanted her to feel safe and comfortable when we talked. I ordered a large black coffee, a large vanilla latte for Ashley, plus a couple of pastries.

Then I stared at the black and white pictures on the wall and waited.

Seeing the bags under Ashley's eyes when she walked in made my heart ache. She wasn't just tired; she'd been crying. Once again, the sinking feeling in my gut screamed she was hiding something. I was willing to listen and help any way I could, but she still didn't trust me.

Not that I blamed her. From her perspective, I was the jerk who lied and led her on before ghosting her.

Ghosting her wasn't by choice, and she seemed to finally understand that.

"Hi, Nina." She waved to the barista.

"Hi, Ashley. You want a decaf again today?" The college-aged girl behind the counter asked.

She glanced at me. *Interesting*. Her red-rimmed eyes opened wide while a blush crept up her cheeks. Like she'd been caught with her hand in the cookie jar. *What the hell is that all about?*

I pointed at the second cup on the table.

"I'm good, thanks." I stood as she approached the table. "Hi," she said.

"Hi. I got you a vanilla latte. I hope that's okay."

A sad look crossed her face as she glanced at the cup. Her big fake smile didn't match her soft tone. "Thank you."

Something was definitely going on, but it wasn't my place to ask. At least, not yet. First, I had to repair the damage I'd done a year ago. Then, maybe I'd have the right to stick my nose in her business.

Ashley took a small sip, closing her eyes as she savored it. When she licked the foam off her upper lip, I had to tell my body to stop reacting. Thank God for the table, because my body ignored my command. I'd been dreaming of Ashley in my bed for a year, and now that she was flesh and blood again, my body was eager for the dreams to become a reality.

"What?" she asked, her voice laced with impatience.

"Nothing." I cleared my throat. "I'm just glad you're enjoying your coffee."

Her irritation fled as understanding dawned. She looked away, but not before a hint of desire flashed in her eyes.

"Why'd you let me believe you were an accountant?"

She's skipping the small talk. Good to know.

I took a deep breath to steady my nerves and reminded myself I'd faced far worse than a pissed-off woman and survived.

"Honestly—"

She cut me off. "No, please lie to me again."

After last night, I'd expected her to be less angry, but this morning Ashley seemed determined to stay mad, making apologizing a challenge.

"It was easier than making up a different lie."

"Seriously?"

"Yes. Like I said, I was deep undercover and couldn't tell you the truth."

Ashley sat back and crossed her arms over her chest. Several emotions—frustration, understanding, sadness—warred for dominance.

Frustration won.

"Then why'd you hook up with me?"

"If I remember correctly, you hit on me."

My attempt at humor missed the mark. Her expression was definitely anger this time. My instincts screamed at me to retreat.

Before I could apologize, she grumbled, "You didn't have to flirt back."

She was right; I didn't. And I shouldn't have.

"You're right, but only an idiot would ignore a gorgeous woman hitting on him."

"You're an idiot for making me believe we had something special."

"I am." But I couldn't bring myself to regret it. "We did. Why do you think I asked you out?"

"How should I know? Maybe it was all a game, and you got a thrill standing women up."

A game? It'd never been a game for me. Even when I picked up random women, I acted with respect.

"Ashley." I missed the carefree side she'd displayed when she walked up to me, a man lost deep in thought and scowling at his beer, and dropped a cheesy pickup line like she owned the world.

"It wasn't a game. You have no idea how badly I wanted you." *Still do.* "Wanted us." I'd wanted it since our first kiss, but forced myself to walk away. The second night, my strength failed me.

"You didn't ask for my number."

"No, and I couldn't give you mine." I admitted, knowing it'd start a new argument.

"Why the hell not? I assume you had two."

I did, but one was in a locker along with my real ID, credit cards, a stack of cash, and a gun. In case I needed to make a fast getaway. It'd come in handy after I killed the Perpura Brothers.

"Ashley, I understand how difficult this is for you to accept." I paused as she made a face, giving her time to follow it up with a snarky comment.

She didn't disappoint. "Don't patronize me." She leaned back and crossed her arms over her chest. Her body said, I'm pissed. Her eyes said, I'm sad. I addressed the sadness, knowing the windows to her soul displayed the deepest emotion.

"I'm not." I tried a different tactic. "Are you familiar with Black Op groups?"

"Only what I've read in books."

So, probably nothing real. "What do you know?"

Her stare gave me the impression she wanted to punch me for asking.

"Humor me. Please?"

"They exist in the shadows, sometimes they do bad stuff for the right reasons, and no one is supposed to know about them," she finally answered.

I nodded. She wasn't far off. "When we met, I was deep undercover for a civilian black ops company. When I became Scott Miller for the op, Nathan ceased to exist. My survival depended on it, and it protected the people I cared about."

She looked at my scar before reaching forward and grabbing her coffee. She held the tall paper cup under her nose, inhaling deeply before taking a sip.

Waiting out her obvious delay tactics while maintaining eye contact wasn't easy, but I reminded myself that if I could go a week without sleep, I could wait another minute for Ashley to speak.

"Tell me about it."

I'd get to that, but first, I circled back to her previous statement. "I couldn't risk carrying Nathan's phone." God, it felt weird talking about myself in the third person. "It was in a locker with some other stuff I'd stashed, in case of an emergency."

I could see her thinking as she played with the cardboard sleeve on her cup while she processed the extremity of my circumstances. Finally, she nodded, seeming to accept how complex the situation was.

"I had no right getting involved with you. It was stupid."

"What the fuck does that mean? You think talking to me was stupid?"

How could one man fuck up so badly while trying so hard?

"No, no. That's not what I meant." I ran my hand down my face as anxiety started rearing its ugly head. "Talking to you, meeting you, was the best thing that happened to me in a long time."

"You're not making any sense."

"I'm trying to, but you keep interrupting me." I bit back. Once again, I wondered if this was a bad idea.

"Fine." She dragged her pinched thumb and forefinger across her lips, zipping them shut.

Leaning forward, I reached for her hand like I had the night before. Only this time, she didn't let me take it.

Hiding my disappointment, I continued. "It was stupid to risk your life. When you hit on me," her eyes narrowed, "I thought I'd hit the jackpot. A one-night stand with a bold, gorgeous woman."

I paused to let her respond, but she didn't. Blood rushed south as I watched the sexiest shade of pink crawl up her neck and spread across her cheeks. Then I did what I knew I shouldn't. I looked down to enjoy the same color spreading across the tops of her gorgeous breasts.

I couldn't help myself; her curve-hugging, low-cut tank top framed them perfectly.

"My eyes are up here," she said.

Reluctantly, I dragged my focus back to her face. "But the more we talked, the more we connected, the more I wanted."

Her expression softened, confirming she'd wanted the same thing. Something I'd suspected from her tongue-lashing the night before.

"When I left your room, I didn't think I'd see you again. I didn't ask for your number because I couldn't risk it being in my, in Scott's phone."

Ashley wasn't stupid; she'd find her way to the reality of the situation without me drawing a map.

The next night, I'd broken my routine and returned to the same bar two nights in a row. It was stupid, and I shouldn't have, but I hoped she'd come back. I trusted myself to play it cool, acting like all I wanted was sex, at least in public. Not willing to risk her safely, I'd kept a watchful eye out for my associates. If I'd spotted any of them, I would've called the whole thing off.

Sitting at the bar, I felt like I was being watched. When I turned, I saw Ashley staring at me. Her smile widened as sauntered over and plopped down on the empty stool beside me. Pride straightened my spine as my own smile grew. If I'd been a peacock, my tail feathers would've been on full display.

The doorbell chiming brought me back to the present.

"I shouldn't have returned to the same bar. But I did, hoping you would too." I sipped my coffee to buy myself a second before admitting, "I was torn between the desperate need to see you, and the sincere desire to keep you safe."

Images of what they'd do to her, each one worse than the last, flooded my mind. My hands trembled. I ground my teeth. My heels bounced up and down.

It wouldn't be long before my anxiety developed into flashbacks and panic.

I gripped the edge of the vinyl bench cushion. I pinched the fabric of my jeans. I picked up my coffee cup.

"What happened? Why'd you stand me up?" Ashley leaned forward, resting her arms on the table.

"My cover was blown."

"So you had to leave?"

I could hear soft music, someone steaming milk, and Ashley's foot tapping on the floor. I was doing things out of order, but I felt desperate.

"Nathan?" Ashley's soft voice cut through the building anxiety.

"I never got the chance," I said, staring at my coffee cup.

Ashley waited for me to say more, but I couldn't.

"Ashley, I can't." Nausea took over. My stomach revolted.

"You can't, or you won't?"

My breathing sped up. "I can't." I gripped my coffee cup too hard, and the lid popped off.

Concern replaced anger. "Are you okay?"

Clearly, I wasn't. "I'm fine," I said through gritted teeth, sounding more angry than panicky.

"Fine? Really?" Now, frustration laced her voice. "I shouldn't have bothered trying." She stood up.

The fear of Ashley leaving spurred me into action. *I'm a fucking SEAL, I can fight through this.* I stood and reached for her arm.

"Please," I didn't ask, I begged, reaching the other hand to caress her cheek.

Her eyes widened, but to her credit, she didn't flinch.

Did she trust me? Or was she too scared to move?

I took two quick deep breaths to calm down, searching her eyes for the answer. No fear.

To my surprise, she waited patiently. Watching. Analyzing.

Our eyes stayed focused on each other as I found my voice. "Ashley," I growled as I placed my forehead against hers and wrapped my hand around the back of her neck. "Please don't go. You have no idea…"

I still couldn't tell her the details of what had happened. Hell, just telling her the summary of the cliff note version resulted in an anxiety attack as memories flooded my mind. Our conversation the night before had caused nightmares that haunted me most of the night.

"Then tell me," she whispered. "Help me understand why you ghosted me."

Taking a deep breath in, I said, "The FBI set a trap, but it didn't work. I was outed as a mole in the organization I was trying to tear down."

She put her hand on my arm but didn't pull it off her neck. Her touch was gentle and sympathetic. "How bad?"

Images of chains, knives, and brass knuckle-covered fists flashed before my eyes. The snap of a whip cracking filled my ears. The tangy, metallic scent of blood filled my nose.

My chest rose and fell too fast as I lost control of my breathing.

"Nathan?" Ashley sounded like she was underwater.

Two hands grabbed my face, tilting it down. "Nathan. Are you okay?"

She sounded closer. I shut my eyes and started counting as I forced my lungs to slow down.

She waited, her soft, warm hands holding my face. When I opened my eyes, I was staring into the depths of the most beautiful honey-brown eyes I'd ever seen. Eyes I could get lost in, if she'd let me.

The depth of compassion radiating from them almost dropped me to my knees.

"I'm sorry."

"Are you okay? Should I call someone?" she asked.

There was no one to call. Well, maybe Kroup, but I'd recover before he got here.

I rested my forehead against hers. "I'm okay. Can we get out of here?" My need for fresh air was sudden and all-consuming.

"Yeah. Sure."

On our way out, I counted five things I could see, including a dark blue sedan with tinted windows. It wasn't the one I'd seen yesterday, but it still made my gut scream loud enough for me to shove down the anxiety and switch to protector mode.

I was already between Ashley and the potential threat, but that didn't feel like enough. I asked Ashley to stop and pretended to tie my shoe so I could look for the license plate. My nerves tingled as alarm bells went off in my head. *No front plate.*

Not that it'd matter. Doug had found out that the car from the previous night was a rental. The renter had reserved it with a stolen ID and paid in cash. Doug was exploring other avenues of getting information, but hadn't found anything yet. I expected the same result if I had a plate to run from this car.

I stood and placed my hand on the small of her back. To my surprise, she didn't pull away. *Good.* I didn't care if it was Finn or his hired hand watching.

I wanted whoever they were to know Ashley was protected.

Chapter 19

Ashley

I'm an asshole. I shouldn't have pushed him. At first I thought he was being evasive, but then he had an anxiety attack. The hand he'd wrapped around my arm had trembled just enough to scare me.

I wasn't scared of him. I was scared for him. Nathan wouldn't hurt me. I don't know how I knew, but I believed it with every fiber of my being. Watching as a Navy SEAL's eyes disconnected from reality as he struggled to breathe was unnerving, and I hoped never to experience it again.

"Where do you want to go?" I asked as he knelt to tie his shoe. Tension poured off him as his eyes focused on a parked car.

His concern was contagious, and I couldn't help but look too. Nothing about the car stood out, but I figured it was safer to trust Nathan's intuition than my own.

"Is it okay if we just walk around?"

"Sure."

When he stood, Nathan put his large, warm hand on my lower back.

I didn't want to like it, but I did.

I told myself to move away, but I didn't.

But I should. I was pregnant with another man's baby. There was no way Nathan would forgive me for keeping my secret, a lie of omission, after I yelled at him for the same reason.

Even if he forgave me, I couldn't imagine him wanting to raise another man's child. Especially when the father was a self-centered psycho who'd make our lives miserable. Once again, I prayed the result was wrong.

"You okay?" Nathan asked.

"Shouldn't I be asking you that?"

"I'm fine. Just needed some air." He brushed it off like he hadn't just freaked out in Grannie's.

"Right. Of course you won't tell me the truth." I shouldn't be mad, but I hated that he wouldn't talk to me. He was switching between open and closed off faster than I scrolled through ads on my social media accounts.

"It's complicated." He ran his hand down his face before turning and scanning behind us.

"And I couldn't possibly be smart enough to understand."

"That's not what I said."

"You think I'm not capable of understanding." That felt more accurate. God only knew I'd been acting like a bitch instead of showing compassion or patience.

He dropped his hand. "Jesus Christ, Ashley, stop putting words in my mouth."

Walking away from him, I doubled down on my bitchiness. "Just tell me."

Nathan did this to me. I was known for my snark and sass, just like Gran, but I wasn't a bitch. How did he draw out the worst in me?

Because he hurt me in ways no one else ever had. Because he was here, but miles away. Gone were the easy smile, the playful teasing, the snappy banter I'd witnessed in Vegas.

In its place were secrecy, shadows, and scars.

He stepped in front of me and turned, stopping so fast I almost ran into him. His hands on my shoulders stopped my momentum.

One hand stayed on my shoulder, holding me still with nothing more than gentle pressure. The other hand grabbed my chin and forced me to look at his face.

"This happened." He didn't need to point. "When I fought my way out after two weeks in captivity." He dropped both hands, his chest rising and falling too fast for how calm he sounded.

Two weeks in captivity.

"And this," he pointed this time, "isn't the worst of it."

Not the worst? What else had they done to him?

"I'm sorry." My apology felt as lame as it sounded.

He stared at me. "I don't need your sympathy."

I deserved that after pushing him so much.

"I shouldn't have been such a pushy bitch."

His smile didn't reach his eyes. "Three hours before I was supposed to meet you, I was called into a meeting." He paused, taking a deep breath while dragging his hand down his face. "I didn't see the light of day again until I escaped."

Two weeks. Jay and Cate were held and tortured for four days. The few things I'd heard were horrific. I could only imagine how much worse it was for Nathan.

I couldn't say I was sorry again, so I stepped closer. When Nathan flinched, I said, "Stand still." I wrapped my arms around his waist and used my body to comfort him instead of my words.

His chin rested on my head as he pulled me closer. "Thank you," he whispered into my hair.

I nodded against his chest and pressed my hands into his back as I squeezed tighter, pouring my forgiveness and sympathy into the hug since he didn't want my words.

Chapter 20

Nathan

I'm a fucking mess. The last thing I expected after our conversation was for Ashley to hug me. The only thing more shocking was my racing thoughts calming to a crawl as I wrapped my arms around her and held on for dear life.

The only worrying thought still taking up space was the fucking sedan. It hadn't moved, but that alone didn't mean anything. Maybe the person I'd seen moving around inside got out while we walked. My gut doubted it.

I couldn't tell you why, but I sensed it was a threat, and I'd learned at an early age to always trust my gut. It served me well in the foster care system, and it'd saved my life and the lives of my teammates in the Navy.

No way would I doubt it now.

My thank you came out rough, my breath moving her hair. The words weren't strong enough, but they were all I had. Half of my brain was shocked stupid by how quickly my anxiety had halted; the other half was focused on keeping Ashley safe. During our brief walk, I'd memorized the names of the stores on this side of the street and mapped out three escape routes.

I'd probably have to pick Ashley up and carry her, given her reluctance to listen to me, but I was ready and more than capable of doing just that.

"Let's get out of here," I finally said.

"Okay, but I have to be home for lunch to check on Gran."

"I'll make sure you get home on time." I chuckled. "I wouldn't dare upset your grandmother."

Ashley's laughter was music to my ears and a spear through my heart.

It felt like she'd forgiven me for what happened in Vegas, but that didn't mean she'd give me a second chance. Given how fucked up I was, I couldn't blame her.

We didn't talk as we walked to my truck. Her lips curled up in the tiniest of smiles when I opened her door and helped her up.

After getting in and making sure her seatbelt was buckled, I asked, "Okay if we just drive around for a bit?"

"That's fine." Her tone agreed, but her eyes didn't. I couldn't shake the nagging feeling that there was something else going on.

I shifted in my seat to face her. "Are you sure you're okay?"

"I'm fine, really. It's just been a rough few weeks."

I couldn't argue with that. Not only had I shown up unexpectedly, but she'd lost her job and her apartment in short order, and that was on top of her ex harassing her.

My gut warned me there was more to the sadness, but there was nothing else I could do if she wouldn't talk to me.

Not that I wouldn't keep trying.

I started the engine and turned the radio down to a respectable volume.

Exiting the parking lot using the street that didn't have a suspicious blue sedan with dark windows parked on it, I asked, "How's your grandmother?"

"She's fine," she answered, a wrinkle forming between her eyebrows.

"Sorry, what I meant was, is the walker temporary while healing or a permanent fixture?" It wasn't the most PC phrasing, but it worked.

"She fell and broke her hip; with any luck, she'll only need it for a few more weeks."

"That's good. She seems like a spitfire." It was obvious where Ashley got her feisty, no-nonsense attitude.

"She is." Ashley turned towards me. "She didn't grab your ass, did she?"

I laughed. She hadn't, but the question piqued my curiosity. "Has she grabbed other guy's asses?"

"I don't know. She talks about it, but I'm never sure if she's saying it to shock me or if she'll really do it."

"Has anyone confessed?" I was dying to know just how many asses Gran had touched.

"So far, just AJ, but I think he was lying to fuck with me."

AJ? Why was AJ at her place? Once again, the green-eyed monster woke from its slumber when it had no business existing.

"Did you date AJ?"

"No," she answered.

"No?"

"No, we never dated."

I'd swear there was more to it. "But?"

"But we were friends with benefits before he met Blake."

My growl was a visceral response.

"Did you just fucking growl?"

More than anything, I wanted to lie, but she'd obviously heard it.

"And if I did?" I asked instead of answering.

She rolled her eyes. "Men."

Ashley sounded disgusted with my gender, but she had a spark in her eyes and a grin on her face.

Seeing her reaction to my jealousy gave me hope we could be more than friends.

Having watched the rearview mirror the entire ride, I knew we weren't being followed, so I parked near the park. A crowd gathered at a kid's baseball game, and others strolled through the park, but everyone was busy doing their own thing, which meant we could walk and talk with a modicum of privacy.

"Ashley, can I ask you a question?"

"You just did." She laughed. "Sorry. Ask away."

"Do you think you can forgive me for ghosting you?" I had a feeling she had, but I still needed to hear her say it.

She stopped, taking her sweet time to think about it while I waited in agony.

"I forgive you."

Oh, thank fuck. The breath I'd been holding whooshed out.

We walked in silence while I gathered the courage to ask my next question. I was pushing my luck by asking, and if she said no, I'd work on building our friendship instead.

"Do you think you can give me a second chance?" My voice sounded like it came out of a small child, not a six-foot-two battle-hardened Navy SEAL.

Again, she took her time answering. When she put her hand on her belly, I figured it was to steady her nerves.

"I don't know." Her voice sounded as foreign as my own. "I. I'm sorry. I can't do this right now." She turned around and walked towards my truck. "Can you take me home?"

Recognizing the deer-in-the-headlights expression on her face, I agreed.

"Of course."

My gut screamed, *you're missing something.* Luckily, I had a ton of resources at my disposal, and I'd figure it out, one way or another.

Chapter 21

Ashley

I wanted to say yes when Nathan asked if I'd give him a second chance. But how could I? My life was a disaster, and I was fucking pregnant.

The drive back to Grannie's was eerily quiet. Like graveyard-at-night quiet. Like I'd just laid to rest the last chance I had with Nathan.

"Thanks," I said when he parked near my car.

"Wait." He got out and walked around to open my door. "Careful," he said, helping me down. His big black truck suited him, but wasn't so big that I couldn't get in and out on my own.

Usually I'd have a snarky comment about being able to open my door but, not wanting to add to the tension between us, I held it back.

I wasn't sure we could be friends, given our history, but maybe we could manage a friendly acquaintanceship. My best friends' husbands were his bosses, so it was inevitable we'd see each other. We'd need to co-exist, tolerate the awkwardness, or skip group events.

"Thank you."

"You're welcome." He shut the door, walked me to my car, and waited until I pulled away before he got back in his truck.

So this is what it's like for Meg, Emily, and Blake. I had only experienced it a few times when AJ and I went out. Which wasn't often. Usually we'd meet up, hang out for a few minutes, then rip each other's clothes off.

I wondered if Jay acted the same way with Cate. That girl was seriously badass and didn't need a guy taking care of her. Thinking back to the times they'd hung out with us, I knew he did. He didn't always open her door or pull out her chair. His support and protection were more subtle, but they were there. Jay was at his most gentlemanly when Cate, who wasn't used to our boisterous group, felt overwhelmed. He'd simply walk up beside her and put his hand on her back. It was such a simple, sweet way of supporting her.

When I got home, there was a package on the front porch.

No return address. No stamp. Just my name scrawled in big capital letters in thick black marker. I wrapped my arms around my waist as a chill ran down my spine.

I spun, searching up and down the street. *Did I really expect whoever had hand-delivered it to be standing on the sidewalk watching?*

Thinking back to Jamie and Jack's reaction to the black flowers, I left the package on the porch and went inside.

Shit. I'd forgotten to tell them about Red Flag Finn's texts.

Gran was napping in her room with Prince, who glared at me for daring to disturb him when I opened the door to check on her. Hopefully, she'd stay asleep long enough for me to call Nathan.

Nathan? *Why'd I even think that?* I couldn't call him. I meant to think, call Jamie.

A soft knock at the door interrupted me.

I ran to open it before the noise woke Gran. As I reached for the handle, I remembered getting blindsided by Finn.

Check the peephole.

What the fuck was Nathan doing here?

"Ashley, I know you're there. Please open the door." His voice wasn't loud, but it carried through the closed door loud and clear.

Opening the door, I hissed, "What are you doing here?"

"The same thing I was doing last night."

"I told you, you don't need to watch my house."

"The mystery package indicates otherwise." He nudged it with his foot. "Unless you know who it's from?"

"I don't. That's why I didn't touch it. I was getting ready to call Jamie when you knocked and scared the crap out of me."

"Right, sorry. Go inside, lock the door, and call him. I'll deal with the box." He scanned the street, searching the same way I had.

Nathan's tone scared me, so I did what he asked. I watched him snap several photos before running to his truck. He slid blue rubber gloves on before picking up the box and examining the outside.

Holding my phone to my ear, I opened the door to watch him.

Nathan opened his mouth and then slammed it shut. He ground his teeth and exhaled before asking, "Can I take this out back?"

"Go around the side." I didn't want him waking up Gran, and I sure as hell didn't want to give her a reason to worry. "I'll meet you back there."

"Lock the door," he ordered before walking off the porch, holding the box at arm's length. I locked the door, checked on Gran again, and then went to the patio.

Jamie answered as I slid the patio door closed. "Hey Ashley, is everything okay?"

"I'm not sure. There was a box on the front porch when I got home. No return sender or stamp."

"Did you touch it?"

"No, but Nathan did. He took it out back."

"Good. Tell him not to open it."

Holding my phone to my chest, I said to Nathan, "Jamie said not to open the box."

"Copy that. Do they have a bomb specialist at SSI?" Nathan stepped away from the box he'd set on the edge of Gran's brick patio. Her tall wooden privacy fence would serve its purpose today. But would it protect our neighbors from an explosion?

"How the hell would I know?" I asked.

"You could ask Jamie." He pointed at my phone.

"Right. Sorry." I pulled it up to my ear to hear Jamie ask if I was still here.

"Yeah, sorry, Nathan wants to know if anyone at SSI is a bomb specialist." I felt like a poser for asking.

"Not really. The closest we have is Jay, but he's out of town."

"Okay, I'll tell him." When had my life become a fucking action movie? *And how the hell do I opt out?*

"We'll be there soon. Don't touch the box."

"Yes, sir." Jamie told me not to call him sir before hanging up.

"What'd he say?" Nathan asked.

"Jay is the closest they have, but he's out of town." I quoted Jamie.

Nathan nodded. "Do me a favor and keep your distance. Just because I don't hear anything ticking doesn't mean it's not dangerous."

"Yes, sir," I said, laying the sarcasm on thick. It wasn't like they needed to keep reminding me; I was the one who left it on the porch untouched.

Nathan tapped his phone screen before holding it to his ear. "Hey man, how's it hanging?"

He listened, never taking his eyes off me.

"Good to hear."

Pause.

"Good so far, but it's only been a week."

Another pause while he listened.

"Sounds good. Listen, any chance you're free to come to Weatherford? We've got a bit of a situation and could use Havoc's nose."

Who's Havoc? And what kind of name was that?

"Thanks, man, we'll wait."

He hung up and tapped the screen before putting the phone back to his ear.

"Who was that?"

Nathan held up a finger, indicating I should wait. Normally, I'd be angry at getting shushed, but I recognized his demeanor. He was in full-blown work mode, and it scared me.

"Jamie, I've got a friend in the area with a SEAL-trained dog."

He paused.

"He's trained to sniff bombs, among other things."

Nathan nodded as he listened.

"Yeah, that's him. He's on his way."

As he ended the call, I asked, "You have a friend with a bomb-sniffing dog?"

"I was a SEAL; most of my friends have unique skill sets." Nathan's scar caused his soft smile to be lopsided.

"Like what?" I asked, needing to talk about something other than the box he thought required a bomb-sniffing dog.

Before Nathan could answer, his head snapped up as the familiar metallic sound of the patio door opening filled the air.

I was right behind him as he rushed to intercept Gran. "Good afternoon, Violet," he greeted her.

"How lovely to see you again. Ashley, you didn't tell me we were having company," Gran scolded me as she patted her silver, sleep-disheveled hair.

"Sorry, it was a surprise visit." And not a good one.

"Well, don't just stand there; offer our guest something to drink." Gran started towards the patio.

"I'm afraid you'll have to stay inside for a—"

"Young man, don't tell me what to do in my own home."

Nathan's eyes widened as she stood her ground. At five-foot-three, and hunched over her walker, Gran looked downright comical facing off against Nathan.

Nathan's expression softened as he stared down at her.

I couldn't wait to watch him try to charm his way out of this.

"You're right, and I'm sorry. It was rude, and it won't happen again."

Damn him. He backed down too fast, and I wouldn't get to see her tear him a new asshole.

"That's better. Why do you think I need to stay inside?" Gran wasn't stupid. She would've picked up on the tension and known there was a reason Nathan gave the order.

"Some of the guys from SSI are coming over to talk shop. It's about a case, and it'll be easier if we don't have to worry about watching our language while we work." His lie was smooth as silk.

Gran put a hand on her hip and stood a little taller. "You think I'm afraid of a few curse words?"

"No, ma'am." He dug his hole deeper. "I'm sorry I didn't ask before offering your backyard as a meeting place. I'll call the guys and ask them to meet somewhere else."

Well played. She loved having guests, especially tall, dark, and handsome men, and he knew it.

"That's not necessary. I'll make a pitcher of lemonade unless you'd rather have beer."

"Lemonade sounds good. Thank you."

Gran eyed the box, then looked at me.

Turning to Nathan, she looked him in the eyes, squinted. I knew that look. Gran was opening daring him to lie when she asked, "Is Ashley in danger?"

Nathan's eyes flared before he looked at me, a question in his eyes. I appreciated him letting me control how much we'd tell her, so rather than letting him squirm, I put him out of his misery.

"We think Finn sent the flowers and that box." I said, pointing to it, even though she'd seen it.

Nathan finished the explanation. "SSI is coming over in case he sent something the police need to handle." He smiled, his scar wrinkling. "It's always better to be safe than sorry."

"Why didn't you just say that?" Gran asked. "I'll go make the lemonade. Ashley, come help me."

Nathan nodded when I made eye contact, answering my silent question.

"I'll be right back," I said.

While we made lemonade, I apologized for hiding things from her.

"Do you really think Finn wants to hurt you?"

"I wouldn't have thought so, but he won't accept that I broke up with him." At first, I figured he'd eventually get the message if I kept ignoring him, so I hadn't told anyone he was still contacting me. I meant to tell them when I got the stalker-ish texts, but then I saw the positive text result and forgot all about it. I didn't respond, and since I hadn't heard from him, I'd forgotten all about it.

Until today.

At least I'd kept all the messages, knowing from Emily's experience they'd be useful, and maybe even evidence.

After Nathan got in his face, I expected Finn to leave me alone. And he did, but only for a day. His first text was polite, asking how I was, but they quickly escalated to claiming we were still a couple and asking me to return to Dallas. The angriest messages came after I didn't meet him where he'd told me to.

"Well, I'm just glad you have friends who can help you," she said as she cut slices of lemon and put them in tall colorful glasses filled with ice.

Me too, Gran. Me too. I didn't think Finn would escalate like Asshat Craig had, but glancing outside had me rethinking my previous evaluation.

I fought back the tears threatening to spill. *Lucky me, I'm having his baby.*

Chapter 22

Nathan

Jack and AJ arrived first, but Jamie wasn't far behind.

"I didn't expect him to call in the team."

"Ashley's family," AJ said.

"Dad's waiting to hear what we find," Jack said. "Doug's on his way to the office. He'll check if any neighbors have cameras and get permission to access them." Damn, he really had called in the entire team. Well, everyone who was in Weatherford.

"ETA on your guy?" Jamie asked.

I glanced at my watch. "Twenty minutes."

"Don't get me wrong, I'm glad you were here, but why?" AJ asked.

I looked at Jamie, who nodded. "I'm providing unofficial protection until we figure out how big a threat Finn is."

"Oh," he said. "Oh!" he repeated with a chuckle as it hit him. "How long have you loved her?" He asked.

Not if, but how long.

No way would I open that can of worms. "I'm just worried."

"He doesn't lie any better than you do, Janerek."

"Shut up, Sheppard," AJ snapped at Jack. I didn't know the details, but apparently AJ fell for Blake after assigning himself as her bodyguard.

I ignored the implications of the coincidence.

"Knock it off," Jamie said. "We all know what it's like, so let's give Nathan some space." I nodded my appreciation, but he wasn't done. "While he pulls his head out of his ass."

One wouldn't think it was acceptable to glare at one's boss, and that one would get one's ass handed to them for doing it. But Jamie only laughed.

AJ got close, like nose-to-nose, way too fucking close for comfort. "If you hurt her, I will kill you."

I held his stare, contemplating my response. I couldn't lie and say I wouldn't. And he was threatening me for all the right reasons, so challenging him was out of the question.

"Understood."

He narrowed his eyes, driving home the threat. "Good." He nodded as he exited my personal space. "What's the deal with the box?"

We examined it from a distance while I filled them in on my assessment, scant as it was. The box was lighter than I'd expected, and evenly balanced with the weight distributed along the bottom.

"No rattling as I carried it."

"So your fingerprints compromised the evidence," AJ accused.

"No, they didn't. I wore gloves." And because I needed to regain some of the power I'd lost in the stare-down with AJ, I added, "And I only used my thumb and trigger finger on opposite corners." I pinched the two digits together on each hand and then rolled my wrists and flipped him two birds.

He laughed.

"This isn't my first rodeo, Janerek." I spat out.

"Right, sorry, Bro."

My phone buzzed. "Kroup's here." I went around front to meet him.

"Hey brother," I said, shaking his hand before pulling him into a hug and slapping his back. "It's good to see you."

"Right back at you."

"Hey, Havoc, how you doing, boy?"

Havoc barked in response as I scratched behind his ears.

Pleasantries finished, Kroup asked, "The box in the back?"

I stood. "Yeah, this way."

Ashley and Gran were handing out glasses of lemonade when we arrived. Having them so close to danger wasn't ideal, but there was nothing I could say to control Gran. Or Ashley.

"What a pretty dog! I bet Prince would love to play with him." Gran said enthusiastically.

"This is Havoc," Kroup answered.

"Nathan, don't be rude. Introduce me to the tall Greek Adonis standing next to you," Gran ordered. Good God, she reminded me so much of Ashley with her zero fucks to give attitude.

"Just go with it," I whispered to a wide-eyed Kroup before saying, "Violet, this is my friend, Jon Kroupa. Jon, this is Ashley and her grandmother, Violet."

"Nice to meet you, ma'am."

"None of that ma'am stuff. Call me Violet, like Nathan does. Or Gran, like I told him to."

I closed my eyes so she wouldn't see me rolling them.

"Noted." Kroup humored her with a smile. "Everyone calls me Kroup."

Kroup made a hand signal, and Havoc trotted to his side and sat. He released the dog when he introduced him to Violet, so she could give him love and attention. "Who's Prince?" he asked.

"My cat." As if on cue, a black cat sat in front of the patio window and glared at Havoc. At least I think he glared. I wasn't familiar with cat expressions, so, for all I knew, Prince could've been bored or in love.

"Violet, thank you for the lemonade, but I think it's best if you and Ashley go inside now," Jamie said, adding a please at the end.

"Alright, but only because you said please. You boys let me know if you want lunch. Ashley makes a mean ham and cheese sandwich."

After they went inside, Kroup said, "She's a hoot."

"You have no idea," Jamie and Jack said together.

After introductions, Kroup put Havoc to work. Watching him obey Kroup's subtle hand commands was poetry in motion.

It took all of five seconds for Havoc to sit at Kroup's left side, signaling he hadn't sniffed anything worth warning us about.

"I can't guarantee the box is safe to open, but it's not giving off a chemical signature," Kroup said matter-of-factly. "Open at your own risk."

We discussed theories before Kroup asked, "Do you need me to stick around?"

"We're good, thanks for your help." Jamie stuck out his hand.

After they exchanged business cards, I walked Kroup back to his truck. Havoc hopped into the back seat after I gave him a pat goodbye.

"Thanks for coming. I owe you one."

"It's good for him." He nodded toward the back. "And don't think I won't call to collect."

We shook hands and hugged again. "Let me know what you find. And Blaze."

"Yeah?"

"Don't be such a stranger."

"Copy that."

They'd already cut the tape on the box by the time I returned. Apparently, AJ wasn't a patient man. Jack and Jamie filmed from opposite sides as AJ's large, blue-gloved hands lifted the flaps.

We held our breath as he slowly lifted the last flap.

All we could see was brown packing paper.

"Step back," AJ said. His voice was thick with concern. We didn't know what we'd find when he pulled the paper out.

"We're good," Jack replied. Jamie and I nodded our agreement. Their actions confirmed my initial impression of SSI—they were good men and wouldn't leave their teammate to face the risk alone, regardless of the risk to themselves.

AJ grabbed a corner of the thick brown paper and slowly lifted it. It didn't change shape as he lifted it out of the box in one rumpled piece and set it on the ground at arm's reach. A thin decorative stone, glued to the bottom of the four by six-inch box, explained the weight distribution.

After confirming there was nothing under the stone, we shifted so Jack and Jamie could record AJ opening the wadded-up paper.

We held our collective breaths as AJ slowly, methodically unraveled the packing paper.

Wrapped inside was a plastic black rose. All that build up. All that worry. All that caution for a rose. Essentially, for nothing.

Well, caution was never for nothing, but it felt anticlimactic.

"Who the hell sends a rose in a box?" AJ asked.

"We need to ask Ashley about the black roses. The first delivery could be construed as an insult for breaking his heart, but this," Jack paused, running his hand through his hair, "this was meant to scare her."

"That's fucked up," AJ added.

A chill ran down my spine. This wasn't the game of a jealous ex. It seemed like someone was testing us. Testing Ashley's protection.

"We need to increase Ashley's protection," I blurted out.

If this was done on behalf of her ex, it meant he was a bigger threat than we'd anticipated. If it wasn't, we needed to figure out who and why. And we needed to do it yesterday.

"She won't like that," Jack said.

"I don't care," I growled back. "This." I kicked the box. "This was a test."

AJ's knowing smile irritated me, but I was glad he wasn't arguing.

"Sum it up, Blaszek," Jamie said. He was a cop before starting SSI with his father and brother. He'd have his own ideas, so it surprised me he'd asked for mine first.

"The flowers were delivered when Ashley wasn't home. We," eyebrows raised, so I corrected, "I responded by camping out in front of the house."

"They delivered the box while Ashley was out, too," Jack said.

"Exactly. Whoever left it knows we aren't watching the house when Ashley's not here."

"We need coverage for Ashley and Gran," Jamie said.

"She's really not gonna to like that," AJ repeated Jack's sentiment.

"I really don't fucking care," I growled at him.

"Good. Because she'll fight you every step of the way," Jack said.

"Me?"

"Dude, don't even pretend that you won't be with Ashley twenty-four-seven from this point forward," Jamie said.

He was right. I'd already planned to ask someone to stay while I ran home and grabbed some clothes and my gear.

"We'll write up the official paperwork and have Gran and Ashley sign it."

"Bill it to me," I said, knowing they couldn't afford SSI's rates.

"We aren't billing her. Ashley's family. The paperwork is to cover our ass," Jamie said.

"It also allows us to dig deeper into Finn," Jack added. "I'll start tonight, see what I can dig up."

"Can someone stay while I run home?"

"I'll stay. Gran loves me," AJ said, earning a low growl. "Relax, dude, I'm happily engaged."

Relaxing wouldn't be on my to-do list anytime soon.

"Try to convince them to let Doug install cameras at the front and back doors," Jamie said.

"Will do, boss man." AJ saluted.

I went inside to talk to Ashley while the guys bagged up the box, paper, and rose. John would use his local contacts at the PD to have a chemical analysis run and check for prints, but I already knew they wouldn't find any.

As soon as I walked in the door, a little black fur ball wound itself around my legs, almost tripping me. I squatted down and petted his head. "You must be Prince."

"Look, Ashley, Prince adores Nathan," Gran said from her seat at the table, her smile far too mischievous for my liking.

Chapter 23

Ashley

I almost gagged when Gran gushed over Prince plopping down and letting Nathan scratch his belly. She wasn't even trying to be subtle with her matchmaking.

Nathan's head snapped up when I said, "He's an attention whore." I clarified, "The cat, not you."

He stood. "Can I talk to you for a minute?" He tilted his head to indicate he wanted to do it away from Gran.

"It's okay; you don't have to hide from me," Gran said.

I agreed. "She knows Finn's been," I paused to find the right word, "bothersome." I'd filled her in on Red Flag Finn's persistence while they opened the box.

Not bothering with kid-gloves, he nodded and said, "There was a single black rose in the box. We're looking into Finn, but we're keeping our minds open to other possibilities." I could tell he was choosing his words carefully.

"What does that mean?" Gran asked.

I didn't need to ask. Not after what happened with Emily.

"Ashley, do the black roses mean anything to you? Can you think of anyone else who might want to scare you?"

They didn't. I couldn't. I wasn't perfect, but I was a decent person, and I tried not to hurt people. And other than Finn, no one had ever given me a reason to think they'd want to hurt me.

"Not that I can think of." No one from my past was unhinged enough to harass me. *That you know of.*

"If you remember anything, let us know." He looked down at his phone.

"I know you won't want to hear this, but we're not comfortable leaving either of you unattended, so SSI will be providing around the clock coverage—"

"Oh, hell no," I said. When I stood, the movement sent my pine chair crashing behind me. Prince tore from the room in a black streak.

"Let him finish," Gran said, as Nathan stood and righted my chair.

"Thank you, Violet." Nathan held my chair out for me.

"I'll stand." If only my eyes could shoot laser beams of death.

"Jamie said SSI won't charge you." He put one fear to rest. "I'll be with you twenty-four-seven." He confirmed my second fear.

This was way worse than I expected. Nathan would camp out in front of Gran's house all day, every day. When would he sleep? Eat?

"What about Gran? You can't leave her alone to follow me."

"Someone from SSI will be outside anytime we leave."

"So you're just going to sit in your truck twenty-four hours a day? What happens if you fall asleep?" I challenged.

"I won't be outside." His voice was flat, hard. Like he had the final say in the matter.

I'd swear my eyes opened so wide they almost popped out of my head.

Gran, the traitor, smiled.

Ignoring her, I said, "We don't have a bed for you." I crossed my arms and smirked. *Let's see him solve that problem.*

"I can sleep on the couch, or on the floor if necessary."

I dropped my arms. Why hadn't I thought of that?

"I'll get you sheets and blankets for the couch. Though it'll be a bit short for you."

Ignoring my protests, Nathan said, "Thank you, Violet."

At the same time, I said, "That won't be necessary."

"Ashley, if the guys from SSI think you need protection, you should graciously accept it," Gran said before asking Nathan. "How concerned should we be?"

"You need to be cautious, but let us do the heavy lifting. We're here so you can go about your normal business." Like we could do that knowing we had a full-time bodyguard. "I'll go over safety protocols when I get back."

Having clearly lost the battle, I asked with an exaggerated sigh, "Starting when?"

"Starting now. AJ will stay while I run home to pack my bag."

Maybe I can talk some sense into AJ.

Nathan stood. "I won't get in your way. You don't have to entertain or take care of me while I'm here."

"Don't worry, we won't," I said.

"Don't be rude," Gran chastised me. "I assume it's okay for you to have meals with us?" she asked Nathan.

"It is, but only if you let me help with cooking, cleaning, and buying."

"That won't be necessary, dear."

I rolled my eyes at Gran's over-the-top sugary-sweet performance.

"I insist" was all he said.

Nathan asked for a piece of paper and wrote down his number. "Call me if you need anything."

What I needed was for him to leave me alone. I wanted him, but couldn't have him. Nathan's presence would be a constant, painful reminder of that reality.

AJ must've waited near the door, because he came in as Nathan left.

He walked over and gave Gran a gentle hug. When it was my turn, he said, "Sorry this is happening, but we'll figure it out."

"Thanks," I said, racking my brain for a way to convince him we didn't need Nathan here.

AJ narrowed his eyes, studying my face. "I know this is disruptive, and you're already searching for a way out, but there isn't one." He crushed my hopes. "We won't risk your safety."

"But—"

"No buts. It's a done deal unless your grandmother kicks us out." AJ turned to Gran. "Gran?"

"You can stay."

It wasn't fair that I didn't have a say in any of this. Or that they were using my grandmother against me. No matter how well-intended their actions.

"Thank you. We want to install cameras at the front and back doors. Is that okay?"

"What?" I yelled more than asked. "Nathan didn't mention that."

"We thought you'd be more reasonable if the request came from me." AJ's calm, all-business tone made me more nervous than Nathan's overly aggressive one. No, aggressive wasn't the right word. He was matter-of-fact, protective and pushy, but not aggressive.

Finn was aggressive.

"We don't want a repeat of what happened with Craig."

Gran gasped. She knew about Emily's abusive ex, and his actions that led to his death.

"You told her?" he asked.

"I don't keep secrets from Gran," I said. My hand went to my belly, knowing I was keeping the biggest secret of them all. But only until I saw Dr. Greenfield and confirmed the positive test result. An internet search said a false positive was less likely than a false negative, but I was hoping and praying, none-the-less.

AJ's eyes followed my hand.

"When you guys helped Em, you rotated shifts outside the house."

"And we failed her."

"But she didn't have cameras; we will," I argued.

"Ashley, I know you're upset, but this is the best way. And it's happening." AJ crossed his arms.

"Ashley, I think it's best if we follow their advice. They wouldn't suggest this without a good reason," Gran added.

My resignation escaped with a sigh. "Why does it have to be Nathan?"

He raised an eyebrow. "Don't play stupid, Ashley. It doesn't suit you."

Leave it to AJ to call me out.

"Jamie or Jack could assign him a different job."

"Why would they do that, dear? It's clear that boy is crazy about you," Gran said.

That was the problem. I wanted to give us a second chance but couldn't. Nathan hovering, being nice and charming while protecting us twenty-four-seven was more than I could handle.

"He volunteered for the job. Well, volunteered isn't quite the right word." He winked at Gran. "He pretty much told us he was staying."

My heart skipped a beat. *He told them?* I dropped my head in my hands. Nathan was doing all the romantic things I fawned over in romance books, which made resisting him harder with each passing minute.

How will I survive with my heart intact?

"I'm sorry, I shouldn't have said anything." He rubbed my back.

"No, it's okay. This is just a lot, you know?"

Prince chose that time to jump onto my lap. Instead of shooing him off, I stroked his silky-soft fur. His loud purr rumbled against my lap.

"He's a good boy, giving you comfort when you need it," Gran's pride showed in her eyes. I wasn't sure why she was so proud; she didn't find the cat-he found her. *Found us.*

"If you want, I'll talk to Jamie and Jack and see if I can get them to schedule me to share shifts with Nathan," AJ offered.

"No, I don't want to cause trouble." If Nathan was determined to stay, if SSI let him assign himself, and Gran supported their decisions, who was I to argue?

AJ scoffed, not believing me for a nanosecond.

A part of me, the part I wanted to ignore but couldn't, wanted Nathan here.

"Are you good with Doug installing cameras?" AJ asked.

"Yes, we'll do whatever you suggest if it'll keep Ashley safe."

It's not just about me. My eyes blurred as tears filled my eyes.

"Okay. I'll tell Jamie. Anything you want me to add?" His question offered me a chance to change my mind about Nathan.

"No." I shook my head in defeat. I'd deal with seeing Nathan twenty-four-seven to protect my grandmother. "Gran?"

She shook her head no.

AJ's knowing grin made his dimples pop.

"He's a good man," Gran said after the door slid shut. "I'm happy he's found someone who makes him happy."

"Me too." I smiled. AJ'd had a rough childhood and had sworn off love until Blake wiggled her way into his heart.

"You know who else is handsome and tall?"

Please don't say it.

"Nathan." She said it. "He reminds of AJ."

She wasn't wrong. "Gran, it's not gonna happen."

"Why not? I see how you look at each other." How could I explain without revealing my secrets?

"I'm not sure what you think you saw, but it's not what you think." *That would certainly clear things up.*

"What kind of nonsense answer is that?"

The only one I had, unless I confessed.

"It's complicated," I answered.

"Is it because of the scar?"

"What? No, of course not." I didn't care about the scar. I sighed. "It's because we tried, and he lied to me."

"Hmmm." She thought about it. "Because he told you his name was Scott when you met in Vegas?"

I hadn't made it hard to figure out.

"Yes."

"And you've never given someone a fake name?"

Of course I had, but not someone I wanted to date.

He said he wanted to come clean. But then he never got the chance because his cover was blown.

It didn't matter. The reason it wouldn't work was my current secret, not his previous lies.

Not waiting for me to answer, she said, "Well, Prince likes him." As if hearing his name summoned him, Prince jumped on the table and sauntered over to Gran.

Prince had a lot of pull in Gran's small ranch home, but he didn't get a say in my love life. "Gran…"

"Cats have a sixth sense about these things."

The adorable spawn of Satan meowed his agreement before knocking a spoon off the table.

"Prince and I think Nathan's a good man. And he's easy on the eyes." She turned her attention to the cat. "Plus he gives good scritches, doesn't he?"

I sighed as I leaned over to pick up the spoon. There was no point in arguing.

Chapter 24

Nathan

After packing my bag, I went to the office to grab my laptop and protection duty gear, including my vest and rifle. As I approached Jamie's office to ask about vests for Ashley and Gran, should we need them, I overheard him talking.

"I'm not sure what we can do." He sounded tired. After a pause, he said, "I promise, Em, I will personally accompany her any time Finn wants to see the baby. If that's what Ashley wants."

I shouldn't have eavesdropped, and I certainly shouldn't have barged into his office looking like I was ready for a fight. But a different kind of panic had washed over me. *Ashley's pregnant?*

That's the problem I couldn't figure out. All the times her hand went to her belly weren't because of nerves.

"Listen, Em, I have to go." He held up a finger.

Ashley's pregnant, and the father is the man we suspect is harassing her.

"I promise." He never broke eye contact.

Neither of us blinked when he said, "I love you, too."

He put his phone down and grabbed the back of his neck. "How much did you hear?"

"Is Ashley really pregnant?"

He stood and walked to the front of his desk. Nodding towards the door, he said, "Close it."

After closing it, I turned to face him again.

"It's not my place to tell—"

"Sheppard, do not fuck with me."

To his credit, he didn't flinch or even blink as he crossed his arms over his chest. He stared at me for a good three seconds before laughing.

I clenched my hands and ground my teeth as I counted to ten.

"Relax. I was laughing at myself, not you. I should've known better than to discuss it with my door open, but I'm not used to having secrets in the office."

I held my tongue and waited impatiently.

"I'm only telling you this because I don't expect Ashley to, but you should know. Having assigned yourself as her bodyguard and all." He raised an eyebrow, like the situation amused him.

"Something funny?" I growled out.

"You're having a hell of a start at SSI."

It was true, but now wasn't the time to discuss it. My patience was wearing thin. "Is my job on the line?"

He shook his head. "No, not yet. But you need to stop growling and get comfortable working with a team real quick if you don't want that to change."

"Yes, sir."

"I understand you operated alone a lot at Hawken's, but much like the SEALs, we work as a team. We let you assign yourself to Ashley because it's obvious you have feelings for her."

Before I could deny it, he continued, "Dude, don't. We've all been in your shoes, and we've all watched it happen to each other." When we finished the job, if I was still employed, I needed to buy him a beer and ask about the events behind that statement. "Lucky for you, that means we understand, and we'll let you call the shots. Unless you show us you can't."

That would never happen.

He still hadn't answered my question, so I repeated it. This time with less attitude. Jamie was right. I needed to remember how to function as part of a team. There was no doubt everyone here loved Ashley, and they'd do everything in their power to protect her.

"Yes, she's pregnant, and yes, it's Finn's."

"Fucking hell."

"It's a mess. Even if we can prove Finn is harassing or threatening Ashley, I'm not sure a judge will refuse him his rights as a father."

Hence Jamie volunteering to escort her.

I knew she was hiding something, but never in a million years would I have guessed pregnancy. The need to see

Ashley, to check on her, to comfort her, hit me like a sucker punch. "I have to go."

"Hold up, Blaszek." It wasn't a suggestion.

"What?"

"Don't, and I can't stress this enough. Do not say anything to Ashley. Let her tell you. Understood?"

Instead of agreeing, I said, "I won't rat you out if that's what you're worried about."

"It's not. I'm worried about you charging in there and losing your cool." He held eye contact without blinking. "If you upset her, I will can your ass. Before you argue about not needing to be employed by SSI to help her." Jamie uncrossed his arms, stood to his full five-eleven height, and got in my face. "Know that you're wrong. Have I made myself clear?" His words were a promise, not a threat.

There was no sarcasm in my voice when I said, "Yes, sir."

"Good, because she has enough to deal with, she doesn't need you acting like a fucking caveman." His tone was gentler, but his words weren't.

Taking a deep breath, I nodded. He was right. Ashley needed to be the one to tell me. And I needed to control my caveman instincts. The primal, chest-thumping attitude that took over whenever I thought about someone hurting her. It was like years of evolution disappeared, and I regressed to grunts instead of words.

"If you love her, don't look at me like that."

I hadn't used love in relation to Ashley, not even in my mind. But I was acting like a man possessed—by a Neanderthal, apparently—so it was probably accurate.

"If you love her as much as I think you do, don't be a dick when she tells you."

Given my recent behavior, I probably deserved the warning. But that didn't mean I liked hearing it.

Somehow, Jamie managed to tell me exactly what I needed to hear in the way I needed to hear it. How he knew, I'd never know, but he did. After taking a deep breath and slowly exhaling it, I said, "Damn, Sheppard."

He smiled. "Get used to it. We have an unspoken no-bullshit policy around here."

It was my turn to laugh. "I can appreciate that."

"Good. Before you return to Ashley, my father wants to talk to you."

It shouldn't have surprised me. "How much trouble am I in?" I hadn't exactly been a team player, or played by the rules, or been a model employee.

That changes now. Not because I needed the job—I didn't—but because I was a better person than what I'd shown them. I'd adopted the lone wolf attitude to survive the isolation of deep undercover work, but it no longer suited me. And it wouldn't help Ashley.

"None that I know of. But brace yourself for a lecture."

I rubbed my face, noting the stubble on my normally clean-shaven chin. My silent sigh didn't go unnoticed.

"Don't worry, we've all gotten them. If you're lucky, this will be the last lecture you get."

"How likely is that?"

"Not very. AJ's the overly protective big brother Ashley never had, didn't ask for, but loves having."

"AJ didn't exactly lecture me, but his threat was less than subtle."

"Threatened to kill you?"

"He did. And I believe him."

"No surprise there." Jamie grinned before adding, "Try not to force his hand because he means it, and I'd hate to lose you both."

I was ninety-seven percent sure he was exaggerating, but AJ struck me as someone who could and would kill for those he loved. *Who among us wouldn't?*

"And the rest of the team?"

"Dude, I told you, she's family. She was Emily's maid of honor, and she and Meg have been thick as thieves since the second they met. Doug and Jay don't know her as well, but they'll protect her because—"

"She's family."

"Now you're getting it."

I was. People always said their friends were like family, but they exaggerated. When push came to shove and shit got real, those friends made themselves scarce. But Ashley was right; her friends were her family.

"I expect regular reports, and the more notice you can give us when she wants to leave the house, the better."

Even if no one at SSI was available, Gran wouldn't be unprotected. I'd bring her with us if I had to.

"Yes, sir." I saluted with two fingers.

He muttered. "Why does everyone feel the need to salute me?"

When I didn't answer, he said, "Get out of here and keep our girl safe."

Our girl. I liked the sound of that. But first I had to convince her to give me a second chance, because my conscious mind finally accepted what my primal brain had known all along. I loved Ashley. Her being pregnant with another man's baby wasn't ideal, but I could deal with it. If she'd let me.

"Roger that."

I knocked on John's doorframe. "You wanted to see me, sir?"

"Have a seat." I followed his orders.

"It's come to my attention that you have feelings for Ashley and have volunteered to work for free to provide round-the-clock protection."

"Yes, sir."

He nodded, looking me up and down, assessing. "I appreciate your offer, but we'll pay you."

"Sir, I don't need the money, so it isn't necessary." I kept my voice respectful but firm. "Especially since you're not billing Ashley."

"I'm billing her for legal purposes, but only for a dollar. I have to pay you for the same reason."

Knowing he wouldn't risk the liability of not paying me, I asked him to bill me for the full cost of Ashley's services. "There's no reason for the company to take a loss."

He leaned back, crossed his arms, nodding as he thought about my suggestion. Then he surprised me with a laugh.

"Alright. I'll have Meg add you to the paperwork, but all decisions will be the Yorks."

"Thank you." I'd have my bank mail a check to cover the deposit by the end of the day. "I wouldn't dream of telling Violet what to do."

John's knowing smile didn't last.

"I'm sure I know the answer, but do you plan on sharing the responsibility of providing twenty-four-seven in-home coverage?"

I clarified, "I'll provide coverage wherever Ashley is."

"Noted, Doug will be by this evening to install the cameras."

"Ashley gave you permission?" I didn't hide my shock.

"No, but her grandmother did, and it's Violet's house."

"Good. I'll do what I can to help him."

When I stood up to leave, he stopped me. "Be careful with Ashley. She feels things a lot deeper than she lets on."

I nodded. He wasn't telling me anything I didn't already know, having noticed how often her smile didn't reach her eyes and how she used humor as armor. "Is that all?"

After Jamie's warning, I'd expected more.

"For now." John leaned forward, his elbows on the desk, and his hands steepled. "Don't make me say more."

Message, no it wasn't a message. *His warning was received loud and clear.* "Yes, sir."

"One more thing," he said, circling his desk. "Call me John."

I shook his extended hand. "Will do, John."

Chapter 25

Ashley

When Nathan returned and relieved AJ, something seemed off. I assumed it was because of what they were talking about, even though I couldn't hear them. Nathan's smile looked forced as he stood in the kitchen. And he wouldn't stop staring at me, like I was a riddle he needed to solve.

Instinctively, I put my hand over my belly. His eyes tracked the movement.

Then he squinted, clapped AJ on the shoulder, and marched into the living room.

Does he know? He couldn't. The only people I'd told were Emily and Jamie, and they'd never tell him.

He smiled when he spoke to my grandmother. "Doug will be here soon to install the cameras."

"You can wait here with me." Gran patted the floral sofa cushion next to her, an invitation Nathan couldn't refuse. She played Twenty Questions with him while we waited. To his credit, he was patient as he gave her half answers, using the line "I could tell you, but then I'd have to kill you" more than once.

Gran ate it up.

I watched and listened but didn't participate. Nathan's smile, no longer even, thanks to the scar, never reached his eyes. Gran either didn't notice or chose not to comment, instead patting his knee as she offered sage advice.

Shit. *Is she giving him dating advice?* I'd only been half listening and realized too late she wasn't giving him generic advice; she was providing a road map for dating me. Nathan's focus was absolute, as if he were memorizing every word she said.

Before I could yell at her to stop, the doorbell chimed. A cute, whimsical chime she'd had custom installed.

When I jumped up to answer it, so did Nathan. He held up his hand, saying, "I'll get it."

Although we were expecting Doug, Nathan checked the peephole with his left hand on his gun.

How had I never noticed he's left-handed?

When Nathan opened the door, Doug carried in several boxes. "Blaszek."

"Sharpe." Nathan held the door, asking, "Is that everything?"

"It is," Doug answered. "Hi Ashley, Mrs. York."

She insisted Doug call her Violet or Gran while she, in typical Gran fashion, gushed over his red hair. Doug was the quiet guy at SSI, preferring to observe rather than interact, so her attention made him blush.

Doug had come out of his shell a bit since falling in love with Beth and her six-year-old son, Chase. They'd been engaged for what seemed like forever but had only been a year. They already lived like a married couple, and Chase had recently started calling Doug, Dad, but they weren't in a hurry to make it official.

"No offense, big guy," Gran said to Nathan, patting his muscular bicep. Which was hysterical. At six-foot-two, Nathan was two inches shorter than Doug, and they were equally broad. "But I have a thing for redheads."

Doug humored her with a laugh.

I was too embarrassed to laugh. "Gran!"

"What, I'm old, not dead," she defended herself with a shrug.

"None taken," Nathan said before ushering Doug out the front door to install the shiny, new state-of-the-art surveillance cameras I didn't want.

If it'd been just me, I would have said no, but I reminded myself the security measures were for Gran's safety too.

"You're incorrigible," I said. How many times had I heard that same statement? How many times had I pretended not to care? *Too many.*

It didn't take long for Doug and Nathan to finish. When they came back in, Doug set up Nathan's laptop so he could monitor the feed.

"Ashley, Violet, would you like to see what the cameras see?" Doug asked.

We did. I'd talked to the guys at SSI enough to know they'd never invade our privacy by pointing the cameras inside, but I still felt the need to verify.

Leaning over Nathan's shoulder was a bad idea. He smelled so damn good. Leather and whiskey and him. One hundred percent masculine. One hundred percent yummy.

It was different from the woodsy scent I remembered from our time together in Vegas. This scent suited him better. I took what I hoped was a stealthy deep inhale, before turning my attention to the screen.

The screen showed four views. The top images were from the front cameras; the bottom two from the back. I saw our front porch in the upper left, the street in the upper right, and the bottom sections showed the patio and yard.

"Seems like overkill," I said, ignoring the desire to lean closer and inhale more Nathan.

"I'm sure they know what they're doing," Gran said. Her voice cracked, revealing the fear she'd been hiding so well until now.

Wanting to put her mind at ease, I agreed. "You're right; they're the pros." My smile felt like plastic on my face. I already felt more than enough guilt for bringing this to her doorstep; I wouldn't add more by arguing with SSI.

When Prince stretched to his full length, sinking his claws into Doug's thigh to get his attention, Doug winced and pried the sharp mini daggers out of his pants.

I rolled my eyes when Gran said, "He has good taste." I loved my grandmother, without question, but I needed to get Doug out of here before she embarrassed me anymore.

"Thank you, Doug," I said, as we walked him to the door.

"You're welcome. We'll get this sorted. You'll have your life back in no time."

I appreciated his confidence, but my life was a shitshow, and I wasn't sure I wanted it back. A new and improved, non-pregnant life—that'd I'd take.

Knowing things would go a lot smoother, I decided to play nice with Nathan while he was here. Hopefully, Gran would stop trying so hard to make me like him if I was civil. Plus, I could easily avoid him by hiding in my room. Except for meals.

When I made Gran dinner, I invited Nathan.

When he offered to help me clean, I let him.

When our hands brushed against each other, I ignored the sensation traveling up my arm and settling in my core.

When Gran turned on the TV to watch her favorite show, I stood to go to my room.

"Why don't you stay and entertain our guest?" Gran suggested.

"He's not our guest," I said.

"I'm not a guest," Nathan said at the same time. "You don't have to entertain me."

"Nonsense," I'd swear it was Gran's favorite expression, "you're here, so there's no reason we shouldn't enjoy your company."

No reason except I wanted what I couldn't have. And because I was practically drooling over his heavily tattooed forearms. Forearms he'd hid under long sleeves every other time I'd seen him, even in the sweltering heat of August.

Forearms that should be illegal to cover, no matter the weather, or how plentiful the scars.

"I have to work on my proposal for the Wyatt Foundation." I bent the truth. "Emily and I are meeting tomorrow to go over my ideas."

Nathan's head snapped up.

"What time?"

"Does it matter?" I said without thinking.

"I need to tell Jamie so he can schedule someone to stay with your grandmother."

Right, how quickly I'd forgotten. "Sorry. This will take some getting used to."

"I know."

"You could always stay here with Gran," I said, wanting him to stay but hoping he'd say no.

When it came to Nathan, my heart and brain didn't agree. My heart wanted him. My brain reminded me I couldn't have him.

"Not gonna happen." He attempted to grin. Unlike the Sheppards, whose lop-sided grins were genetic, Nathan's was lopsided because of his scar.

I need to rein it in. There was no point in fantasizing about those gorgeous ice-blue eyes or perfect, kissable lips when I couldn't have him.

"Ashley?"

Damn it. He caught me staring. Again.

"Yes, Nathan." I used my best good-mannered tone.

"What time?" He already had his phone in hand, ready to message Jamie.

I shouldn't have looked at Gran, who stroked Prince's back in lazy strokes. A wicked gleam sparkled in her eyes. *Nathan wasn't the only one who noticed me staring.*

"We're meeting at Grannie's at eleven."

"Thank you."

After thirty minutes of staring at my screen, I took a cold shower to freeze Nathan out of my system.

Chapter 26

Ashley

During breakfast, Nathan told me he'd drive me to meet Emily. Of course he would. I wanted to be annoyed, but who was I kidding? I barely put up a fight when he'd told me as he set a plate of scrambled eggs and bacon, and a cup of coffee in front of me. Knowing I shouldn't be drinking the coffee, I sipped slowly rather than tell Nathan I needed decaf.

He chuckled when Gran snuck Prince a bite of her bacon. I pretended not to notice. If feeding Prince bacon made her happy, who was I to stop her?

I'd just shoved my laptop in my bag when Nathan called down the hall, "Sammie's here, we can leave whenever you're ready."

Sammie, a Weatherford cop, worked part time at SSI. I trusted her to watch the house and keep Gran safe while Nathan and I went to Grannie's.

The ride over was uncomfortably quiet as Nathan and I stole glances at each other. He glanced. I looked. Admired. Tortured myself knowing it could never be.

The first thing I noticed when we walked into Grannie's was Jamie leaning against the booth, talking to Emily. He made eye contact with Nathan and nodded. As I greeted Mary and Beth, Jamie leaned down and kissed Emily on the temple.

"Hey Ashley." He gave me a quick hug.

"Hi Jamie."

"You okay?"

I smiled, ignoring all the things in my life that weren't okay. "Yeah, the big guy here made breakfast for Gran and me this morning," I said, using Gran's nickname for Nathan.

He raised his eyebrows. "Is that so?"

Nathan shrugged. "I was hungry, and Violet was up." He turned towards me and asked, "You want a coffee?"

I'd only had half a cup, so I did, but I couldn't tell him I needed a decaf. At the rate people were buying me coffee, it'd be my kid's first word.

"I heard you're drinking decaf in solidarity with Meg and Em. Is it true?" In that moment, I'd never been more grateful to Emily's husband.

"It's true." I nodded.

"That's quite a sacrifice. Your coffee consumption is almost as insane as the Gilmores."

My eyes rounded.

"Don't look at me like that. Em loves that show, so naturally I've seen a few episodes."

"Do you like it more or less than Outlander?"

Nathan's laugh saved Jamie from having to answer. I thought it was sweet that Jamie and Jack watched TV with their wives, even if they'd never choose those particular shows.

"One decaf vanilla latte coming right up," Nathan said, remembering my drink of choice.

"You don't have to buy my coffee," I argued as I sat and slid into the booth.

"I don't have to. I want to," he answered, earning a smile and nod from Jamie.

Nathan being nice as he protected me was making it difficult for me to protect my heart.

When he delivered my coffee, he said, "We're right over here if you need us."

I inhaled the sweet scent of my favorite latte. "Thank you." I wondered if the vanilla syrup was bad for the baby. I'd have to look it up when I got home.

Emily scooted to sit beside me so I could show her my ideas. I should've scooted to her side so we could see the door, but it didn't seem necessary with two bodyguards sitting between it and us.

After taking her feedback notes, the conversation shifted to other topics.

Baby topics.

Specifically, my baby.

"You're still seeing Doc Greenfield Wednesday, right?"

"Yes, I'm hoping I'm not, but Doc said false positives are rare." My heart sank when Doc confirmed what the internet had already told me. Not that I didn't want children; I did. Just not with Finn, the reason I needed a bodyguard.

"Have you taken another home test?"

"No, I'm afraid another positive will freak me out, and a negative would get my hopes up. Neither result would improve the situation."

I'd lost track of how many times a day I prayed the test was wrong.

When Emily asked if I'd considered getting a restraining order against Finn, I said I had but knew it wouldn't help. It could also make things worse, like it had when she got one against her now-dead ex-boyfriend.

I trusted Jamie to tell me if I needed one.

The fact that I might need one, for the father of my child, was a mind-fuck. *It's too much to deal with.* I wanted to hide my head in the sand and pretend this wasn't my life.

My mind spiraled down the rabbit hole. What kind of life would my kid have with Red Flag Finn as his father? How much emotional damage would he cause? Would I be able to maintain custody and minimize the harm he'd inflict with his narcissistic, abusive behavior?

I wondered if an order of protection could prevent him from seeing his baby. Or at least require him to have supervision for visits.

"Do you think I could get one to keep Finn away from my baby?"

"You're pregnant?" The deep voice behind me made me jump.

Nathan. *Shit.* I hadn't heard him walk up.

Feeling like a rat in a trap, I looked at Emily, hoping for help.

She bailed on me like a traitor. "I'll give you two a minute."

My head thunked when I dropped it on the table. How the hell was I supposed to face him?

The leather creaked as he shuffled onto the bench across from me. "Ashley."

"What?" My arms covered my head, muffling my reply.

"Please look at me."

"No."

"Why not?"

"I can't do this right now."

"Yes, you can." His voice was softer, encouraging.

"Can you just go away?" I added "Please" thinking it'd make a difference.

"You know I can't. More importantly, I won't."

Two strong hands gently pulled my arms away from my head, then one hand reached over, pried under my chin, and lifted my face up.

"That's better." He used his thumb to wipe away the tears I hadn't wanted him to see. "Is this why you said no to giving me a second chance?"

No judgement. No questions about the baby or Finn.

"Yes." I had more to say, but was too exhausted to find the right words.

When he held my hand, I didn't pull back.

When my gaze locked on his, he held it.

When Jamie cleared his throat, neither of us looked away.

"I'm taking my wife home unless you need me for something?" Jamie said.

Nathan didn't break eye contact when he answered, "We're good."

Nathan finally blinked, breaking the spell, when Jamie said, "Maybe we'll stay until he's focused again."

My cheeks burned as I pulled my hand away.

Damn, that was intense.

Emily leaned over the bench and hugged me goodbye. "Call me later. I want to hear everything." Her impish grin and sparkling eyes made my cheeks burn a little hotter.

Resisting the temptation to look at Nathan, I said, "Okay."

We sat in silence for a few minutes after Jamie and Emily left. Words seemed inadequate for the heavy emotions swirling in the air around us.

"Can I take you home?" Nathan asked, breaking the silence.

I liked the way the word home sounded on his lips. *No, I can't think like that.*

Sitting there like a deer in the headlights, a million emotions raged inside. My hands shook. My voice failed me. My eyes blinked away more tears.

"Come on, Slick, let's go." He used the nickname he'd given me in Vegas as he stood and took the one step needed to stand beside my bench. When he extended his hand, I took it.

It was as if I no longer had control over my limbs.

Is it too early to blame the hormones?

"Thanks," I mumbled.

When I turned to say goodbye to Mary, she grinned like a cat who'd found the cream. "Bye, Mary." I practically whispered as I lifted my free hand in a half-wave.

"Bye, Ashley. Nathan."

"Have a good day, Mrs. Sheppard."

Mary inhaled deeply, a telltale sign she was repressing her annoyance. "How many times have I told you to call me Mary?"

At the last Craft and Booze Night, she'd complained about all the new hires calling her Mrs. Sheppard. I'd laughed when she praised their good manners while complaining about their reluctance to call her by her first name.

Nathan smiled. "Right, sorry. Have a good day, Mary."

She smiled. "That's better. Now, you two get out of here."

Having embarrassed myself more than enough for one day, I was happy to obey.

Chapter 27

Nathan

When I'd made breakfast earlier that morning, I'd made a pot of decaf but realized I couldn't tell Ashley. Keeping quiet was killing me, and I worried I'd slip up.

Lucky for me, Lady Luck was on my side. Overhearing Ashley mention her baby to Emily at Grannie's solved all my problems.

Well, one of them.

I'd felt bad for startling her, but I couldn't let the opportunity pass, so I'd asked "You're pregnant?".

Then we had a moment. An intense, rock me to my core, turn my world upside down, emotionally charged moment.

So intense that everything around us disappeared.

Until Jamie's badly timed interruption.

Part of me wanted to kick his ass for killing the moment. The other part wanted to thank him for reminding me I was there for Ashley's safety, not my feelings.

Escorting Ashley to my truck, I placed my right hand on her lower back, a choice that was professional and personal. I scanned for any signs of suspicious activity as we walked.

Seconds after I closed my door, Ashley said, "I'm sorry." Her voice was barely loud enough to hear over the country music playing on the radio.

I turned it off. "For what?" There was literally nothing for her to apologize for. Not even for keeping the secret of her pregnancy, which was literally none of my business.

Except I want it to be my business. I wanted everything about her to be my business.

"For not telling you the truth."

She didn't owe me an apology, but I appreciated it.

I nodded. "It's Finn's?" I asked, knowing the answer. Ashley acted as though she played fast and loose, but I knew better.

In a raw moment during our first night in Vegas, Ashley admitted to feeling lonely and wanting what her friends had. I'd felt the same way.

I thought it'd be hard finding a woman to connect with on a deeper level. Until I responded to the cheesiest pickup line and came face-to-face with the most gorgeous woman I'd ever met. One smile, one laugh, one touch, and I was hooked.

If only I hadn't needed to lie.

If only I hadn't been undercover.

If only things hadn't gone so life-threateningly wrong. I gripped the steering wheel as the familiar signs of panic set in and forced myself to focus on Ashley.

Ashley nodded. A tear made a slow trek down her perfect face.

"I don't want his baby," she whispered. "I never want to see him again."

It'd be a nightmare trying to keep Finn away from her and her child, but she had a team of trained professionals who'd protect them, including me.

"Hey, it'll be okay. We'll find a way to make everything okay." I was already talking as if we were a team. A couple.

"How can you say that with everything going on?"

"Because you're tough, Slick. You'll rise above his bullshit. And I won't let him hurt you." I promised, glancing at her still-flat belly. "Either of you."

Instead of thanking me, she cried some more.

"Talk to me," I said, reaching over to put my hand on her shoulder. I wanted to hold her hand, but she was wringing it in her lap. "Tell me what's going through that beautiful head of yours."

She choked out a laugh, clearly doubting my sincerity.

"I'm not beautiful, I'm puffy." She wiped the tears off her face.

"You can be both."

"I'm sorry. I wanted to say yes. To give you a second chance." She sniffed. "But how could I?"

Sensing she had more to say, I waited.

"What man wants to date a pregnant woman?"

Me. Becoming a father wasn't on my radar, but I wasn't opposed to it. A big, loving family was something I'd never had, but wanted. It wouldn't matter if the kids were mine by

DNA or adoption. I'd love them, provide for them, and keep them safe. The way I always imagined my parents would've done, had they lived.

And I want it with Ashley.

We hadn't even gone on a proper date, so how could I admit my feelings without sounding crazy?

Calmly. Honestly. Carefully.

Later.

"Ashley, you're not dumb. I'd still like a second chance, despite how different it looks."

"You want to date someone who's unemployed, lives with her grandmother, and oh, that's right, is pregnant with another man's baby?" The laugh that escaped her lips was a little scary. "Are you insane?"

None of that mattered. I could easily support her. And would, if our relationship turned into more. *If she'll let me.* But that wasn't what she needed to hear. "You'll find another job, and you're taking care of your grandmother."

I felt her staring at me, waiting for me to address the third part of her question.

Taking the time to find the right words proved useless; when I opened my mouth, the blunt truth came out. "You're fucking amazing, Ashley, so, yes, I still want to date you."

She mumbled something, but instead of asking her to repeat it, I asked, "Do you still want to be seen with me despite the huge scar running down my face?" It was a stupid question, since she hadn't shied away from it, but I asked to prove a point.

"What kind of stupid question is that?" she shot at me.

I laughed. "Ashley, how I feel about you doesn't change because of a minor hiccup."

"A minor hiccup?" She laughed so hard she snorted, reminding me of our nights in her hotel room. "A minor hiccup? That's what we're calling pregnancy now?"

"What do you call it?"

"Under the circumstances, a life sentence."

I assumed the life sentence was about Finn, not about being a mom.

"You don't have to go through it alone. Give me a second chance. Let me prove I can be here for you."

She sighed. "Is it really a second chance if you didn't actually do anything wrong?" A soft smile played across her lips.

"In this case, yes. I need a second chance to take you out. To wine and dine you." She laughed. "Okay, just dine you." It was my turn to laugh. "You know what I mean."

"I do." She turned to face me. "Are you sure?"

"I am. But we have to talk. Make sure we're on the same page and set some ground rules."

"Ground rules?" she asked.

"For starters, no more secrets." I set the same rule she had the last time we talked. Now that the big ones were out in the open, I didn't think it'd be a problem. I longed for our return to easy, flowing conversations.

Which meant I needed to find the courage to share more than I had. *More than I feel capable of.*

One step at a time, my therapist's voice whispered in my head.

"Okay. What else?"

"You're not allowed to insult my girl anymore."

"Your girl?"

Yeah, because I already knew I wouldn't give her up now that I had her.

"Is that a problem?"

Her shy smile brought out more of my caveman characteristics as one word flashed through my mind. *Mine.*

"No."

"Anything you want to add?"

"Yes, but can we get lunch first?" Her stomach growled.

I'd forgotten she and Emily had planned on having lunch at Grannie's, but my interruption cut their lunch date short.

"Of course. What do you want?"

She hummed as she thought about it. "Pizza."

"Pizza it is. What toppings should we get?" I didn't get to finish before she answered. Hawaiian.

That had to be the hormones talking. Pineapple on pizza was disgusting.

"Now I'm rethinking things." I squeezed her leg, so she'd know it was a joke.

"What? Pineapple on pizza is delicious."

"It's a crime."

"What do you put on yours? No, let me guess. All the meats." She said meats like it was a bad thing.

"I'll have you know I like sausage, peppers, and onions on my pizza."

"Ew, gross."

"Which part?"

"Sausage. It doesn't belong on a pizza."

"Says the girl who wants pineapple."

Ashley typed the address of her favorite pizza place into my phone.

"I think I'll get wings, too."

There was something infinitely sexy about a woman who wasn't afraid to eat. The image of her devouring the cheese fries we were supposed to share the night we met flashed through my mind. It'd taken every ounce of control I'd possessed not to lick the cheese off her lips or suck it off her fingers.

We rode in comfortable silence until I ruined it. "Can I ask you a question?"

"Sure," she answered, sounding slightly hesitant.

"Do you think Finn's the type of guy who'd hurt a child?" If she said yes, I'd do everything in my power to keep him out of their lives.

"Not physically, but he's so self-centered I don't think he'd hesitate to use our child as a pawn to get what he wants."

"That's not any better." I'd seen too many kids have their childhoods destroyed because one or both parents treated them as weapons to hurt the other.

"I know." She paused, fiddling with her phone. "I need to show you something, but you can't get upset."

Which pretty much guaranteed I would. "I can't promise that."

"Please?" I nodded. "Finn's been texting and calling me." A low growl formed in my throat. Before I could plot his demise, she said, "I meant to tell Jamie, but I kept forgetting because other things kept happening."

She promised to show me the texts later, when I wasn't driving. As predicted, I was upset, but it was directed at Finn, not Ashley.

Upset wasn't quite accurate. I wanted to rip him from limb to limb.

Ashley said, "I have an appointment with Dr. Greenfield on Wednesday." From the way she said the doc's name, I assumed he or she was the family doctor.

"Pregnancy test?" I asked.

She nodded. "Is it bad that I'm desperately hoping I'm not?"

"No." I'd feel the same way in her shoes. "Are false positives common?" I wasn't trying to be an ass, but I knew nothing about home pregnancy tests and couldn't ask the internet while driving.

"No." More tears tracked down her perfect but pale face as she turned away.

"Ashley." I squeezed her thigh. "It's okay to be scared."

She nodded but didn't look back.

I reached over and turned her head so she was facing me. "Please don't hide from me, okay?"

She wiped away her tears. "Okay. Sorry."

"And don't apologize. I can only imagine how overwhelmed you feel."

I insisted on paying when she ordered a large Hawaiian pizza, claiming Gran liked it too, and two dozen chicken wings.

"Did you seriously just order a diet drink?"

"What? I don't want to get fat."

My eyes trailed down her body, taking in every detail. She wasn't fat. She was gorgeous, fit, and...

Ashley cleared her throat.

"Nathan, stop staring and tell me what kind of dipping sauce you want."

"Does that mean you'll share your wings?"

"Maybe." She grinned and tossed her hair over her shoulder with enough sass to make the girl behind the counter giggle.

"Ranch is fine." I said before adding my small pizza to the order.

Lunch with Ashley and Gran was an exercise in patience and control.

Ashley was back to her feisty self, and Violet was even less subtle than before in her attempts to hook us up.

Little did Violet know, we were halfway there.

If I had my way about it, I'd be kissing Ashley before the night was over.

Chapter 28

Ashley

Gran must have sensed the shift. She spent less time trying to hook us up and more time getting to know Nathan. Hearing him cleverly maneuver away from topics he wanted to avoid reminded me of our time in Vegas.

How easily he'd played me.

No, I corrected myself. He did what he had to do. And it wasn't his fault I was too enthralled to notice his shifty behavior.

When Gran asked, "Can I ask how you got your scar?" Nathan's entire body tensed. Gran noticed too and quickly changed the subject.

Instinctively, I put my hand on his arm, offering comfort. I didn't know all the details, but I knew thinking about it caused him to freak out.

Gran didn't miss the gesture, or the tension in Nathan's shoulders draining away as he stared at my hand on his sleeve.

"What I meant to ask is, how do you like working for John and his boys?" Gran asked.

Nathan nodded his appreciation before answering. His voice was rough, like he'd just woken up. Or was holding back powerful emotions. "It's only been a week, but so far, I like it. I appreciate their no bullsh-their no nonsense approach."

Gran laughed. "John was never one for bullshit, got that from his father."

Gran didn't mind the occasional cuss word, which made her the coolest grandmother in Weatherford, maybe even Texas. But she drew the line at fuck. Gran thought the word was unnecessary.

I disagreed. The word had many useful applications, but I refrained from using it in her presence.

"And passed on to his sons," Nathan added.

"At least the oldest one." Gran looked at me. "I seem to remember Jack and the youngest." She paused, trying to remember his name.

"Jaden." I reminded her. It made sense she didn't remember him. Jay was several years younger, so he never hung out with us.

"Right, Jaden. They got in their fair share of trouble."

"Jack wasn't too bad," I said, defending him. We'd hung out in the same circles in high school. Jack wasn't straight and narrow like Jamie, who was a little too perfect, but he wasn't a troublemaker. He questioned rules and tested boundaries, but there was never any ill intent.

"That tracks," Nathan said, at the same time.

Nathan and I cleaned the kitchen after dinner while Gran played with Prince in the living room. The silence should've felt awkward, but it didn't. Our hands brushing as he handed me a plate to dry set my body on fire. When our eyes locked, the same fire burned in his.

When he invaded my space, my heart raced.

My knees turned to Jello when he whispered in my ear, "What time does Gran go to bed?"

His hands on my hips promised more. My hands on his chest asked for it.

We had a lot to talk about, but all I could think about was us spending the night in my bed without my grandmother finding out.

Our desire faded as we hung out with Gran, so after she went to bed, we talked.

In Vegas, we'd bonded over losing our parents young but never finished the conversation because Nathan's lips had begged to be kissed simply by existing, and I'd gladly done so.

"I'm lucky I had Gran and Grandpa to raise me, and the Taylors were like a second family."

"Taylor's?"

"Emily's family."

He nodded. "Have you known the Sheppards forever, too?"

"Pretty much. Chris, Jamie, and Jack played football together, so we saw a lot of them." I laughed. "As kids, Em and I followed Chris and Jamie around like puppy dogs. They hated it, but Em had a crush on Jamie."

"Really? And now they're married?"

"Yup. They went through hell before falling in love with each other." I didn't tell him the details, figuring they weren't mine to share.

"Let me guess, you had a crush on Jack," he said.

I savored the hint of jealousy in his voice, half wishing he'd growl again. There was something sexy about his primal response to another man touching me.

"Nah, I crushed on Chris, but if you ever tell a soul, I'll tell everyone you have herpes." I couldn't threaten anything real, knowing he'd been through far more than any human should endure.

It was music to my ears when he threw his head back and laughed. "I've been threatened with a lot of things in my life, but that takes the cake."

Nathan's heated stare pinned me in place as he raised his hands and cupped my face. "I never stopped thinking about you," was all he said before leaning in to kiss me.

He hesitated, giving me a chance to say no, but there was no way in hell that word would cross my lips.

"Kiss me." My whisper sounded like a plea.

He did. Soft and sweet, and so full of emotion that any lingering doubt I might've had melted away.

"Love when you whimper like that," he said, his lips still dangerously close to mine. "Do I still inspire the kissing scenes in your romance novel?"

My eyes flew open as I pulled away. "What?"

I'd never told anyone I was writing a rom-com.

He grinned. "You don't remember telling me."

"When did I tell you?" It was a stupid question. "Vegas, obviously, but when exactly?" And what else didn't I remember?

"I'd be offended that you don't remember telling me, but we'd had a few drinks, and you mumbled it when we came up for air."

"Then how come you remember?" I asked.

"Because." He tucked a stray hair behind my ear, lighting a blazing trail of desire to my core. "I remember everything about you, Ashley."

We talked. We kissed. When I asked him to join me in my room, Nathan said no.

As joy drained from my body, I stared at my rainbow-striped socks like it was my job.

"Look at me." When I looked up, he said, "I want you. So much it hurts." He adjusted himself to prove his point. "And when I finally have you, there'll be nothing to prevent you from screaming my name. Repeatedly." His hooded eyes, his low, rough voice, and the bulge in his pants, convinced me he meant it.

"But not tonight?"

"No, because tonight I'd have to split my attention between worshipping you and protecting you and your grandmother."

Liking the idea of Nathan worshipping me, I sucked in a gulp of air. My brain started imagining all the things he'd do when we finally stripped off our clothes and let loose.

The thought alone was almost orgasm-inducing.

Chapter 29

Nathan

I woke up early and checked the video feeds. Then I took a cold shower to rinse away the dreams of Ashley. Not that I hadn't enjoyed them, but I couldn't walk around with a raging hard-on.

Enjoying the quiet, I sipped my coffee while waiting for the sun to rise. There was something hypnotic about the world in those last moments before the sun signaled the start of the day.

When Gran joined me shortly after the sun peaked over the horizon, I poured her a cup.

"Cream and sugar?" I asked.

"Yes, please."

"Thank you." The spoon clattered against ceramic as she doctored her coffee.

"My pleasure." Prince's demanding meows caught me off guard. How did one small animal make so much noise? "Is he okay?"

"He wants breakfast. Would you be a dear and feed him?"

I'd do anything to make him shut up. "Where's his food?"

Gran pointed to the tall cabinet beside the white refrigerator.

Anyone wanting to practice the skills necessary to be a SEAL should try feeding Prince. That damn cat used his voice, his body, and his claws to demand my attention. The little fur ball clearly blamed me for starving him, when it was his actions delaying the outcome he so desperately wanted.

"Is he always like that?" I asked after successfully completing my mission with only a few minor injuries.

"No, he must like you."

"I'd hate to see how he acts with people he doesn't like." I shook my head and poured myself another cup of coffee.

Violet pulled a one-eighty and asked, "How'd things go with Ashley last night?" I rushed to cover my mouth so I wouldn't spit out my coffee.

How do I answer that? Our relationship was complex, and her grandmother didn't know our history. Nor did she need to.

What she knew was that I was crazy about her granddaughter.

I answered carefully, "We sat on the couch and talked late into the night." I removed any chance she'd ask about physical activities.

Or so I thought.

"Do I need to have it cleaned?"

My hand didn't move fast enough. It was my fault. I shouldn't have taken a sip after answering.

"Violet!" I grabbed a napkin to wipe up the coffee I'd spewed across the table.

"What'd she do now?" Ashley's sleepy voice sounded weary.

"Nothing," I answered.

When she reached for the coffeepot, I offered to brew a fresh pot. "Fresh is always better." I winked. After emptying the pot into my mug, I brewed half a pot of decaf.

She nodded and plopped down next to her grandmother.

The dark circles under her eyes didn't detract from her beauty. The hint of pink in her cheeks made me think about how she'd flushed when I kissed her.

I didn't miss her eyes darting below my beltline just before I turned.

I needed to take Ashley away for a few hours or I'd have the worst case of blue balls in the history of forever.

Knowing we needed groceries. Or rather, I needed to add to their food supply because I ate more than the two of them combined. Shopping was the perfect excuse.

Maybe I could take Ashley to my hotel room before we went shopping.

Or maybe not. Asking her to my hotel felt slimy, no matter how nice the room was. Once again, I was foiled by my desire to deliver on my promise—to rock her world on our first night together—and my need to be the romantic hero she deserved.

"Ashley and I need to go grocery shopping later today. Do you need anything?"

"We need more tuna," Violet answered.

"No, we don't. You'll make Prince fat if you insist on feeding him tuna all the time."

"Nonsense. He's a cat. It's part of his natural diet," Violet argued.

"Yes, but in the wild, he'd have to hunt for it."

Prince chimed in with what I assumed was a vote for more tuna, making us all laugh.

When I called SSI, John volunteered to stay with Violet.

When I announced John had arrived, she rushed towards the door to greet him.

Safety be damned. When I told her I'd answer the door, she scoffed. "You just said it's John."

"Yes, but I intend to verify that before I open the door."

She muttered under her breath as she waited.

"John."

"Nathan." He nodded in greeting before turning. "It's good to see you, Violet. How's the hip?"

"Still slow, but I'm healing. Nathan, don't just stand there, invite our guest in."

I didn't miss her use of 'our', nor did John. It was useless to argue, so I followed her orders and invited him in.

His uneven grin reminded me of his sons as he accepted. It struck me again how much Jack looked like his father. They had the same wavy brown hair and amber eyes. If they were the same age, they could be mistaken for twins.

After handing John my laptop, I said, "We won't be long."

"Take your time. I have this handsome young man to keep me company."

Ashley rolled her eyes and mouthed "I'm sorry" to John.

"Have fun, kids," John said with a smile and a wave.

With my hand on her back, I walked Ashley to my truck and opened her door. I pretended not to see Violet and John watching from the window with matching smiles on their faces.

"Poor John," Ashley said as soon as I closed my door.

I glanced at the now-empty window. "I think he'll be just fine." John didn't strike me as a matchmaker, but I didn't doubt for a second he'd listen to Violet as she rambled on about Ashley and me. I could only imagine what she'd tell him about us staying up late last night.

Christ. I ran my hand down my face as I imagined what the next lecture he gave me might sound like.

At the store, Ashley suggested we split up so we could finish faster.

"That's not going to happen, Slick." I wouldn't let Ashley out of my sight. I wouldn't even let her out of my reach in an environment as chaotic as a grocery store.

Huffing and rolling her eyes, she squinted at me and crossed her arms over her chest, but there was no bark to her bite when she said, "Fine."

In the canned goods aisle, she set her purse in the kid seat and turned to browse the tuna selection. The little liar pretended to be the voice of reason but was just as inclined to spoil the demon cat as her grandmother.

"Ashley, you shouldn't leave your purse unattended in the cart."

Seriously, how did a woman, whose two best friends had PI/bodyguards for husbands, have no sense of self-preservation?

"It's not unattended. You're right there," she said, not bothering to turn and verify if I was there or not.

"What if I'd turned my back? It'd only take a second for someone to steal it when you aren't looking."

"Fine." She turned, reached over and grabbed it, then made a big show out of slinging it over her shoulder. "Happy now?"

"Blissfully. Let's go."

In Vegas, Ashley had told me she ate out a lot. I assumed she knew how to cook but didn't want to. An assumption she corrected when she started filling the cart with pre-packaged and frozen meals.

"Do you know how to cook?"

"I do, sort of. It seemed senseless when it was just me."

"But you cook for your grandmother."

"I do, but I cheat." She turned back towards the cart to see me removing the frozen meals. "What are you doing?"

"I'm not eating frozen or overly processed food at every meal."

"I make breakfast with fresh eggs." She defended herself.

"Good to know." I smirked.

"Let me guess, you know how to cook." She was laying the sass on pretty thick for someone who'd be enjoying the fruits of my labor.

Steering us to the end of the store with fresh ingredients, I answered, "I know my way around the kitchen." Wanting to open up more, and thinking this was a safe topic, I shared more about my childhood. "I had to learn how to cook in foster care and ended up liking it. I'm not a gourmet or anything, but I can follow a recipe." Wanting to surprise her, I understated my abilities.

"Had to?" she asked softly.

"Sadly, some of my foster parents thought fostering kids equaled free labor and assigned us chores. After getting an ass-whipping for burning a meal, I made it my mission to learn how."

"I'm sorry you went through that." She hooked her arm through mine as I pushed the cart.

"Thanks. It wasn't all bad. And the experience taught me discipline and responsibility. When I wanted to take martial arts so I wouldn't get bullied anymore, I didn't think twice about working to pay for it."

"It's hard to imagine anyone bullying you."

"I wasn't always built like this." I flexed the arm under her hand. "And sadly, foster kids have always been easy targets." Not just in our lifetime, but pretty much forever.

"I'm sorry." She moved closer, wrapping me in an envelope of calm compassion and the delicious scent of her fruity shampoo.

"Thanks."

"Do you remember your parents?"

"No, I was too young. You?"

"Gran and Grandpa told me about them, so I feel like I remember them."

"You're lucky."

"I am," Ashley said before picking up a dragon fruit. "What the hell is this?"

It was exactly the distraction we needed. After having some fun making fun of exotic fruits, we finished our shopping in the dairy aisle, then got in line to pay.

Ashley tried to offer me money when it was time to check out but lost the argument. No way would I let her or her grandmother pay for my groceries. I didn't care that I'd bought far more than necessary. Or that Ashley added six cans of tuna and two tubs of ice cream to the cart. They were on a tight budget, and I had money to spare. Paying was the right thing to do.

On the drive home, Ashley asked me what kind of jobs I'd done before joining the Navy.

"Mostly odd jobs—mowing lawns, raking leaves, the type of thing people are willing to pay young teens to do. During high school, I did construction work in the summers. You?"

"I did the typical teenage girl thing and babysat. When I was old enough, I worked at Grannie's."

"Have you always wanted to write?"

She groaned, causing my head to turn at the sound. Once again, I thought dirty thoughts, and once again I reined them in. Though it didn't stop me from appreciating how cute she looked as she tried to hide her face behind her hands.

"I can't believe I told you that. I haven't even told Emily I'm writing a book."

"Why not?" I didn't know Emily well, but from what I'd seen there was no doubt she'd support Ashley.

"I don't know. We've joked about writing one together with Meg, but it's just that. A joke."

"So tell me again why you're afraid to tell them." I wanted to understand, but she was making zero sense.

She laughed. "I don't know."

"Would you write full time if you could afford to?"

"Maybe," she answered quickly, then changed her mind. "Probably. Being creative was my favorite part of my job, and writing is nothing if not creative."

Back at the house, I let her carry in the bag of tuna, because she refused to get out of the truck unless I let her help. It was easier than carrying her in.

The thought of carrying her, holding her close to my body, had the same effect as actually having her that close. I had to think about Gran and John waiting inside to get rid of the bulge in my pants.

Thankfully, John called Ashley into the kitchen to ask her about her grandmother's habit of cheating at cards, which kept her occupied while I carried in the rest of the groceries.

To justify buying the tuna, after insisting they didn't need it, Ashley made tuna salad sandwiches for lunch. When she invited John, he declined.

But Violet insisted, so John ate lunch with us.

We talked for a few minutes in the living room while Ashley made lunch and Gran spoiled Prince.

"Violet said you're a pleasure to have around."

"Thank you." It probably sounded more like a question because the statement came out of nowhere.

"She likes you." He glanced at the kitchen. "And thinks you're good for Ashley."

If I were a peacock, I would have strutted around showing off my tail feathers. Somehow, hearing it from John meant more than Violet shamelessly trying to pair us up. Maybe because all her attempts were based on physical attraction, but this went deeper.

"How serious is it?"

"We're talking things out." *And I'm dying to drag her off like a fucking heathen and claim her.*

"Good."

"No warning about mixing business with pleasure? No telling me you have a rule against sleeping with a client?"

John laughed. "Would it do any good?"

I smiled while giving a single slow shake of my head.

"Will you be careless with her safety because you're in love with her?"

There's that word again. "Hell no."

"Lastly, do you think I'd dare incur the wrath of Violet York by telling you to stay away?"

It was my turn to laugh.

Chapter 30

Ashley

On Tuesday morning, Nathan checked the video feed before escorting Gran and me to my car, which he insisted on driving.

"Come on, Slick, just give me your keys." He held his hand out.

"Slick?" Gran asked.

Watching Nathan as he realized his mistake was priceless. I was ready to cover for him but wanted to watch him sweat. His comically wide, ice-blue eyes turned to me. Begging. Pleading.

"It's nothing. Nathan thinks he's funny." My shit-eating grin was pure innocence.

He nodded, but not before shooting me a look that promised I'd hear about it later. *I wonder if he'll spank me.* I slammed the lid shut on that thought. Fantasizing about Nathan with Gran in the car would be a fate worse than death.

"Hmm, alright." She looked between us. If I had to guess, Gran was debating whether she should call us out on the lie. "Give him your keys. It'll be fun to have a handsome chauffeur."

Remembering Jamie driving Emily and me around last July made me laugh so hard I snorted. It was either that or cry. Because Jamie had driven that day for the same reason Nathan was driving today.

How the hell did I let this happen?

Instead of taking the keys, Nathan's warm hand surrounded mine. "You okay?"

Damn him for seeing too much.

"Yeah, just remembering when Emily needed protection and Jamie was our chauffeur."

His stare drilled into my soul, seeing what I didn't want him to see. With a quick nod, he said, "Okay then, let's go." He turned to Gran. "We don't want to keep your doctor waiting."

Nathan stood guard while I helped Gran into the back seat. He folded her walker and put in the front passenger seat. When I asked why he didn't put it in the trunk, he whispered, "Quick access."

Hoping my forced smile hid my fear, I slid into the back seat next to Gran. Nathan started the engine, propped his phone in my mounted dash phone holder, and adjusted the mirror.

"What's a good driver name?" Gran asked.

"Mario," I answered without thinking. Then I pictured Nathan as a short, round cartoon figure ducking out of the way of fiery bombs and jumping from box to box. The resulting giggle fit made me snort. I wish I could say my giggling fits were all from humor, but Nathan's tense watchfulness had me on edge.

"What's so funny about Mario Andretti?" Nathan asked.

When I finally caught my breath, I said, "I was thinking more along the lines of Mario and Luigi, you know, the brothers who save the princess?"

"Princess Violet has a nice ring to it." He used the mirror to look at Gran and grinned.

"Nonsense. I'd rather be a queen. Not just any queen. A ruling queen in my own right. Like Queen Elizabeth the First."

Leave it to my grandmother to one-up Nathan.

"Queen Violet it is."

"You can be a princess, dear." She patted my leg.

"I don't know. Princess Ashley doesn't have the same ring to it," Nathan said.

Biting down on my lips was the only thing keeping the words, fuck you, Casper, from flying out of my mouth. But Gran hated the f-word, so I held my lips between my teeth until the urge passed.

Nathan laughed at my frustration.

"Stop laughing, Mario."

It only made him laugh more. And holy shit did my heart do a flip-flop listening to his deep, rumbling, full-on, from-the-gut laughter.

At the doctor's office, Nathan made us wait in the car until he'd opened Gran's walker. He opened my door, then stood guard while I helped Gran out. I could only imagine what people thought seeing us with a bodyguard outside Doc Greenfield's office.

This was Weatherford, not Hollywood. We were the Yorks, not the Kardashians.

Nathan and I kept our shenanigans to a minimum in the waiting room filled with old magazines and children's books and toys. What little talking we did, we did in hushed tones. Luckily, Doc and her team got my message that my upcoming appointment was a secret. The last thing I needed was Gran hearing about my appointment from our doctor.

When a little girl, maybe four or five years old, walked up to Nathan and asked about his scar, her mother scolded her.

"It's okay, ma'am." He turned to the little girl. "Do you know what a Navy SEAL is?"

She shook her head while mumbling, no.

"Well, that's what I am. I had to do a dangerous job, and I got hurt." He lied, but for all the right reasons.

"Does it hurt?" she asked shyly.

"No, not anymore."

She didn't notice him clutching the arm of the small, hard plastic chair, but I did. I laid my hand on his forearm and traced slow circles on his forearm.

The white around his knuckles slowly returned to the natural shade of tanned skin that spoke of long hours outside.

The mom thanked Nathan for his service before ushering her daughter to the kid's table.

"You okay?" I asked.

He reached for my hand. "I am now."

Chapter 31

Nathan

The instant we walked into the house, my body went on high alert. I couldn't see or hear anything, but I sensed something wasn't right.

I drew my pistol and moved them away from the door. My eyes never stopped scanning. "Call John and wait here." I ordered.

Pride filled my heart as I watched Ashley take a protective stance in front of her grandmother despite her hands shaking as she pulled her phone out of her back pocket.

So fucking brave.

The tremor in her voice as she asked for John pierced my heart like Robinhood's arrow. "John's not available," she whispered.

We didn't have time for a game of telephone, so I grabbed her phone. Keeping my voice low, I said, "This is Bravo One. I need backup at Flirty's. Send anyone you can."

As soon as Meg confirmed, I disconnected the call. "Sorry," I apologized as I handed back her phone.

Thankfully, being in a small town meant it only took a minute before Cate called my cell. "We're here. What do you need us to do?"

"Clear the back."

"Clear the back. We're on it."

"Bravo Three, be discreet."

"Roger that."

Using our phones instead of comms wasn't ideal for stealth, but they were all we had.

Before they finished, the rest of SSI arrived. John called for an update and then organized the Sierra team. We kept the line open, so I heard him order Jamie and Doug to cover the front.

I added Jay to the call and ordered him and Cate to stay out back and cover the door.

No one would enter or exit the house without us seeing them.

John, Jack, and AJ would help me clear the inside.

The first thing John did was hug a trembling Violet. "I've got them," he said, releasing us to clear the house.

"I'm on point," I said. If the person terrorizing Ashley and Violet needed shooting, I wanted to be the one pulling the trigger.

For their sake, I prayed the asshole was long gone.

I transitioned to operator mode and signaled to the hall. Jack and AJ drew their guns, lined up behind me, and signaled they were ready.

We searched the bedrooms and bath.

No one.

The last room we needed to clear was the kitchen.

I held up my hand to stop forward motion and pointed.

"Fuck," Jack said behind me.

"Gloves?" I asked.

The black rose petals scattered around the blood stain could be dealt with later. First, I needed to check the mangled, blood-covered mound of black fur on the floor because we hadn't seen Prince yet.

Jack pressed two blue gloves into my right hand. I holstered my gun, snapped on the gloves, and, avoiding the blood drops, dropped to one knee. The closer I got, the faster my breath came. "Snap some photos," I ordered, wanting documentation before touching the bloody mass.

"Done." AJ's response was half growl.

Sending one last prayer to heaven, I touched it.

Thank God. Before I could say "It's stuffed" Ashley screamed.

I was on my feet and ripping off my gloves faster than my brain could think. My arms were around her before I gave myself conscious permission to move. Needing to comfort her, I held Ashley to my chest and whispered "It's not Prince" over and over until she stopped crying.

"We're clear. Call everyone in," Jack said, taking over the lead while I walked Ashley to the living room. John walked the pale-faced Violet to the couch and sat her beside Ashley.

"What happened?" Violet held her head high, but her voice trembled.

"A cruel joke," I answered.

"I thought it was Prince," Ashley said through her sniffles.

Needing to focus on the task at hand, not Ashley's emotions, I transitioned back into professional mode.

"It wasn't. It's a stuffed animal."

Whoever did this wanted to invoke terror. And worse, they knew intimate details about the York household.

Whoever did this had watched the house, waiting for us to leave.

When I looked at John, I could tell we'd formed the same conclusion—the Yorks needed more protection. "I'll arrange it."

"Arrange what?" Violet asked.

"Go, I've got this," I said, dismissing John. It wasn't an order, despite my rough voice, but he followed it.

"One person isn't enough. We need someone outside the house twenty-four seven."

"Isn't that why we have cameras?" Ashley asked.

"Yes, but…" The person who broke in had probably disabled them. "We'll check the feed, but the cameras didn't prevent the break-in."

After making his call, John made tea and delivered cups to Violet and Ashley. Violet made a fuss about being waited on in her own home, but John sweet-talked her. "Let us spoil you a little while we wait for the police to arrive."

"Can't you solve it?" Violet asked.

"We can, and we will, but we still have to report it," he answered. "When the police are done, we'll clean up the mess."

"You don't have to."

"Violet, please don't argue with me about this." John's words asked, but his tone issued an order.

"It's okay, Gran." Ashley held her grandmother's hand. "Just think, watching the handsome SSI guys do housework will be even better than having a chauffeur." Ashley's injection of humor helped convince Violet.

"In the meantime, I have some more questions for you," John said.

"Nathan, got a second?" Cate asked from the kitchen entryway.

"Go, I'll stay here." John took out his notebook, ready to take notes the old-fashioned way.

Cate tilted her head toward the kitchen, so I followed her.

"What's your assessment?" I asked. As a former FBI profiler, Cate's opinion would be invaluable.

"This isn't Finn. Nothing in his profile leads me to believe he's capable of this."

I didn't think so either, but that didn't mean he wasn't involved.

"You think he hired someone?"

"Possibly. If he did, he found a professional who takes pleasure in terrifying his victims. Or it could be someone else entirely."

"Ashley said she can't think of anyone who'd want to hurt her."

"It could be someone who's never made contact." She let the statement hang in the air. Our job would be a thousand times harder if the suspect were unidentified.

I glanced back at the mess. "Any thoughts on the black roses?"

"They symbolize death and mystery, so it feels like a threat. We should research crime reports that include black roses. We assumed Finn was responsible, but after this." She glanced back at the mess. "We have to broaden our search."

I nodded. "Thanks." I looked through the arched entryway towards the living room. "Do me a favor? Type up your assessment and send it to me." I wanted to review the details later with a fresh mind. "Keep me updated on what else you find. Please."

"Of course. And Blaszek," she waited for me to make eye contact, "you're not in this alone, so whatever you need, just ask."

"Thanks, Maxwell." As a team guy, you wouldn't think I'd need to be reminded, but you'd be wrong. My time with Hawken's did more damage than I'd realized.

I was desperate to return to Ashley, but I had a job to do. "Sharpe, anything?" I asked Doug.

"Nothing in front but the back cameras went dark at two-seventeen."

Fifteen minutes after we'd left.

"I scanned the streets before we left. I didn't see anyone."

"This isn't on you," he said.

"Isn't it? It's my job to protect them."

"And you did. They're both fine." We turned our heads just in time to see Prince jump onto Gran's lap. She flattened him like a pancake when she hugged him, praising him for hiding and staying safe while Ashley watched with new tears forming in her eyes.

"Can you replace the cameras?"

"I don't have any with me, but as soon as we're done here I'll get new ones."

"Thank you."

A hand fell on my shoulder. "Blaszek, let us handle this. Go take care of your girl," Jamie said.

My girl. Once again, I had to admit I liked how that sounded.

Glancing back at the mess on the floor, I vowed no one would ever touch a hair on Ashley's head.

It hadn't taken Jack long to figure out the substance on the floor wasn't blood. I felt stupid for not realizing the smell was all wrong, but I'd been hyper-focused on making sure the black fur wasn't Prince.

This is why we work in teams.

The police visit was shorter than expected. They photographed the crime scene, gathered the evidence, took our statements, and released the scene in what had to be record time.

"The Yorks hired us after a previous incident. This it part of our ongoing investigation. We're also providing personal protection," John said. "We'll share intel if you do."

The detective's laugh was devoid of humor. "Do I have a choice?"

He did. He could withhold information, but things would go a hell of a lot smoother for everyone if we worked together.

The detective agreed, and they shook hands before Jamie walked his former brothers-in-blue out.

With Gran's permission, we went through the house and secured all the windows with thick wooden dowel rods we'd found in the garage.

It was hours before everyone finally left. When they did, the kitchen was clean, everyone was fed, and the house was secure.

Ashley pretended she was fine as she read a book on the couch, but she hadn't turned the page in ten minutes. Gran dealt with her fear by showing Prince the video from the cameras and watching for bugs the night vision picked up.

I watched them quietly, giving them the time they needed to process in their own way, but stayed close by.

Prince sat patiently on Gran's lap, like an angel sent from heaven, comforting her.

Thoughts rapid-fired through my mind: Prince's arrival on Violet's doorstep a week ago, Finn's visit, the black roses, Finn's possessive, aggressive texts, the bloody 'body' left in the kitchen today.

What if Prince's arrival wasn't a blessing, but a curse?

"Violet, did Prince have a collar when you found him?" What if someone dropped him off with a tracker?

"No, and I didn't find him; he found me. Why?"

I didn't know why the difference mattered, but it wasn't worth wasting time on.

"Just curious."

"He's not chipped either," Ashley added. "I wanted to make sure we weren't stealing someone's pet."

Knowing it was near impossible to inject a GPS tracker under a dog's skin, I moved forward with the assumption it'd be impossible with a cat. I'd verify, but my confidence level was high.

"He's my little angel," Gran crooned.

"More like a demon," Ashley teased.

"I think he's a little of both."

I texted John my thoughts concerning Prince, trusting him to follow up. *Or tell me I've lost my marbles.*

Soon after, Gran went to bed, and Ashley wasn't far behind.

I read on the couch, with my gun and laptop on a TV tray just to my left. I glanced at the screen each time I reached the bottom of a page.

I'd only read two chapters when Ashley padded into the living room with green fuzzy slippers on her feet. *Fucking adorable.* As my eyes travelled up her uncovered legs, the word adorable stopped applying. I cursed the long strappy top she wore for hanging mid-thigh and disrupting my perfect view.

"Eyes up here, Casper," she whispered as she walked closer.

I didn't have to see her face to know she wasn't okay; the tension in her shoulders spoke volumes.

"What's wrong?"

"I can't sleep." *Not surprising.*

"Sit." I patted the cushion next to me. Not waiting for an invitation, she snuggled up to my side. I wrapped an arm around her and pulled her closer still.

"Whatcha reading?" She asked, her hand settling on my chest, no doubt feeling my heartbeat pick up pace.

"The Hobbit, by Tolkien."

"So not a rom-com?" I missed her hand when she pulled it away to cover her laugh.

"No." I dog-eared the page and put the book down. "Want to talk, or do you want quiet company?"

"Can we talk?"

"Of course." I could hardly blame her for wanting company or needing comfort; the last few days had been hell.

"I can't believe Finn's doing this."

She didn't resist when I lifted her chin so I could see her eyes when she answered my next question. "Why not?"

She shrugged. "I'm not sure. He's always talked tough, but never follows through, you know?"

I did; we shared her opinion. "Do you think he'd hire someone to harass you?"

"He might. How do you find someone willing to do this kind of stuff?"

"It's a lot easier than you'd think, especially if you have a lot of money and no conscience."

"It's a shitty way to try to win me back."

Mine. My arm tightened around her shoulders.

She patted my chest. "Don't worry, Casper, I don't want him."

"Do you think you'll stop calling me that anytime soon?" I didn't hate it, but it reminded me of things I'd rather not think about.

She buried her face in my chest and laughed. "Maybe. Would it help to know I think of you as my gorgeous protective ghost?"

Hers. I smiled before kissing the top of her head. "A little." I was totally and completely hers.

"Can I ask you a question?"

"Sure," she mumbled into my chest.

"How'd you end up with a guy like Finn?" I sounded judgmental, but was legitimately curious. She'd dated AJ and was attracted to me. Ashley clearly had a type, but Finn was so far from it he might as well be a different mammal.

"I wanted to try something different. He seemed nice and was easy on the eyes."

My free hand lifted to my scarred face without conscious thought.

"You have nothing to worry about, my ruggedly handsome ghost." She ran the back of her fingers down my scar. Her gentle caress had the dual effect of calming my nerves and exciting my body.

"Thank you."

"Sadly, Finn isn't the first ass in my life."

I growled as I ground my teeth hard enough to crush stone. If I hadn't, I would've demanded the name of every asshole who'd dared to touch her. My mind was already thinking up creative ways to make them pay.

"Breathe, Casper," Ashley whispered. She reached over, her fingers forcing mine to unclench. She laced hers with mine and squeezed.

I needed to know. "Who hurt you?"

"No one." My left eyebrow lifted in disbelief, so she added, "I swear."

I tilted my head and waited for her to explain.

"They were assholes, and I refused to put up with their shit. I kicked them to the curb once I saw their true nature. You don't need to worry about me."

My free hand lifted, caressing the side of her face. "Just because I don't need to doesn't mean I won't." I saw her pupils dilate before I glanced at my laptop.

Ashley bragged about her independence, but she liked that I was worried, and when I got jealous. *Good.* I just hoped she'd like it when I acted on that concern.

When she started yawning, I stood and offered her a hand up. "Let's get you back to bed."

"Will you stay with me until I fall asleep?" Hearing her sound small and scared again invoked two feelings: empathy and anger.

My anger wasn't directed at her, so I choked it down and focused on the empathy.

"I'll stay as long as you want."

Chapter 32

Ashley

Asking Nathan to my room felt risky, but I felt safer with him close by. I promised myself I wouldn't sleep with him with my grandmother across the hall. Especially not with my emotions running so high. *No matter how badly I want to.*

I blushed as he surveyed my still pastel pink and green room, his eyes lingering on the boy band posters.

"Gran didn't redecorate after I left for college."

"You liked pretty-boys." Nathan nodded absentmindedly while pointing at a poster.

"I did, but I grew out of it."

Once again, he nodded. This time erasing the distance between us before saying, "Good." His warmth wrapped around me like a hug. He lifted my chin with his hand until I had no choice but to make eye contact. "Because I'm not a pretty boy."

His lips crushing mine cut off my reply.

It didn't last long, but when he pulled away, I could barely stand.

"Come on, Slick, let's get you to bed."

I scooted back to lean against my white headboard and asked him to sit with me. "I'm not ready to fall asleep yet."

He put his laptop and gun on the table beside my bed before sitting. The mattress sagged as he scooted up beside me, his long, muscular, black cargo pant clad legs stretched out in front of him.

"Are the tats on your arms your only ones?" I asked, thinking it was a safe topic. I'd seen the art on his forearms but figured he'd have more.

"No."

"How many?"

"Hard to say."

Why was he being so difficult? "Are you seriously playing Mr. Mysterious with your body art?" I asked.

He shrugged. "Do you have any?"

"I'll show you mine if you show me yours." I meant to tease him, but he had two polar opposite reactions. His pupils dilated two seconds before his shoulders tensed, and his teeth clenched.

"That's not a good idea."

Shit. "Because of your scars?"

"Yes." I could see him warring to control his emotions as he turned towards me. "And because I can see most of your skin. For me to see your tattoo, you'd have to remove what little you're wearing." His heated gaze roamed down my body and back up.

"Nathan?"

"Ashley."

"Please?"

"Please, what?"

"Please don't hide from me." I repeated his words back to him.

"You're not playing fair."

"No, I'm playing to win."

He laughed. "Bold. I like it." He rolled up his sleeves and showed me his forearms.

No way would I allow that. "That's cheating. I've seen those."

He held my gaze, his intensity a probe straight to my soul. I refused to back down.

"Are you sure?" His raspy voice was barely above a whisper.

"Yes."

Nathan leaned forward and peeled off his blue long-sleeved shirt, revealing drool-worthy, tattoo-covered arms. The scars stopped at his elbows; the ink continued under his T-shirt.

Knowing I was staring, he flexed his biceps to break the spell.

I felt the heat of his gaze as I traced the scars on his right forearm. He trembled at my touch. Then, I followed the lines of ink up to the hem of his black shirt.

Pushing up the sleeve, I asked, "How far does it go?"

His Adam's apple bobbed as he swallowed. "All the way."

"Can I see?" If he said no this time, I wouldn't push.

The silence stretched so long I worried I'd crossed the line.

"I'm sorry, Nathan. I shouldn't have asked."

His chest rose and fell with a giant breath. "It's okay. I just need a minute." He leaned forward, grabbed his T-shirt behind his neck and pulled it up over his head.

I may have drooled over his six-pack abs. The patches of small, circular, discolored skin didn't detract from his beauty. Without thinking, I reached out to touch one.

He flinched back, his shirt covering his face as he continued to lift it off.

"Sorry."

He jerked the shirt off his head. "Give me a second." His eyes stayed closed as he took a few deep breaths. "Sorry, I wasn't ready for that."

"I should have waited."

Nathan's chest was covered in a blend of color and thick black lines that didn't extend to his stomach. The black design reminded me of Celtic or Viking knotwork. The light smattering of hair on his chest begged to be touched. My hand was halfway there when I remembered his reaction and pulled back.

"Go ahead. You just caught me off guard last time."

I closed the distance, feeling his soft hair under my fingertips as I traced the thick black lines below his collarbone. "What does it mean?"

"The symbol on my left pec is my SEAL Team logo; the others are Celtic tribal symbols."

He was so fucking sexy that my brain short-circuited.

"And this one?" When my fingers trailed over his shoulder, towards his back, he leaned forward and swung his legs over the side of the bed.

My gasp at the sight of the crisscrossed slashes across his back was involuntary. His muscles tensed, his hands gripped the edge of my bed, his lungs stopped moving.

I leaned forward and rested my cheek on his back while wrapping my arms around his waist. "Breathe."

His back heaved under my cheek. I waited until his breathing returned to normal before leaning back to look.

The long lines of torn flesh blurred as my heart broke for him and the hell he'd endured.

Guilt followed closely on its heels. While I was cursing Nathan's name, someone was whipping him. I knew then I'd never call him Casper again.

"I'm so sorry, Nathan."

Chapter 33

Nathan

I started counting the instant my feet hit the floor. Showing Ashley my tattoos meant exposing my scars. Exposing my scars brought back memories. Those memories induced anxiety attacks.

Knowing I couldn't hide forever, I fought every urge to run. My knuckles ached as I held on to the bed to prevent myself from pulling away.

When I felt Ashley's wet cheek on my back and her arms around my waist, things started settling. When I heard her say, breathe, I filled my lungs with air.

Slowly but surely, my breathing returned to normal.

I let go of the bed, leaned forward and rested my elbows on my knees and my head in my hands.

Ashley's quiet presence calmed me faster than the countdown ever had. Her touch healed wounds deeper than the scars left by the barbed whip.

Hearing her apology brought me fully back to the present.

I spun, grabbed her and dragged her onto my lap before she could protest.

One hand fisted her hair while the other supported her back. She wasted no time adjusting and straddling my lap.

When my mouth claimed hers, I poured my soul into the kiss.

Time lost all meaning while I clutched her to me, kissing her like my life depended on it.

When we finally came up for air, Ashley's lips were red and swollen from my stubble. *And sexy as hell.*

She rested her forehead against mine as we caught our breath.

Ashley's hands grabbed my face as she pulled back. When I met her eyes, she said, "Mine."

No argument there. I'd been Ashley's since that first night in Vegas. "Yours." I swear I felt a thousand pounds lighter when her lips lifted in a smile.

I tugged her hair, looked deep in her eyes and whispered, "Mine."

"Yours."

We were finally where we were meant to be. Together.

Eventually, we settled back against the headboard, Ashley's head resting on my chest. I didn't doubt she could see the effect she had on me, but neither of us acted on it.

I anticipated needing more cold showers until we figured a way to get some alone time. Not a simple task, given the current circumstances.

As much as I wanted to spend hours learning every inch of Ashley in my bed, I was reluctant to keep her away from her grandmother too long. They needed each other, and I'd be selfish to deny them that.

When Ashley fell asleep halfway through the movie she chose, I turned my phone off and let her cute, soft snores lull me to sleep.

We stayed that way, Ashley curled up with her head on my chest while I reclined on the headboard, until four sets of sharp claws landed on my thigh.

"What the fuck!" I yelled, bolting upright and accidentally knocking Ashley away when I brought my hands up, ready to fight.

I probably cost Prince one of his nine lives, but he deserved it for scaring the shit out of me.

Ashley laughed as I cursed the cat. I wasn't amused. That stupid demon cat had ruined the best night's sleep I'd had in a long time.

Chapter 34

Ashley

During the short ride to the doctor's office, Nathan asked me more about my job before bringing up my writing again.

"What would you do if money wasn't an issue?"

"It's a big issue, since I don't have a job."

"Humor me."

"I'd probably volunteer to do the social media marketing for the Wyatt Foundation and write my novel."

"How would you feel about having a man support you?"

"Why?" I asked wearily. I'd worked my whole life, so while the idea of having a man support me seemed appealing, the reality wasn't so simple. Having a man support me meant giving up control over my choices, and I didn't want to do that.

I turned the question back on him instead of answering. "What would you do?"

"Nice deflection, Slick." He smirked. "I'm doing it."

"Really?"

"Really. I've always wanted to help people. And protecting them is the best use of my skills."

I considered teasing him about being an accountant, then changed my mind. And then changed it back again. "So, not working in an office crunching numbers."

"Ashley." The way he said my name was a warning.

"Nathan?"

He sighed and relaxed his white-knuckled grip on the steering wheel.

"I'm sorry." I'd meant to tease him, not upset him.

"Forgiven, now answer the question you tried avoiding."

"I'm not sure I could give up my freedom."

"Why would you need to do that?" He sounded genuinely confused.

"It'd be expected, wouldn't it?"

"No. At least not from me."

"Are you offering to support me?"

"I'm saying I could, if you wanted me to."

"Well, it's not just about me. I have to support Gran, too." I argued. Gran only needed help financially while she recovered, and she'd kill me if she heard me using her as an excuse, but I wasn't ready to have this conversation yet.

"I can afford it." It didn't sound like he was bragging, just stating a fact.

"Just how much is SSI paying you?" I joked.

He laughed. "I made smart investments and saved most of my money while serving in the Navy."

I bit my tongue instead of telling him he sounded like a banker.

"If you finished your book, you could make money, right?"

"If people bought it, yes."

Marketing was the difference between two equally good books making the bestseller list. And I'd be able to market the hell out of my book. I just had to write one people wanted to read.

"So you'd have an income." He turned his head and grinned. "Plus, you could hold off on volunteering for the Wyatt Foundation until your book made you money."

"Where are you going with this?" The Wyatt Foundation paycheck wouldn't pay the rent, and unless I got a publishing deal, it could take years to make any real money if I self-published.

"Would working part time give you the financial safety net you seem to think you need?"

My head whipped around to stare at him. He'd hit the bullseye of my fear, despite my not actually saying I was afraid.

"Don't look so surprised. I get paid to hear the unsaid."

"I don't know. I've never thought about it."

"Fair enough. Will you? Think about it?" He paused.

"Let me get through today first." I still wasn't sure how either of us would feel after Doc confirmed my pregnancy.

I'd taken a play out of romance books and claimed him last night. He hadn't hesitated to accept and return the favor. But that was in the heat of the moment.

Would he still feel the same watching me get fat with another man's baby?

Nathan insisted on coming into the clinic with me. Thankfully, he agreed when I said he had to wait in the lobby. No way would I let him in the exam room.

"I love this building," my voice shook as I made small talk.

"What do you like about it?" he asked, reaching over and resting his arm behind my chair.

The move reminded me of awkward dates as a teen when the guy would yawn and throw his arm around me hoping to cop a feel. Only Nathan played with my hair in the most distracting way, while offering comfort.

I appreciated his steady support, offered without thought or need for credit.

"It's not sterile like most doctor's offices. And Doc Greenfield takes her time with her patients. That's why I had Gran's care transferred as soon as it was practical."

He looked around. "No white anywhere."

"Nope. The exam rooms are pale pastels. Only the cabinets and sinks are white."

"You like Dr. Greenfield?"

"I do; she's been our family doctor forever." I laughed. "You'll get to know her soon enough; she treats a lot of SSI's injuries." The only time she didn't was if the injuries required an ER visit. Like when Jack got shot rescuing Meg. Or after Jay and Cate were held hostage and tortured.

"Good to know." He laughed. "Do the guys get hurt a lot?"

I regaled him with some stories that involved SSI needing some medical support. It was usually for minor things, like stitches.

"And when they rescued Blake, John got shot. Mary almost had a heart attack. But luckily it wasn't too bad."

"Ashley?" The medical assistant called my name. I stood, squeezed Nathan's hand, and followed her to the back. I prayed the entire time. *Please don't let me be pregnant.*

After taking my vitals and weighing me, Sheila left me alone with my thoughts. I scrolled on social media to keep my mind busy so I wouldn't freak myself out.

A soft knock preceded the door opening and Dr. Greenfield walking in, a tray with a plastic jar in one hand.

"Ashley, good to see you. I hope your bladder is full."

"Full enough." We talked for a few minutes before she sent me to the bathroom, jar in hand.

I doubled my prayer efforts during the few minutes it took for me to fill the jar, wash my hands, and walk back.

My heels bounced on the floor at a pace that'd make a hummingbird jealous as we waited. Noticing it, Doc asked about Gran. It was enough to distract me for the next three minutes. Not completely, but at least my legs bounced a little less.

I held my breath as she checked the results.

"Good news, it's negative."

"Negative?" I squeaked out, still holding my breath.

Doc smiled. "You are not pregnant." She spelled it out for me so there'd be no misunderstanding.

I sucked in air as tears filled my eyes, and my body sagged. I would have fallen off the exam table if her reflexes weren't so fast.

"You okay?" she asked.

I nodded. Relief robbed me of my words.

It wasn't until she handed me a tissue that I realized I wasn't just teary-eyed; I was crying. Who knew relief could induce tears?

"I thought false positives were rare," I said after calming down enough to form a sentence.

"They are, but that doesn't mean they don't happen. The test may have been faulty, or you may have a condition that interfered."

Condition? I'd just recovered from the pregnancy scare; I didn't need a health scare. "What kind of condition?"

"Ovarian cysts are a common one. Have you had any pelvic pain or pressure in your lower abdomen?"

I thought about it for a second. "No."

"Any unusually heavy periods recently?"

I shook my head.

"Then the test was probably bad. I'm sorry you had to go through this."

"I'm just relieved I'm not pregnant." My life, and my relationship with Nathan, would be so much easier.

She answered my next question before I could ask. "Chances are, you're late because you've been under a lot of stress lately."

She knew I'd lost my job, and with it, my insurance. And I'd told her I had to move in with Gran. I hadn't told her about Finn, but she knew I'd broken up with the father.

No, he's not the father because I'm not pregnant.

"Take a second. When you're ready, Sheila will sign you out."

"Can I get some fresh air first?" I needed a few more minutes to recover before seeing Nathan, and the fresh air would feel good after so much time spent holding my breath.

"Sure. Turn left when you exit the room. Just don't take too long."

"Thanks." I hopped off the table, grabbed my purse and walked out the door. The red exit sign made it easy to find the back door.

My eyes closed the instant I walked outside. The sun had barely warmed my face before a voice interrupted my tranquility.

"Thank you, Ashley, for making my job so much easier."

A chill ran down my spine, and the hair on my arms stood up at the snake-like quality of his voice.

I forced my eyes open and asked, "Do I know you?"

"No." He stepped closer. "But I know you."

Shit! He wasn't alone, and he had a gun. I looked at the back door, wondering if Nathan would hear me scream.

"Scott, or should I say Nathan, can't save you."

Vegas.

Before I could scream, a wet cloth covered my mouth.

My last thought as my consciousness faded was that I had to warn Nathan.

Chapter 35

Nathan

I checked emails on my phone. I checked in with Dean, the SSI part-timer with Violet. I glanced at my watch.

Twenty minutes. My knees bounced up and down as I grew restless.

According to the internet, a pregnancy test only takes a few minutes. The rest of the appointment could last ten to thirty minutes, depending on the patient's needs.

I'll give it another ten minutes.

I lasted five before going to the counter and asking how much longer it'd be.

"I'm not sure, sir. Dr. Greenfield said Ashley wanted some fresh air. That was about ten minutes ago."

Every muscle tensed. Blood roared in my veins.

"Show me." She didn't deserve my anger, but my fear overrode my ability to be polite or patient.

"Sir, I can't—"

I kept my voice low, but authoritative. "Her life is in danger, and I'm her bodyguard. Now. Show. Me."

"What's the—"

"Doc, I need to find Ashley."

"She hasn't come back?" Concern filled her voice as she opened the door. "This way."

"Thank you," I said. I'd apologize to Sheila later.

I couldn't reach the back door fast enough. The instant the doctor stepped out of the way, I shoved it and raced out. With my hand on my gun, I scanned the backyard.

"Ashley!"

"I'm so sorry. I didn't know," her doctor apologized.

Nothing. That was when I noticed the single black rose on the ground next to Ashley's purse.

Without turning, I asked, "Do you have cameras back here?"

"No, we've never had a need."

Fuck. "Clear your schedule; your office is now a crime scene."

I stayed outside and dialed the main number for SSI.

"Hey Nathan." Meg's cheerful voice felt like sandpaper on my frayed nerves.

"Flirty's missing."

Meg gasped and then yelled, "Jack!"

A few seconds later, Jack called my cell from his.

"Jack's calling," I said before hanging up on Meg. I'd owe her an apology too.

"Where are you? What happened?"

"Greenfield's office. Flirty went out the back for air, and now she's gone."

"Jamie's with a client, but AJ, Cate, and I are leaving now."

"He left another black rose." I picked up her purse. "Her phone's in her bag." I didn't care if Jack heard my fear and desperation.

Dr. Greenfield's office was searched twice; first by SSI, then by the WPD detective investigating the break-in at Violet's.

Luckily, no one asked why Ashley was at the doctor's office. Her doctor couldn't tell them, and I wouldn't. Neither would Jamie, since this had nothing to do with the pregnancy.

Or did it?

I had to hand it to John; he handled the WPD detective with ease, despite stepping on his toes and refusing to stop our investigation.

Back in my office, the first thing I did was locate Finn. He was at work and about to have a very bad day. That fucker would pay. He may not have taken Ashley, but he most likely hired the guy who did.

Dallas was only ninety minutes away. Less if I ignored the posted speed limits. "I'm going after Finn."

"Wait," Jamie said.

I stopped, looked at his hand on my arm, then into Jamie's intense hazel eyes. He said, "You can't just go after him—"

"One. Take your hand off me. Two. I quit."

He was either extremely stupid or exceptionally brave because he gripped my arm tighter.

"One, I'm not accepting your resignation. Two, shut the fuck up and let me finish." He gave me one and a half seconds to nod my compliance. "AJ and Jack will go with you. You may question Finn. You may not attack Finn. Have I made myself clear?"

"Crystal." I barked as I yanked my arm away. Turning to Jack, I said, "Let's go."

"AJ?" Jamie asked.

"I got him," AJ answered, stepping in behind me.

Great, I have a fucking babysitter. Not that I blamed Jamie. Left to my own devices, I'd rip Finn's arms off and beat him with them until he talked.

Jack drove. AJ called shotgun. I crammed my body into the backseat of the company sedan.

"Nathan, we've all been where you are. I won't make empty promises, but we won't rest until we find Ashley," Jack promised.

Before I could ask about Jack's experience, AJ turned in his seat. "Were you followed?"

"What kind of dumbass question is that? No, we weren't followed."

"How'd he know where to find you? Who else knew about the appointment?"

"Emily and Jamie. As far as I know, Ashley didn't tell anyone else."

"They wouldn't have said anything." Jack's defensiveness was unnecessary.

"Did we sweep her phone for a tracking app?" AJ asked.

"No," I said. *I'll beat myself up later for not thinking of it.*

"Let's talk through it," Jack said. We filled the time on the ride to Dallas talking through every idea, no matter how ridiculous it sounded.

Had Finn hired someone? Was the suspect operating with or without Finn's knowledge? If Finn wasn't responsible, who the hell was?

We'd have some of those answers soon enough.

The air in the car felt thin. My chest rose and fell in rapid succession. I clenched my fists and my teeth.

I will not have a panic attack.

I will hold my shit together.

I will not fail Ashley.

When I started my countdown, my focus was on Ashley. How she'd looked curled up in my arms. How soft her skin felt. Her laughter, which was always followed by a snort if it lasted too long. The fruity scent of her hair. The taste of her lips.

When Jack parked, he reminded me of the mission before turning off the engine.

Focus on the mission. I'd done it a thousand times before and could do it now for Ashley.

"We're looking for Finn Bentley," Jack said to the receptionist.

"Who may I say is asking to see him?" To her credit, there was only a slight tremor in her voice.

"I'm Jackson Sheppard from Sheppard & Sons Investigations. We think he can help us with a missing persons case."

"Have a seat, Mr. Sheppard." She looked at the rest of us before continuing. "I'll see if he's available."

I positioned myself so I was out of the way, but could block Finn if he tried to run.

My scowl and laser-beam focus probably spooked the receptionist. I added her to the growing list of people I'd need to apologize to.

"What's this about?" Finn asked as he sauntered into the lobby. The second he saw me, he started backpedaling. "Oh no. You need to leave."

He backed away fast. I moved faster. "Let's have a little chat in your office," I said, putting my arm around his shoulders like we were old friends. Jack and AJ were right behind us.

Finn looked like he wanted to piss his pants when AJ closed the door behind us.

"I'm calling the cops."

"No, you're not." I snatched his phone out of his hand.

"Blaszek."

"Sheppard."

"Let me talk to him."

I stared Finn down before stepping back.

"Mr. Bentley, we're looking for Ashley York. Have you seen her recently?"

His eyes widened in surprise. Not the reaction I was expecting.

"Not since this asshole threatened me."

I smiled; he'd deserved it.

"You haven't been to her house? Left any gifts for her?"

"Why would I give that bitch—" Finn's eyes tripled in size when I lunged forward. The only reason he wasn't sporting a black eye or bloody lip was AJ's speed.

"Go on," Jack said, pretending like nothing had happened.

"Why would I give gifts to an ungrateful ex? She refused me even after I promised to get her job back."

"She didn't work for you. How could you guarantee that?" I asked, wanting to verify my theory.

"My uncle was her boss." He paused, his eyes flicking between the three of us. "I have sway."

I was right. He got her fired and probably played a part in getting her evicted too.

"If I were in your shoes, it would've pissed me off when she said no," Jack said.

Finn hesitated, sensing the trap. "Whatever. I thought I'd made a mistake dumping her, but obviously it was the right move."

Dude was rewriting history, but it didn't matter.

"Who told you about Prince?" Jack asked, referring to the texts Finn had sent.

"Who's Prince?" His question was a lie.

"Her cat," I barked.

"I, um, I heard it from a…" He trailed off, fidgeting with his pinky ring as he glanced between us.

AJ grew impatient and answered for him. "You spied on her."

"No, I didn't. I stopped by to talk to her, but I changed my mind and left. I saw the cat in the window."

Tired of playing games, I asked, "What's the significance of the black roses?"

"The what?" His genuine confusion didn't mean he was innocent; it only meant they weren't his idea.

Taking a calm step forward, I asked, "Who'd you hire to harass Ashley?"

"What the fuck are you talking about?"

Jack and I shared a look. No one could act this well. He might convince one of us, but he couldn't convince all of us at the same time.

"Thank you for your time, Mr. Bentley." Jack held out his hand, but Finn refused to shake it.

"We'll show ourselves out," AJ said, holding the door open for me. They wouldn't leave me alone with him. Smart choice.

At the door, Jack said, loud enough for everyone to hear, "Thank you, Mr. Bentley. Your help could help us save a life."

I rolled my eyes. Dude was less than helpful, but Jack's statement fed Finn's ego and made him look like a hero, not a suspect.

Chapter 36

Ashley

My mouth felt like a desert, and the light hurt my eyes. *Where am I?* Memories flashed through my mind. The guy in the backyard. Him calling Nathan, Scott. Passing out.

The rhythmic thump-thump-thump sound of tires on the road told me I was in a moving car. With who? And where were they taking me?

Rap music assaulted my ears, but I couldn't cover them because they'd tied my hands behind my back. Too bad it wasn't duct tape; John had taught me how to break free from that.

Not that I could do it lying down in a moving car.

"She's awake," a male voice said.

"Hello, Ashley," the driver said. It was the voice I'd heard at the doctor's office.

"Who are you? Where are you taking me?"

He laughed.

"How do you know Nathan? What do you want with me?"

"Funny you should ask." He paused as he turned off the main road onto an uneven dirt road.

"I met Nathan when he called himself Scott Miller."

My breath caught in my throat. *He must be someone who used to work for the guys Nathan killed.* The driver was probably in charge now, or working for whoever was.

"You'd think you'd be happy. Now you can be the mob boss or whatever it is you call yourself."

"I'm a merchant." He made sure I was making eye contact in the mirror before winking. Nathan had called them terrorists because they sold weapons to our enemies, but I didn't think I'd earn any brownie points by correcting my captor.

"Whatever." I exaggerated my eye roll. "Why do you need me?"

Just then, he drove over a rough patch, making the car bounce and almost knocking me off the seat.

"Can you untie me so I can brace myself?"

"I'm sorry, gorgeous, but I can't do that." His use of endearments made my skin crawl.

Be brave. Play it smart. You can get through this.

"Why the hell not? I assume you don't want me to die yet, or you would've killed me already."

He yanked the wheel, causing the car to jerk violently and making me slide, which resulted in my head hitting the door.

"Asshole," I mumbled.

He must've heard because when he laughed, it sounded like a death sentence.

"This is gonna be fun," the driver said. The passenger agreed with a laugh that made my stomach turn.

"If your beef is with Nathan, why didn't you grab him?"

"We would've grabbed you both, but you walking into my arms was too good an opportunity to pass up."

"I'd hardly say I walked into your arms," I spat at him. "Why do you want me?" I had a feeling I was the bait, and would probably regret asking if he confirmed my suspicion.

"Because he cares about you."

"What's that got to do with anything?"

We were driving deeper into the woods. But I didn't know which woods. *How long was I out?* Hopefully not too long.

"Will you let me have a pass at her after you're done with her?" the passenger asked. His leer showed off his stained teeth.

Bile rose in my throat, and my hands trembled. How long would it take before Nathan realized I was missing?

I prayed. *Sorry God, I know I've been asking for a lot lately, and you already came through with the whole not-pregnant thing but if you could do me one more favor, I'd really like for Nathan to find me sooner rather than later because these guys scare me.*

"Sure. I think Nathan would enjoy seeing that," the driver answered.

My stomach dropped out.

My lungs stopped working.

My bladder threatened to let loose.

Digging deep, I found some courage. "What makes you think he cares about me?"

"Don't play dumb, Ashley. I've seen how he looks at you."

When? How?

"It was you."

"What was me?"

My voice only shook a little when I asked, "Who's playing dumb now?"

His smirk turned to a thin flat line, and his nostrils flared.

"The black roses, the fake blood on the floor." I couldn't bring myself to bring up the black fur. "Why?"

"Why not? I'm especially proud of the stuffed black cat idea." He chuckled.

He's proud? "You're sick," I said. This time my voice shook a lot.

No reply. When he turned off the bumpy dirt road, he said, "We're here."

Up ahead, I saw a small cabin. I didn't see the other vehicles until we got closer.

"Take her to the kitchen." He looked back at me. "And gag her. I'm tired of listening to her."

Calling it a kitchen was a stretch. It was a space off the open area with a cooler, a camping stove, and several cases of water stacked in the corner.

"Who's your decorator? I want to make sure I never hire her."

"Shut up and sit down."

When I didn't, he pushed me. Sitting wasn't optional when the back of my knees hit the edge of the folding chair.

After securing me to the chair, he put a knotted cloth into my mouth and tied it behind my head. It was impossible to move my tongue, but at least I could still breathe.

Chapter 37

Nathan

"Finn's not behind it. He's carrying a grudge, but his reaction was genuine surprise," I told Jamie via the car's Bluetooth.

"We're scouring the video feeds, but so far nothing," John said.

"Whoever's behind it is a professional, but why target Ashley if it's not on Finn's order?"

"Has she ever mentioned having issues with a different ex?" I asked. Ashley wouldn't have told them, but she wouldn't told Emily or Meg.

"I'll ask the girls," Jamie said. His rapid footsteps filled the silence in the car as he left John's office.

"Could be an unknown stalker," AJ said. "Don't bite my head off when I ask, but did anything else feel off at the house or Greenfield's?"

I narrowed my eyes but didn't answer. Reminding myself this was how teams worked, challenging each other and making sure no stone was left unturned, I answered calmly. "No. But it isn't my neighborhood. John, could you talk to Violet? Maybe she saw something without realizing it."

"Dean's bringing her here now. They would've been here sooner, but Violet refused to leave Prince behind after the scare, and Dean had a hard time getting that stupid cat, as he called him, in his carrier."

"That sounds about right," I said. I hadn't known Violet for long, but she was made of sturdy stuff. And she raised Ashley to be just like her.

Hold on, Slick. I'm coming for you.

"I'll let you know what we find out." John disconnected the call.

When we arrived back at the office, Violet was watching the video feeds with Doug. Prince rested quietly in his carrier on a chair next to her.

"How are you holding up?" I asked as I entered the room.

"I'm doing okay. Just trying to help Red here find my granddaughter."

She was doing her best to sound strong, so I pretended not to see her hands shaking or the tears she blinked back.

"Good. I'll be in John's office if you need me." I couldn't imagine Violet needing me, but I didn't know what else to say. Being in love with her granddaughter didn't automatically make me a part of the family.

"Nathan. You'll find her. I know you will."

I hoped. I prayed.

But I didn't know.

"John and his boys," she patted Doug's shoulder, including the non-blood boys, "they won't rest until they do."

Her confidence in the team was humbling.

My new team. I embraced my role as the familiar comfort of having a team washed over me. They had my back. I had theirs.

"Thanks." With a nod in Doug's direction, I left.

"Blaszek, this is your case, so the lead is yours," John said when I walked into his office.

"Sir, I appreciate that, but this is your town. You know it and the Yorks better than I do, so I'll follow your lead."

"Damn, I wasn't expecting that," Jay said. "I'd be going batshit if I were in your shoes."

I was one-hundred percent losing my shit, but I knew how to lock it down. "That's why SEALs are better," I said.

"Before you two get into a pissing match, let's get to work." John said before handing out assignments.

Jamie would coordinate with Weatherford PD and file the missing person's report. Jack and AJ would ask businesses near the clinic if they had street-facing cameras. Cate offered to jump over the heads of the local authorities and contacted her friends at the FBI to get traffic cam footage.

"Jay and I will scour them."

Each of them clapped me on the back and offered support as they left. I didn't realize how much I'd missed having a team at my back until that moment.

John waited until everyone had left before giving me my orders.

"How are you holding up?" He asked the same question I'd just asked Violet.

"I've compartmentalized it, sir. But when we find the bastard responsible, I want his head on a pike."

"Understood." He walked to the front of his desk. "Welcome to the team." He held out his hand. After I released his hand, he said, "When this is over, will you please stop calling me sir."

"Not insisting on it now?" I asked with a choked laugh.

"No, you're relying on your SEAL training to hold it together. Barely. I won't mess with that."

I nodded.

"I've contacted the Parker County Sheriff's Office and the Texas State Police; they've issued area-wide BOLOs for Ashley."

It wouldn't do much good since we didn't have a single shred of information about the getaway car.

"Coordinate with Doug. His attention is divided between the footage and Violet, so a second set of eyes will help. I'll have you work with Cate when she gets access to the traffic cams."

"Yes, sir."

Using AJ's chair, I worked alongside Doug and Violet watching surveillance footage.

We hadn't been at it long when Meg called out, "Nathan, did you order a pizza?"

Chapter 38

Ashley

"Smile pretty for your boyfriend." The driver said, gripping my chin and forcing me to look at the camera.

The gag prevented me from saying fuck you to the cameraman, but my eyes got the point across.

Click. Flash. The camera spat out a black square that would magically become a photo of me. The guy holding me let go with a laugh and grabbed it.

He shook it as it developed. "It'll do." He wrote on it with a black marker and put it in a box. He dug around a bit, and then added a note and a black rose.

Nodding to his buddy, he said, "You know what to do."

I had questions, but because of the gag, I couldn't ask. I stomped my foot to get his attention.

"The worm wants attention," a random dude said.

Worm?

"Remove her gag, but don't go far."

After he, none too gently, removed the knotted cloth, I licked my lips.

"Who the hell are you?"

He laughed, sounding like a cartoon villain. All he needed was a long, curly mustache, and the image would be complete.

"I'm Alan Perpura."

"Should that mean something to me?" I had a feeling I knew who he was, but I wanted to confirm.

"I suppose confessing to murder doesn't make good pillow talk, so he probably hasn't mentioned me."

He had, but not by name. Shouldn't he be dead?

"Your boyfriend killed my brother."

It was in self-defense, but this guy clearly had a different opinion.

"And he shot me." He pointed at his chest. "If he were a better shot, I'd be dead."

His statement confirmed my guess.

"If only." Remembering the scars crisscrossing Nathan's back, the burn marks on his stomach, and the scar on his face, I thought they got what they deserved. "The world would be a better place if he hadn't missed your heart."

I expected to get hit. Instead, he smiled. Somehow, it made him seem a lot scarier. "Gag her and take her to her room."

"Can I go to the bathroom first?"

"Take her, but don't let her out of your sight."

"My bladder is shy, so you'll need to wait outside," I informed the guy holding the gag.

"Fine, but I should warn you. There are men with guns everywhere. They have orders to shoot you if you try to escape."

"Then you have nothing to worry about."

The knotted fabric was shoved between my teeth before the same guy untied me from the chair. His vice grip on my upper arm was unnecessary, but I couldn't complain.

Needing the bathroom wasn't a lie; fear made my bladder overactive. I took the gag off for comfort while I used the outhouse they called a bathroom.

I 'accidentally' dropped my gag in the pit before I left.

Al was waiting when we walked back into the cabin. "Take her to the bedroom and chain her up."

"Is this your cabin?" It'd be easy for SSI to find me if it was.

No, it wouldn't. They don't know who kidnapped me.

"And get her another gag." His wide smile displayed his crooked yellow teeth.

"Really? It's not like anyone can hear me scream."

"I can hear you, and I don't want to listen to your smart-ass mouth anymore."

"Better than being a dumbass." My comeback was lame, but I didn't care.

His eyes roamed down and back up my body. "You're hot, I'll give you that, but annoying. What does Nathan see in you? Beyond a good fuck, that is."

My first inclination was to say "I'm a great fuck", but I was afraid they'd want to test the theory.

Instead, I clenched my teeth and glared at him, wishing I could shoot daggers out of my eyes. I'd shoot a million at him, cut him into tiny pieces. Hurt him and make him bleed like he did to Nathan.

"And here I thought you'd have a snappy comeback."

"You're not worth the energy."

He slapped me. Not as hard as I would've expected, but it still stung my cheek. "You should probably remember who's in charge."

"What are you going to do to me?" I wasn't sure I wanted to know, but I needed to.

"You? Nothing. You're not worth the energy." He threw my insult back at me. "You're the bait. The worm I'm dangling in front of Nathan so I can get my revenge."

"So you'll just let me go after you get your sick revenge."

His eyes roaming my body again turned my stomach sour. "I didn't say that," Al said as he nodded. Two hands reached around my head and shoved the gag back in my mouth.

In the bedroom, the guy cuffed me to a chain wrapped around an exposed beam in the wall.

After he closed the door, I tested the chain and the beam. No luck. I had neither the strength nor the skills needed to escape.

It didn't matter. Even if I could escape the cabin, I wasn't a capable-of-surviving-in-the-woods kind of girl. Especially not with night coming and a psychopath and his henchmen chasing me.

Idiot. I took out the gag and, afraid they'd use it again no matter where I put it, stuffed it in my pocket.

The cabin couldn't be a residence. It didn't have electricity or running water.

I regretted not wearing a watch, so I'd know how much time passed as I waited.

Trying not to panic. And failing.

Telling myself not to cry. And failing.

Thinking of ways I could be my own hero and escape. And failing.

They left me alone until it was time for dinner. My stomach rumbled when Al brought me a sandwich and a bottle of water. I ignored him as he set them down on the cot and moved out of reach. He sat on the only other piece of furniture in the room, an old wooden chair that squeaked when he dropped his weight on it.

"What time is it?" I asked. The metal cuff on my wrist chafed my skin, so I rubbed it.

"Just after six. Why, you have a hot date?" He laughed.

I didn't. Instead of celebrating my negative test result with Nathan, I was chained in a room and talking to a madman.

Don't let him know you're scared. I shrugged. "Just curious."

"I know you're hungry. Eat."

My stupid stomach wouldn't shut up, so there was no point in lying. But that didn't mean I'd eat.

"We didn't drug it, if that's what you're thinking." He crossed his arms over his chest and stretched his legs out.

That's when I saw it. The black rose tattoo on his forearm.

"Why would I trust you?" I asked.

"I told you. You're not my target, so you're safe."

For now. He wasn't subtle when he suggested I was fair game for his men once he'd exacted his revenge.

"What'd Nathan do to you, anyway?" I knew the answer, but wanted to keep him talking and maybe find a weakness I could exploit.

"He was a mole." Al touched his right thumb to his index finger. "He brought the feds to my doorstep." Thumb to middle finger. "He shot me." Thumb to ring finger. "He killed my brother in cold blood." Thumb to pinky.

"You mean in self-defense."

Al leaned forward slowly, put his hands on his now bent knees, and glared at me. "He slit Tommy's throat."

He had to be fucking with me. Did he really think it was acceptable to torture Nathan for weeks and then label him the bad guy for fighting back?

It was foolish to argue, but I wanted to know what he'd say. "So you think it's okay to torture someone, but not for them to defend themselves."

This time he stood, closed the distance between us in two fast steps, and grabbed my face. He squeezed my cheeks so hard that tears formed in my eyes. "Nathan deserved what he got. He's a liar. A rat who tried to ruin our business." He whipped my head to the side when he released my face. "And he deserves what he'll get for killing my brother."

Tears rolled down my face as I curled my lips between my front teeth. Anything I said would piss him off more, and I didn't dare push him.

"Nothing smart to say?" He sneered.

I shook my head back and forth; the motion caused more tears to roll down my cheeks.

"About time. Eat your fucking dinner or go hungry until lover boy shows up."

How long before Nathan finds me? Had Al left clues behind?

When will Nathan get the box? The one with my picture and a black rose. Al didn't strike me as the patient type, so I'd bet he put the address in there.

Chapter 39

Nathan

A teenage girl stood in the lobby holding a pizza and a small sealed brown box.

"Did you order pizza?" Meg asked again.

"No."

My volume was polite, but my tone wasn't when I asked, "Who sent you?" The girl went from bored to nervous in the blink of an eye.

John, Cate, and Doug joined us in the lobby.

"He didn't say." She took two steps back. I couldn't blame her; she wouldn't know the box on top of the pizza might contain a ransom note.

John asked Dean to take Violet upstairs, so she'd be out of hearing distance.

Then he stepped forward and took over questioning the girl. "Russo's doesn't deliver this far out."

Her eyes skittered between us, looking like a cornered cat.

"Dude paid me an extra hundred bucks." She held out the boxes. "Look, I'm just the delivery guy. Can you take these so I can leave?"

John stepped forward and took the boxes. "You're not in trouble, but I'd like to ask you a few more questions."

She swallowed so hard I practically heard it before nodding.

John set the boxes on the lobby table and walked her towards Meg's desk. "Did you see the guy who placed the order?"

She nodded. "But he was wearing a hat and sunglasses."

Nothing odd about that in early August.

"Did he use a credit card?" As expected, he'd paid in cash.

"What did he tell you to say about the extra box?" John asked, tilting his head towards the table. I was taking pictures of the boxes from all angles and looking for clues.

"He said it was a surprise for his old friend, Scott."

My head snapped up. "What did you say?" My stomach dropped as fear and rage burned through my veins. *It can't be. I killed them.*

It could be someone who'd stepped up and taken the reins. But then, why all the games? Why not just kill me?

Knowing what they'd done to me, blind rage filled my head, making me see red at the thought of them touching Ashley.

"Can I go?" the delivery girl asked.

When John looked at me for confirmation, I nodded.

Cate followed the girl to the door. "Lock it," John ordered as soon as the door closed. He turned his attention back to me. "Blaszek?"

"Vegas." I didn't recognize my voice. Images of the warehouse flashed before my eyes. The sound of a whip cracking filled my ears. The tang of blood filled my nose.

My scar itched. My back burned. My lungs struggled to take in air.

When Ashley replaced me in the chair in my mind's eye, my heart stopped beating as seconds that felt like hours ticked by.

Until rage replaced panic.

My lungs sucked in air. My mind locked down.

"They have her." I reached for the box.

"You should wait," John said.

"Who?" Cate asked at the same time.

"I don't know exactly who, but I've only done one op using the name Scott. When I was deep undercover with the Perpura brothers in Vegas."

Ignoring John, I used my pocketknife to cut the tape after handing my phone to Doug. "It's recording."

He nodded and stepped back to give me room.

Rage allowed me to share my story without fear. "They held me for two weeks, torturing me non-stop, after learning my real identity." A chill ran down my back as I opened the flaps.

"I killed the brothers, so I don't know who's responsible for taking Ashley, but it's someone from their organization." It had to be.

After putting on the blue latex gloves John handed me, I carefully removed the single black rose, exposing a folded piece of paper.

I held my breath as I unfolded the paper, then laid the note flat on the table.

Doug moved to get a better angle for recording as I read the note out loud.

Scott Miller, or should I call you Nathan now?

Your brain must have leaked out of your face when Tommy slashed it open because it's taking you and your PI buddies far too long to figure out who's been taunting you via that pretty lady of yours.

The next time you kill someone, make sure they're really dead.

It couldn't be Tommy; I cut his throat and watched him bleed out. Al. It had to be him. I'd shot him in the chest and assumed he was dead. *But I didn't check*. There wasn't time. There'd been no news suggesting Al survived. I knew because I'd checked religiously the first few months. Once I was confident he wouldn't reappear, I stopped.

There was no reason to keep torturing myself with the past while planning for the future.

Taking too long?

"It's been Al all along."

"I thought he was dead," John said.

"So did I."

"Call everyone back," John ordered Cate before picking up his phone. "What name do I give for the BOLO?"

Ice ran through my veins. "Alan Perpura, of the Perpura Syndicate." They never made the FBI's top ten most wanted list, but they were in the top twenty. Until I killed them. Or thought I did. "Call the FBI, too. But I'm not waiting for any of them."

I dug through the black plastic rose petals knowing there'd be more.

An envelope. Inside was a Polaroid of Ashley. She was bound and gagged, a hand forced her to face the camera. *For Tommy*, was written in black marker across the polaroid's white strip.

The image of Al raising his right arm flashed in front of my eyes. The black rose tattoo on his right forearm was larger than life in my memory.

"How could I be so stupid?"

"Blaszek?"

"The black rose." I handed the photo to John. "Al had a black rose tattoo on his right forearm. They wore long sleeves most days because they kept the room I was in cold as fuck, but I saw it when I shot him."

"Can you be sure it's him from just the arm?"

"Yes. Plus the note says, The next time you kill someone, make sure they're really dead. It has to be."

Knowing Al was behind recent events explained the level of cruelty. Using a stuffed cat to traumatize the Yorks was something he'd take pleasure in doing.

I sank onto the couch. My elbows landed on my knees as my head dropped into my hands. "How?" The why was obvious, but how?

"How'd Al survive? How'd he find me? How'd he find out about Ashley? How the hell do I find her?"

I didn't realize I was talking out loud until John answered me.

"This isn't on you."

"But it is." I lifted my head. "I didn't finish the job."

"I can't speak to that, but you aren't responsible for a madman's actions." He put a grounding hand on my shoulder. "Tell me what you know about him. Where is he most likely to hold her?"

A deep breath in. "He'll want seclusion." Hold. "He won't be alone." Deep breath out. "He's a weapons expert." Hold. "He likes to inflict pain." Involuntary shudder.

I stood and dug into the box. Taped to the bottom were coordinates. Singularly focused, I was typing them into my phone before remembering the team.

"He gave me coordinates," I said, still typing.

"Us. Unlike last time, you're not in this alone."

My thumbs paused while I looked him in the eye, nodded, and said, "Hooyah."

Because the rest of the team returned without me realizing it, the round of "Ooh Rahs!" and "Hell yeahs" as they chimed in caught me off guard.

Calm washed over me. *I was never meant to be a lone wolf.* Falling back into a leadership position and issuing orders felt like coming home.

"Sharpe, can you pull up satellite footage for the coordinates?"

"On it. I'll get the drone ready, too," Doug answered.

"Thanks. Sheppard," four sets of eyes turned to me. "Right." I huffed a half laugh at my mistake. "John, can you bag all this?"

I was issuing the next order before he finished nodding.

"Jaden, we need an entry plan."

"Obstacles?"

"Expect booby traps and an ambush."

I heard Meg gasp.

"Just another Tuesday, right, Jack?" AJ asked with a grin, holding out his fist.

"Except it's Wednesday." Jack bumped AJ's fist before hugging Meg to reassure her.

I put the team to work, knowing that together, we could save Ashley.

I hit speed dial. When I got Kroup's voicemail, I left a brief message. "Perpura's alive. He has Ashley. Meet us at SSI."

Chapter 40

Ashley

I'd just finished wiping snot on my shirt when the door opened.

"You ever heard of knocking?"

Al laughed. "Why would I do that?"

"Because you called this my room." The chain rattled on the floor when I brought my hands to my hips.

"You're sexy when you're mad. Has Nathan seen this side of you?"

The predatory look in his eyes as they roamed up and down my body made me shudder. Stepping back, I sat down on the cot and crossed my legs. I held the chain in my free hand. I didn't stand a snowball's chance in hell of winning a fight against him, but if he tried to touch me, I'd go down fighting.

The heavy chain could do some damage.

His eyes lingered on my hands. "Do you really think that'll work?"

"What?" I asked, practically batting my eyelashes to seem innocent.

"Using the chain to attack me?"

"Do I look that dumb?"

He laughed. "You look that desperate."

I was. "I'm not. It's dragging on my wrist, and it hurts." I held up the chain. "This helps."

"Whatever you have to tell yourself."

When I didn't respond, he continued. "Your boyfriend should be here soon."

"He's not my boyfriend." I lied.

"Fine, your lover."

"Never slept with him." Sadly, that wasn't a lie. And wouldn't it just piss me off if I died before I could?

"Seriously? The way you look at each other, I figured you were fucking each other's brains out."

"How romantic." I rolled my eyes. "How'd you connect me to Nathan?"

"That was easy. I followed him when he moved here. He's spent half his time at your place. It doesn't take a genius."

"Why'd you wait so long?"

"In general, or since he moved to your podunk town?"

"Dealer's choice." I hated how high my voice sounded.

"It took me months to recover and rebuild. When I finally went looking for him, he was a fucking lump on his friend's couch." He chuckled. "There's no fun in killing a man who looks like he'd greet Death like an old friend, so I watched and waited."

That didn't sound like the Nathan I knew.

"The next thing I knew, he'd packed up and moved to your crappy little town. I thought about just killing him, but changed my mind when I saw him staring at you like a lovesick puppy. It's more fun to fuck with him."

Al liked hearing himself talk.

"It was fun playing cat and mouse, but I never expected the mouse to be so stupid."

"He's not stupid."

"And yet he missed all the clues I sent."

"I thought they were from my asshole ex who couldn't take no for an answer."

"You didn't really think that loser would send black roses or break into your house, did you?"

No. "He could've hired some random psychopath. You can't be the only one out there."

He laughed. "I'm not a psychopath. I'm a businessman who's willing to do whatever it takes to get what I want."

"How'd you know I was at the doctor's office?" Nathan was paranoid about us having a tail, so there was no way he'd followed us.

"I employ some exceptionally gifted people. One of them hacked the GPS on your phone. I knew your location every minute of every day." He smirked.

He probably hacked Nathan's too.

"He'll find you," I said with a smug smile.

"I'm counting on it." His tone erased my smile and made my skin crawl. "And I'm sure he'll bring your PI friends along to help."

"Don't guys like you usually tell the good guy to come alone?" I asked.

"They never listen, so I didn't bother."

"You'd hurt innocent people, people you've never met, just to get to Nathan?"

He smiled, and I'd swear his eyes sparkled at the idea of killing them all. "Yes."

I shivered despite the warm room.

God, it's me again. Please don't let this lunatic kill my friends. They're good people, and they don't deserve it.

"Don't worry, my gorgeous little worm, it'll all be over soon."

What the fuck was with the nickname? "Worm?"

I thought, duh, just as he said, "It's what you use as bait to catch a fish."

Chapter 41

Nathan

The coordinates marked a clearing in a wooded area thirty minutes east of Weathford. Cate called the FBI and asked for access to any surveillance in the area.

Jamie and Doug mapped access routes to the small, rundown cabin.

Jay planned our entry.

Dean occupied Violet in the break room.

"I don't see anywhere for Jamie and me to set up nests. We'll go in with the teams."

"Copy that. Kroup will join us on Bravo. We'll get him up to speed when he gets here." I wasn't worried about him fitting in with the team.

"Have you heard back?" Jack asked.

"No, but he'll be here." Kroup had my back as a SEAL. He had my back after the Perpura op went south and I needed a place to lie low and recover. He'd have my back now.

Five minutes later, my phone rang.

"Hey Kroup."

"Dude, are you fucking serious?"

"Yes."

"Details."

"You'll get them. ETA?"

"Havoc and I are twenty out."

"Kitted?"

"Full kit and ready to rumble."

"Drive safe." I hit the end button. "He's on his way."

"It's been a hot minute since I've worked with a dog," Jaden said.

"Havoc is one of the best."

Jay looked at Cate and wiggled his eyebrows. "Should I worry about you with all these Navy SEALs around?"

She slapped his arm and said she'd take a grunt over a taxi driver any day. Jay smiled and pulled her in for a hug. Watching as he kissed her temple before letting her go made me desperate to hold Ashley again.

We'd finally started our second chance less than twenty-four hours ago, and now she was gone. In Al's psychotic clutches.

"Jamie, can I talk to you?" I nodded my head towards his office.

"Sure." He followed me and closed the door behind him. "What's up?"

"Ashley's pregnant."

"I know." He leaned on his desk. "Have a seat."

Needing a pause, I did.

"I don't want to betray her trust, but the team should know."

"I'll leave it up to you, but I don't think we need to tell them yet."

"They need to be careful."

"Nathan, they'll do everything in their power to rescue her without hurting her."

"What would you do?"

"I'd wait. Knowing might make them worry more. They're already giving a hundred and ten percent; I wouldn't put that on them."

He was right; there was no reason to reveal Ashley's secret yet. "Thanks."

"Anytime. Anything else?" He stood.

I shook my head and stood. "Actually, there is." I held out my hand. "Thanks for not kicking my ass to the curb when I deserved it."

He shook my hand and laughed. "You're welcome. Can I assume your willingness to work with the team is long term?"

"Yes, sir. The lone wolf thing sucked."

"Good. Let's go get your girl."

We were setting up comms when my phone buzzed.

Kroup's text was one word: Here.

After letting him and Havoc in, I introduced him to anyone he hadn't met.

"Do you have something of Ashley's with her scent?" Kroup asked once the introductions were over.

"In my truck. Jay, bring him up to speed while I go get it."

Chapter 42

Ashley

"I made a special throne, just for you," Al said as he walked in without knocking. "Want to see it?"

"I'll pass."

"Not an option." He waved, and a second asshole entered the room. "Cuff her before unchaining her. Then bring her out."

His asshole friend was none too gentle when he yanked my arms behind my back and closed the handcuffs too tight.

"Ouch."

"Shut up or I'll gag you again."

The cuffs dug into my wrists, but at least my left arm felt ten pounds lighter when the steel cuff fell off. Dude pushed me out of the room so I could see my throne.

Al stood proudly behind a big, boxy, wooden chair with a metal plate on the seat.

"It's brilliant, if I say so myself."

"What's that?" I asked, using my eyes to point at the plate.

"This?" He reached down and lifted it up. "This is a pressure plate. When Nathan and his friends get close, I'll make you sit on it. If you move." He dropped the plate with a clang. "Boom!"

I jumped at the sound, my entire body trembling as I realized what the black box under the chair contained. "It's…" I couldn't bring myself to say the word, but Al had no such issues.

"A bomb? Yes. So even if Nathan gets by me and my guys, he'll blow you both up when he tries to save you."

My knees gave out, and I landed with a thud as I sank to the floor. "No."

"Yes." *God, I hate him.* "If Nathan surrenders, and his friends don't do anything stupid, things will be easier for you. I might even keep you around for a little while. The guys think you'll be fun to play with."

I dropped my head forward and cried. *How foolish of me to think this could end well.*

Even if Nathan killed Al and all his men, he couldn't save me. He couldn't save us. Al had made sure he'd get his revenge no matter what.

"Take her back to her room."

The guy yanked me to my feet and dragged me back without a word.

The click of the thick metal cuff locking on my wrist had a finality to it that drained the fight out of me.

How do I warn Nathan and the guys at SSI?

I'd never be able to steal a phone, and it wouldn't matter anyway. Everyone's phone number was saved in my phone. I couldn't even remember the last time I'd memorized a phone number.

Except Grans and Ashley's parents, because they still had the same landline phone numbers from when we were kids. I could call them and ask them to warn Nathan and everyone at SSI.

How the hell can I steal a phone if I can't leave the room?

Chapter 43

Nathan

"How'd they find Ashley if you didn't have a tail?" Kroup asked. He wasn't the first person to ask, and I still didn't know the answer.

"I don't know. The only thing I can think of is they bugged my truck, but we searched it."

"What about your phone?" he asked.

"It's clean," Doug answered. "Ashley's too."

"He could've hacked it, which wouldn't leave a physical trace," Kroup suggested.

"Fuck! Why didn't I think of that?" I ran my hand down my face. "Sharpe?"

"I can try, but it'd take more time than we have. Let's assume he did," Doug answered.

"Then we leave all cell phones here and use comms from now on." I asked, "John, will you collect them?"

He pulled his phone out of his pocket and asked Meg for a bag. After collecting the phones, he put them in his office.

"I don't want Meg staying here alone. If he tracks the phones, it'll lead him to her."

"She and Violet can stay with Mary. I'll call from the office phone and have Mary pick them up before we leave," John answered.

"Thanks. And tell Ma I said thanks too."

"Kroup, you need to call the missus before handing it over?"

"No, she's made of granite. Kissed me goodbye and told me not to call until we'd saved your girl."

She was a seasoned SEAL wife and knew the drill. Don't give your man more to worry about before a mission.

"Then gear up."

We put on black clothes, applied greasepaint to our faces, tossed on our body armor, and loaded our gear.

"You look like you're going to war," Mary said as she hugged John goodbye.

"Nah, just a little manhunt. I'll be home before you know it."

"You were supposed to be done with this shit when you retired from the police force." Mary buried her face in his plate-covered chest. "You lied."

"Mary, look at me." She lifted her head, tears in her eyes. "I'm sorry I lied, but it wasn't intentional. How could I know we'd see so much action?"

Jamie walked up beside them. Jack and Jay followed. "We won't let anything happen to him, Ma," Jamie promised.

"You see, your sons have my back. There's nothing to worry about," John said while rubbing her back.

"But who'll make sure nothing happens to you?" She asked, turning to each of her sons.

"We've got their backs, Mrs. Sheppard," I answered.

She sniffled and wiped her eyes. "It's Mary." She straightened her shoulders and pinned me with a look. "Don't make me tell you again. Now, get your asses out of here and bring Ashley home."

My jaw hit the floor. She'd flipped a switch and turned badass in the space of a heartbeat.

"What, you've never seen a wife or mother have a moment of weakness seeing her family geared up like warriors?"

"Yes, ma'am, I mean Mary." I'd just never seen them turn it off so quickly.

"Something about this mission feels different from the others." She looked around the room. "You will all come home safely. Do you understand?"

Being my first mission with SSI, I couldn't speak to it, but the looks shared between everyone else told me it wasn't different. Mary just didn't know it.

"Yes, ma'am." The room answered as one.

"Meg, let's get Violet and go home. We'll plan a feast for when they return."

Meg hugged Jack. "Come home to me, Charming; our little one needs a dad." She addressed the rest of the team. "That goes for the rest of you, too. Don't you dare get hurt."

Another round of, yes ma'am, filled the room, making Meg laugh. "I kind of like it when they do that."

"Want to know a secret?" Mary asked before saying, "So do I."

John and his boys escorted them to the car. At the door, Mary turned and said, "Be safe."

When the Sheppards returned, I said, "Let's go earn our feast."

Chapter 44

Ashley

"Looks like I was wrong. I figured your Prince Charming would rush over to save you, but it appears he's waiting until tomorrow."

I stared at him with scratchy eyes, no doubt red from all the crying I'd been doing. My plan to steal a phone was a joke. Al left me alone for hours while he and his guys got ready for Nathan.

"I'd hate to think all the traps we set were for nothing."

I couldn't stand looking at him another second, so I stared at my feet.

"I expected a smart-ass remark. Guess the chair scared the snark right out of you."

"Fuck you," I whispered without moving my head.

He laughed. "Not all of it. Maybe I should call Nathan and let him hear you scream."

My head snapped up as my heartbeat doubled in speed and my breath caught in my throat.

The whimper I tried suppressing, escaped. "I don't know his number," I said, trying to be brave.

"That's okay, little worm, I do." He turned his phone towards me. "And he's still at the SSI office."

I didn't doubt they'd come for me, but apparently it wouldn't be tonight. The sun was already low on the horizon, and it'd be dark soon. It'd be a hell of a lot harder to rescue me in the dark.

"Maybe I misjudged your usefulness." He scratched his chin, making himself a caricature of someone thinking. Al tapped his phone screen a few times then held it out so I could hear.

"Blaszek. Leave a message." Nathan's voicemail was short but not sweet.

"I never pegged you as a coward. Come get your woman before I start sending her back to you in pieces." He hit the screen.

If I'd been standing, I would've fallen. Al's mood grew darker with each delay keeping him from his revenge. It didn't take a genius to see Al had expected this to be easy.

"Boss. Lookout 1 called. We've got company."

Could it be them? But Al said Nathan's phone was still at the office.

"He must've left his phone behind. Not so stupid after all." He smiled. "Looks like it's your lucky day."

I didn't feel lucky; I'd have to witness Nathan and my friends get killed.

"Cuff her and tie her to the chair. I'd tell you not to move, but I don't trust you not to sacrifice yourself to save your lover."

I gulped in air as panic set in. *I'll be sitting on a literal fucking bomb.*

I definitely didn't feel lucky as I stumbled on boneless legs to the chair.

"Sit." He pushed me, forcing my knees to hit the edge of the wood, and I fell back.

He tied my ankles to the thick legs, ran a rope over my thighs and under the chair, then secured my arms at the wrists and elbows.

"Try to stand," Al ordered.

What the fuck! "I'll blow up if I do."

"It's not armed yet. Now stand."

I tried, but the rope cut into my thighs and arms, holding me secure.

Satisfied I couldn't move, Al said, "Arm it."

Every prayer I'd ever said in my life paled in comparison to the non-stop string of pleas I sent to God asking him in incomplete and run-on sentences to help us.

Chapter 45

Nathan

Kroup drove the Bravo team, while John drove the Sierra team. We'd enter from the west; they'd enter from the east. Our plan was to park and hike in. We packed our night-vision goggles in case the sun set before we made it to the cabin.

"Bravo One to Sierra Two. You copy?"

"Sierra Two. Loud and clear," Jamie answered.

"Keep your eyes open and be ready to go without warning."

"Copy that."

We split at a fork in the road three miles from the cabin. The rest of the drive would be on dirt roads.

"Thank God for bulletproof vehicles," Jay said from the back seat. He scanned the trees on the left. Cate and I scanned to the right.

"Never thought we'd do this again," Kroupa said, holding his fist up.

I bumped it. "Just keeping you in fighting shape, brother."

He laughed. "You do understand what the word retirement means, don't you?"

It was my turn to laugh. "Retirement is for officers."

"Ooh Rah," Jay added his two cents.

"Hooyah," Kroup and I answered the call.

"Men," Cate said from the back seat.

There was nothing small or incapable about Catelyn Maxwell, but she looked tiny compared to the three giant special forces guys on her team. The guys at SSI swore she could handle going in with us, but I had my doubts.

To make things worse, I had to worry about Jay taking himself out of the fight if she needed help.

"You good back there, Three?" I asked Cate.

"Other than having to listen to the dick-measuring contest between you three, I'm right as rain."

I laughed, still scanning the area to the right of the car. "Just checking. Did you do anything like this in the FBI or Marines?"

"Yes, and no. I've raided buildings with a team of agents. But nothing this complex."

"Just keep your eyes open, your ears peeled, and if something clicks under your foot, don't move."

"Asshole." Jay smacked the back of my head without taking his eyes off the surrounding forest.

"Jay, it's his job to make sure I'm ready. And as the only non-spec op guy on the team, I can't blame him for being worried."

"Who said I'm worried?" I asked.

"Your tone. Your body language. You checking on me every fifteen minutes."

"More like ten," Kroup corrected her.

"Way to have my back." I shot him a look to convey my annoyance. Which he didn't see because his stayed focused on the road and trees.

When Jay said "I've got movement" Kroup tapped the brakes, slowing us to a crawl.

"What do you see?"

The SUV came to a full stop. Havoc's head popped up over the back seat, ready for action.

"Vehicle," he pointed, "through the trees, about thirty yards." A clearing provided us with a line of sight.

Jay lowered the window, lifted his rifle and aimed in. "He's armed. I have a clean shot. Awaiting orders."

Kroup drew his pistol and watched in front of us. Cate and I did the same. I scanned to the right while she watched behind us.

"Even if he lets us pass without engaging, he'll warn Perpura." If he hadn't already.

Kroup was right. There was no reason for a man to park along the road, holding his rifle at low ready.

"He spotted us."

"Send it."

The silencer minimized the percussive blast, but the sound still filled the cab.

"Target down." After waiting to make sure the guy was alone, Jay pulled his rifle in and rolled the window back up.

"Bravo One to Sierra Two."

As soon as Jamie acknowledged, I filled him in.

"Assume Tango knows we're coming," I reported over comms. If the dead guy warned Perpura before dropping, we'd lose the element of surprise. *But the Sierra team might still arrive unnoticed.*

Chapter 46

Ashley

Al's expression when he turned to me was so vicious that I pulled away. At least I tried, but I couldn't move anything except my head because I was tied to a chair with a bomb under my ass.

"Your boyfriend decided to be a knight in shining armor, after all."

I never doubted it.

Al issued orders, and his remaining men left. From what I could tell, they wanted to stop SSI—everyone except Nathan—from getting to the cabin.

My hands turned white and cramps set in as I gripped the arms of my throne, as Al continued to call it.

"You think he'll behave to save you?"

"Does it matter? You'll kill me no matter what he does."

"True, but it'd be a shame to kill you before getting my revenge."

"It'd be a shame for you to kill me at all." I barely recognized my voice as I replied.

"You're right. I'd love to give my boys a shot at that sexy body. I bet you're a tiger in bed." His eyes roamed my body and settled on my hands, still gripping the arms for dear life.

I tried relaxing my hands, but they were so tense and my grip so tight, I couldn't. There was no way for me to hide my fear; it was obvious in my grip, my sweat, my high-pitched voice.

If I'm going to die, there's no point in playing nice. "I hope I get to see you die."

He laughed. *Not the response I expected.* "If I die, you die."

My eyes widened. *How?*

He answered my unasked question. "Did you really think I wouldn't have a back-up plan?"

"You mean other than the bomb I'm sitting on?" I clung to the hope that the guys could free me without setting it off.

"I suspect things won't go the way I want, so I may not have the pleasure of seeing his face when I kill you. But I can live with that." Al looked at the door. How had I not noticed the wires and explosives?

"You're trapped in here. One way or another, I'll have my revenge."

My stomach sank. There was no way I'd survive this, and worse, my friends wouldn't survive either. How do I warn them that the door is booby-trapped?

Bravery, even the facade of it, faded as fear consumed me. I had nothing left to say. Even thinking was hard as my impending doom occupied every brain cell.

My stupid, creative brain easily imagined seeing the door explode and watching everyone die a painful, violent death.

Would anyone survive long enough to free me? Would I starve to death tied to a bomb chair? Would crying non-stop hasten my death because of dehydration?

Could I find the courage to get off the chair and end my suffering? If I found the courage, would I be able to break the ties?

Chapter 47

Nathan

"Sierra One to Bravo One." John's voice came over comms as the sun hovered just over the horizon. Less than an hour of sunlight remained, but the clearing would feel dark sooner because of the trees.

I didn't love the idea of finishing the rescue mission in the dark, but we couldn't wait until morning. The Bravo team could easily carry out the mission in the dark. I had to trust the Sierra team could too.

"Go ahead, Sierra One."

"Parked and ready to move."

"Move. Watch your backs." Sierra would enter from the back of the clearing, relative to the cabin's front door.

"Copy that. Sierra One out."

Perpura wouldn't kill Ashley. *Get used to calling her Flirty.* A call sign I loved and despised in equal measure.

"It's not much farther before we can park," Kroup updated me.

I nodded. We'd park in the dense forest and walk in. Perpura would expect us to come in guns blazing, so we'd sneak in instead.

Not that it'd matter. Perpura would've staged men, ready to engage, the instant he knew we were coming. If he didn't know, bonus. But we had to assume he did as we moved forward.

After we parked, Kroup prepped Havoc with his body armor, goggles, and Ashley's scent. If Perpura hid Ashley, Havoc was our best hope of finding her.

"Bravo One to Sierra One."

"Go Bravo One."

"Bravo is on the move," I said.

"Copy that. We're almost in position."

"Observe and report from there, but don't engage." I didn't have to add, unless necessary.

Kroup led with Havoc sniffing his way to the cabin.

Time stood still as we inched our way to our destination, where we'd spread out and observe before finalizing our plan of attack.

We knew there'd be a firefight. We expected booby traps. We didn't allow ourselves to think about failing.

Failure wasn't an option.

Prepping took minutes but felt like hours as shadows danced between the trees. Every rustle of the leaves, every croak of a frog, every branch snapping underfoot had our heads scanning for a threat.

When we were in place, I contacted the Sierra team.

"We're in place. What do you see?"

"Sierra Five has the drone ready to go."

"Let it fly."

The drone barely cleared the forest before a single shot rang out.

"The drone is down." John confirmed. "We're going in blind."

At least we still had thirty minutes of natural light.

"Copy that." I sent one last prayer to heaven. "On my mark."

Chapter 48

Ashley

The first gunshot, mere minutes after Al left me alone in the cabin, made me flinch.

SSI was here. But what would happen to them? Al seemed confident he'd win. Even if he didn't, he'd made sure we'd all die.

Tears rolled down my cheeks, and snot dripped from my nose. Unable to move my wrists or elbows meant I couldn't lift my shoulder high enough to wipe either away.

I'm going to die a slobbery mess.

Not that it mattered. I'd end up blown to kingdom come or eaten by wild animals before anyone found me.

Thump thump thump.

I looked up toward the sound. Someone was on the roof.

Then it was eerily quiet. The only sounds were my sniffles and mumbled prayers.

A few more shots sounded.

Noise came from the roof.

People yelled.

Then it got quiet again. There was no way the fight had ended that quickly. I held my breath and waited.

When the sound of gunshots surrounded the cabin—lots of it, like in war movies—I flinched, squeezing my eyes shut as I shook uncontrollably and lost control of my bladder.

Chapter 49

Nathan

We made it to the perimeter without setting off any booby traps. Unexpected, but not surprising. Al would want me alive so he could exact his revenge, and booby traps couldn't distinguish between targets.

"He wants to engage. I can't speak for his men, but Primary Tango is an expert marksman," I whispered to the teams.

"Copy that," everyone answered.

"Sierra, they know we're coming, so let us fire first. We'll test their reactions."

"Copy that. Sierra, stand by." John's voice cracked over the comms.

"Bravo Two, are you ready?"

"Target in my crosshairs."

"Bravo Three?" I asked Maxwell.

Everyone had a bad guy in their sights. On my order, we fired and removed four obstacles in the blink of an eye. A few people fired blindly into the woods, but we'd already moved from our shooting positions and taken cover.

"Movement in the back. They're turning to the front, but not moving." John updated us.

"Movement on the roof," Jay said.

"Has to be the primary target." I was ninety-nine percent sure it was Al. Taking the high ground gave him a tactical advantage. Knowing we might need him alive if Ashley wasn't in the cabin, I didn't give the order to kill him. Al was a sick fuck who didn't care who he hurt, and there was no telling what he'd done to Ashley.

"Awaiting orders." John's voice broke the silence and brought me back to the present.

"Sierra Two, you have a clean shot to the roof?"

"Affirmative," Jamie replied.

"Pin him down, but don't kill him."

"Copy that." There were shuffling noises before he said, "Ready."

"Sierra, take out the men in the back."

"You heard him," John ordered two seconds before the percussion of rapid-fire gunshots filled the air.

"Bravo. On my mark, we storm the castle. Bravo Four, send Havoc to the roof."

"Copy that," Kroupa responded. He prepped Havoc.

"Three, two, one. Go! Go! Go!" I yelled as we charged out of the woods, raining gunfire down on them like the wrath of God, as we moved.

Screams of anger, pain, and aggression filled our ears and bled into the comms.

"Sierra Two, cease fire. I repeat, Sierra Two, cease fire," Kroup ordered.

As soon as Jamie confirmed, Kroup released Havoc. He was a brown blur as he raced to the cabin, using a car to leap onto the low roof with ease. He moved too fast for anyone to shoot him.

"Joining the team."

"Sierra Two, hold your position, stop runners."

"Holding," Jamie answered.

I couldn't hear Havoc growl as he attacked Perpura and dragged him off the roof, but I knew what it sounded like after years of serving together. Al didn't stand a chance against Havoc.

A pained scream came through the comms, too clear to be anyone but one of ours.

"Sierra Four is hit," Jack confirmed.

"I'm fine. Get Flirty!" AJ yelled into the comms.

"Bravo Two, Bravo Three, cover us. We're retrieving the Primary Target."

"Copy that." Jay and Cate took up their positions and covered the front while we moved to the back.

"Bravo One and Bravo Four are circling the cabin."

"Copy that."

I heard Jack talking to AJ while he applied a tourniquet. AJ laughed. "Aurora's going to kill me."

"She'll be happy you're alive. Now stand up."

I heard AJ grunt before shutting them from my mind.

Chapter 50

Ashley

The sound of gunshots slowed down, but there was more pounding and yelling coming from the roof. Someone was fighting.

Is that a dog?

When I heard the yelp, I knew. Nathan's friend, whose name I couldn't remember, had a trained dog. To distract myself from the fear of Al killing the dog and my friends, I focused on remembering their names.

Screams of pain and frustration cut through my thoughts. All I could do was listen.

Did the dog kill him? Did he kill the dog? *What's happening?*

There was shouting outside the cabin. It sounded like it was coming from behind me, so I tried turning my head. The ties holding me in place meant I could only see the small dirty window in my peripheral vision.

Mor yelling and Al's wicked laugh carried inside.

"You brought a fucking dog?" That was Al.

"Where is she?" *That's Nathan.* My heart soared at the sound of his voice. Then it sank faster than the Hindenburg.

He'd die trying to save me. We'd both die.

"She's inside, waiting for her knight in shining armor."

Knowing there was only one way to save him, I sucked in a deep breath and screamed at the top of my lungs.

Chapter 51

Nathan

Havoc stood on Perpura's chest, blood dripping down his left front leg as he growled, a mere two inches from Al's neck. One wrong move and Havoc would rip Al's throat out.

Fuck, Perpura cut Havoc during the fight. It was hard to tell how bad the injury was, but I had to assume it wasn't life-threatening since Havoc showed no signs of weakening.

I sent Doug to help Jay and Cate cover the front and left the rest of Sierra to cover the back. "If anyone moves, shoot them."

Seeing Al again brought back memories. My skin itched, and my breath came in short bursts.

I can't afford to have a panic attack right now.

"Breathe," Kroup said beside me. "We've got him."

We did. I counted as I breathed in and out. In and out.

Kroup ordered Havoc off Al's chest. Havoc stood near Al—eyes glued to Kroupa—ready to attack the instant the command was given.

John zip-tied Al's hands behind his back. Al complained about the nasty dog bites on his arm, groin, and ankle. From the looks of it, he'd fought hard. But Havoc fought harder.

Kroup gave the command for Havoc to stand down once John and AJ had rifles pointed at Perpura's head.

"You can't ignore my wounds. You're the good guys."

I glanced at his bloody, torn arm and broken fingers. Not life threatening. No doubt the bites to his thighs and groin hurt like hell, but if those injuries were going to kill him, he'd already be dead. I couldn't see his ankle wound through his bloody, torn pants, but he'd live. I almost said, you'll live, but if I had my way, he wouldn't. "Those wounds won't kill you." I turned towards Sierra One. "Don't get close enough for him to touch you."

Perpura's laugh grated on my nerves. "Dude, I'm all tied up." It didn't matter. Knowing I wouldn't kill him until Ashley was safe, he'd kick and bite just to inflict pain.

When I asked where Ashley was, the fucker had the nerve to cackle.

"She's inside, waiting for her knight in shining armor."

A second later, a piercing scream came from the cabin.

Ashley!

I turned and sprinted to the window. Sure enough, Ashley sat in a chair, ropes dangling off the back and sides. She faced the door, so I couldn't see her face, but it was definitely her.

When her head moved, confirming she was alive, I released my breath.

Please God, let them be unharmed.

As far as I could see, she was alone. Unfortunately, I couldn't see everywhere, so we had to assume someone was in the cabin.

I turned back to Perpura. "What'd you do to her?"

"Nothing. I was waiting for you before having my fun."

Before torturing her. In front of me.

Repressing the urge to kick him, I growled instead.

"Bravo Four, you and Havoc are with me." I ordered John and AJ, "If he moves, shoot him."

"My pleasure," AJ answered.

"I can't wait to see the look on your face—"

AJ cut him off by stepping on his throat. "Shut the fuck up."

Perpura's eyes widened before he complied with a grin.

"Sierra Two and Three, with us."

"On your six," Jack said.

Jamie jogged over and stood next to Jack. "Let's go."

"We're coming around," I said into the comms.

"Copy that," Jay answered.

When I rushed towards the door, Kroup pulled me back. "Havoc, search."

Havoc barked and sat at the door, letting us know something was wrong.

"The door is booby-trapped!" The door muffled Ashley's warning, but her message was loud and clear.

"Fuck!" I scrubbed my face. "We'll find another way in. Hold tight," I called through the door.

"We'll use a window." The bedroom window was to the left, so we checked it first.

Unlike the door, the explosives in the window were readily visible.

There was only one other window—the one I'd looked through earlier.

When we walked around back, Perpura taunted me. "Fucking bitch ruined my surprise."

AJ made sure he wouldn't say anything else by pressing his bloody boot into Perpura's throat until his eyes rolled back in his head. "He won't be out long. Go save your girl."

We checked the window but couldn't see any obvious signs of tampering.

"Is the window safe?" I hollered my question.

"I think so," Ashley yelled back. "He climbed out of it."

The window was our best option.

Havoc whimpered and sat down, licking his wounded leg.

"Is he okay?" I asked.

"Yeah, give me a second to bandage it." Kroup grabbed a roll of gauze from his IFAK and wrapped the leg, soothing Havoc with praise the entire time. When he finished, he said, "Let's go."

The window opened on a hinge and would be a pain in the ass to deal with. "I'm breaking it off," I said.

The others stepped back in case the glass shattered.

"Ashley, we're breaking the window," I warned before slamming the butt of my rifle into the window frame and breaking the hinges. Jamie caught the frame when I tossed it back.

The small window redefined the term 'fatal funnel'. I'd be a sitting duck the instant I put a body part through it until I had my rifle back in my hands.

"Are you alone?" I asked Ashley.

"Yes." She nodded as she answered. Hearing the terror in her trembling voice erased any relief I felt knowing she was alone. This ends now.

"I'm going in feet first," I said to the guys.

Ashley said she was alone, but that didn't mean there wasn't someone hiding that she couldn't see. I'd take a bullet to my lower legs over a hit to my head any day of the week. "Help me up."

Jamie and Jack stood on either side while I explained what we were doing.

"On the count of three."

On one, I used the brothers' shoulders to lift myself while I jumped and shoved my feet through the window. They pushed on my back and shoulders to help me get through faster.

As soon as my feet hit the floor, I brought my rifle up and scanned the room.

"Clear."

When Ashley said "It's a bomb" I forced myself not to respond. It wasn't an issue. We'd leave the same way I'd come in.

Fighting the impulse to rush to Ashley, I held my rifle on the only internal door in the space. I wouldn't risk her life, their lives, by not clearing all the rooms first. And for that, I needed my team.

Chapter 52

Ashley

Thud! Nathan landed. Then silence, until he yelled, "Clear."

Thank you God.

"There's a bomb," I warned him, but he didn't respond.

Two more people entered, then I heard Havoc yelp. *I remember his name.* Another thud echoed as someone else came in through the window.

"Clear the bedroom," Nathan said.

"On it." That was Jamie's voice.

"Jamie?"

He didn't answer.

I turned to see Jack with him.

"All clear," Jamie said, exiting the room.

"There's a bomb," I said again.

They looked at the door.

"Bravo Two, Sierra One, we're inside."

"Why are you ignoring me?" I screamed.

"We're not." Nathan's gruff voice pulled my attention away from the brothers. "Are you hurt?" His hands were already checking for injuries.

"No, did you hear me?"

"Yes." Nathan still hadn't made eye contact. "Help me untie her," he said to his friend.

"Fucking listen to me," I screamed again.

"Hold up," his friend said. Havoc walked over and sniffed around the chair. He barked once and sat.

Nathan stopped moving. Stopped breathing, from the sounds of it.

He'd untied one arm, so I used that hand to lift his face.

I stared him in the eye, making sure he heard every word when I said, "There's a fucking bomb under the fucking chair. If I move, it'll fucking explode."

His eyes rounded. Then he blinked twice before sucking in gulps of air.

Nathan's chin dropped to his chest as he whispered, "Fuck."

"Fuck is right."

"I'm going to run my hands along the seat to see what we're working with."

I really didn't want him doing that because my ass was wet from losing control of my bladder. "I'm sitting on a pressure plate. Fucknut wasn't shy about sharing the details."

Nathan nodded, his eyes glued to the bottom of the chair. "Fucknut?"

"Fucknut," Jack said, chuckling. "Glad you're okay, Flirty."

I wasn't. Okay and I weren't in the same state. "I'm going to be blown to smithereens or starve to death in this fucking chair. I'd hardly say I'm okay."

"That won't happen," Nathan growled. "We'll find a way."

"You keep being feisty. Let us worry about the chair," Jamie said, resting his hand on my shoulder.

I wanted nothing more than to believe them. Literally nothing. "Easy for you to say."

"Kroup, think you can disarm it?"

"We'd have to dismantle part of the chair, and it might be rigged."

Nathan dropped his head before looking at me, his hands resting on my knees. "Do you know if Al rigged the chair?"

"He didn't mention it."

"Doesn't mean he didn't." It'd be typical for him to give her most of the details and leave a major one out.

"He really hates you," I said.

"I know."

"He's a fucking psychopath."

"I know."

"Did you kill him?"

"Not yet."

Al still might see his plan work. I could die in front of Nathan, or we could die together. Either way, Al would live to have his revenge.

"You can't let him win," I said.

"He won't. We'll get you out of here. I promise."

His words sounded like false hope, but the conviction in his eyes convinced me.

"Then get to it, Cowboy."

His eyes flared, a small smile formed on his lips before he stood up. "I won't risk it. I think we have to do this the Indiana Jones way."

"How?" Jamie asked. "We can't move fast enough to replace her and prevent the bomb from exploding."

I groaned. That wasn't comforting. Not one bit.

"Sorry," Jamie said.

Jack walked behind the chair. "We put pressure on the plate. Nathan pulls Flirty off. We put a dead body on it. It won't be hard to find one heavy enough to replace her."

I appreciated the compliment but couldn't let them do that. "I, um, you um, you can't do that." I'd die of embarrassment, knowing their hands were wet with my pee.

"Why not?" Nathan asked, tilting his head.

"Come here." When he leaned in closer, I whispered, "I sorta peed my pants." If the bomb didn't kill me, the embarrassment might.

Nathan threw his head back and laughed. "Is that all?" He looked over my head at Jack. "Glove up."

He didn't tell them why, but I had to assume they'd heard me because Jack didn't hide his laugh.

If I don't die, I'll have to change my name and move to another country.

"Problem solved." He squeezed my knee. "Trust me, we've all been there."

I made a mental note to ask him about that later. *If I don't die.*

Chapter 53

Nathan

When Ashley said we couldn't use brute force to hold the pressure plate to get her off the bomb chair, I thought for sure Al had done something else to prevent us from saving her.

But no. She didn't want her friends finding out she'd peed her pants when they put their hands under her ass.

My relief was so intense, all I could do was laugh as I watched Jack and Jamie put on medical gloves. Maybe she could blame it on the baby. They both had pregnant wives, so it'd be the perfect excuse.

"Bravo Two, Sierra Five, we need a dead body in here."

"You wanna repeat that?" Doug asked.

"I'm not leaving Bravo Three alone," Jay said before Doug finished. I couldn't blame Jay for not wanting to leave his fiancée alone.

"Damn it," I hissed.

"This is Sierra Four," AJ chimed in. "I'll help Five."

"You stay with Sierra One and watch the target. I've got this," Doug said.

A few minutes later, Doug shoved a body through the window to a waiting Kroup, before hauling himself in. The smell of blood and death quickly filled the cabin, making my eyes water.

"Let's get this over with," Doug said as he lifted the dead guy.

I finished untying Ashley in relative silence. The sound of our hearts beating too fast, the sound of our labored breathing, the sound of Ashley's sniffles meant the room wasn't silent, but no one was in the mood to talk.

"You ready?" I asked.

"Yes, get me out of here," Ashley said, wiping tears off her face.

Doug stood to my left, holding the dead body in a bear hug.

I'd roll back and to the right after pulling Ashley off the chair.

"You should get out of here." I told Kroup off comms.

"You stay. I stay," he answered and clapped me on the shoulder before giving us space.

Squatting, I nodded to Jamie and Jack, who leaned over behind the chair. "We're putting our hands under your ass to hold the plate down."

"If you try to cop a feel, I'm telling your wives," Ashley tried to laugh, but it came out as a whimper. *God, she's so fucking strong.*

"Noted," they answered together.

I waited for them to get into position, the veins in their necks standing out as they put their body weight behind their efforts.

"Ready," Jamie grunted.

"Ready," Jack groaned.

Ashley tried looking behind her.

"Ashley, eyes on me."

Her eyes whipped to mine. *Good girl.*

"Ready," Doug said.

I snaked my hands under Ashley's armpits, hooking my forearms behind her shoulders. When I said "Let me do all the work" she nodded.

"On three."

With a grunt, I yanked Ashley off the chair and fell back. I immediately rolled her under me, shielding her in case the bomb went off.

Chapter 54

Ashley

With Jack and Jamie's hands under my pee-soaked ass, and Nathan's hands under my sweaty armpits, I wanted to die from embarrassment. Thinking about that instead of the bomb that might explode made it easier for me to stay calm-ish as Nathan counted.

When he reached three, I squeezed my eyes shut. He yanked me off the chair, and the next thing I knew, he was crushing me, his arms wrapped around my head.

I held my breath and waited. No explosion.

There was a lot of thudding and grunting, then Jamie said, "Tie him so he doesn't fall off."

"On it," someone answered. It must be Nathan's friend, because I didn't recognize the voice.

I'm alive. We were all alive. I no longer cared about the tears flowing freely down the sides of my face or my pee-stained pants.

When Nathan finally got off me, my lungs moved a little easier. He sat back on his heels, my legs trapped between his.

"Flirty is safe. Bomb is secure," Jack said. He and Jamie hugged me as soon as Nathan released me from his bone-crushing hug.

I ignored my shaking legs and weak knees and acted like I didn't need them to hold me upright.

"Thank you," I said, sounding more like a maniac than a damsel in distress.

"You didn't think we'd leave you here, did you?" Jack asked.

"No, but I was terrified you'd all die trying to save me and I'd starve to death in a chair full of piss and even the raccoons wouldn't want to eat me," I babbled.

Nathan pulled me back into his chest, his arm around my back supporting me. "Never gonna let that happen."

"Let's move," Jamie said. He and Jack climbed out the window first.

Nathan's friend picked up Havoc, who had a bandage around his front leg, and handed him out the window before jumping out.

"Is the dog okay?" I asked, more tears falling at the thought of Assfucker hurting an innocent puppy.

"Havoc will be fine. It's just a scratch." He wiped tears off my face. "Let's get you out of here."

Nathan picked me up like I weighed nothing before handing me out the window, where Jack caught me. He held me until Nathan landed on the ground beside us.

Doug was the last one out.

Nathan picked me up again as soon as Doug's feet hit the ground.

"I can walk." I argued. *At least I think I can.* My legs still felt a little wobbly.

"Please? Let me do this," Nathan begged.

I was ready to argue, but I turned and saw Al. My legs turned to jelly. If it hadn't been for Nathan scooping me up, I would've landed on the ground in a heap of trembling Ashley.

"Thanks," I whispered as I wrapped my arms around his neck. I lifted both hands off Nathan's shoulder and flipped the assfucker who tried to kill us two birds.

When a gun went off in front of the cabin, I flinched.

Nathan crushed the air out of my lungs when he folded me in half, holding me tight to his chest.

Chapter 55

Nathan

Two rapid gunshots, a short pause, and then another shot split the air following the unexpected gunshot.

Cate's high-pitched voice came over the comms. "Tango down. Bravo Two hit."

Guns were up, and everyone turned towards the perimeter, watching for incoming threats.

Kroup and Havoc were already in motion, moving towards the front of the cabin.

"It's just a scratch," Jay said, putting everyone at ease.

I heard John release his breath and turned my attention back to Perpura.

Fuck.

He'd slipped one hand out of the zip ties while we were looking for threats. The next few seconds happened in slow motion.

Perpura grabbed John's knife. Feeling the pressure on his belt, John turned.

Perpura shoved the knife under John's armor.

"Dad!" his sons yelled as they rushed forward.

Perpura yanked John's pistol out of its holster and, using John as a human shield, pointed the gun at me.

"For Tommy!"

I spun so my armor would protect me, and I'd protect Ashley.

Protect them.

It was my only thought as the sound of gunshots echoed through the clearing.

Fire burned through my inner right thigh. Then tore through my right side.

Protect them.

I stumbled and fell to a knee. Warm blood soaked through my clothes as the scent of copper overpowered the smell of burned gunpowder.

"Are you hit?" I asked, still clutching Ashley to my chest as my other knee hit the ground.

Protect them.

The telltale crack and crunch of a neck breaking cut through the chaos erupting around me.

None of it mattered.

I clutched Ashley to my chest as my vision blurred.

When I fell to the side, I rolled over her.

Protect them.

"Nathan!" Ashley yelled and pushed at my chest. "Get off me."

"Not safe," I mumbled.

"Let go," someone said as a hand landed on my shoulder. I didn't know who it was, and it didn't matter.

Protect them.

"I'm okay." Ashley's voice sounded funny. "But you're not." She squirmed in my arms.

My hold loosened as my vision blurred. The background noise faded as I focused on Ashley's voice.

"Please, Nathan. Let them help you."

Ashley yelling at me not to die was the last thing I heard before the world went dark.

Chapter 56

Ashley

"Y ou can't die, Nathan. I won't let you." I yelled while struggling against the person trying to pull me away.

"Ashley, you need to give them room," Jay said. He yanked me off the ground and carried me away from Nathan. When he put me down, he held me tight so I couldn't go back.

Not that I stopped trying.

"What's he doing?"

"Kroup's applying a tourniquet to his leg and Cate's bandaging his side."

Al shot him. Twice.

I looked around Jay to see Jack and Jamie bent over John. "Oh God. Is your dad okay?"

"He will be." He sounded confident, and I wanted to believe him, but Jamie and Jack looked scared. "Fucker stabbed him and shot Blaszek before AJ snapped his neck."

"We need to get him to a hospital," Cate said.

"Search Perpura for keys," Kroupa ordered.

AJ bent and reached into the dead man's pockets. "Got 'em," he said, tossing the keys to Kroupa.

"Sheppard!" Three heads turned to Kroupa, who seemed to be the one in charge. "I'm taking Blaszek and Ashley in Perpura's SUV. I've got room for one more. Sharpe, you good to drive everyone else?"

"Yes, sir," Doug answered.

"I'll ride with you," AJ said.

"Stay on comms. Cate, call 9-1-1 and have them meet us on the main road. Send the coordinates as soon as you have them."

"Yes, sir," Cate said. AJ dug in Al's pockets, found his phone and tossed it to Cate.

"Sharpe, help me lift him. Sheppard, help Ashley to the car."

"I got her," AJ said, picking me up without effort despite the bandage on his leg. "Jay, go see your dad."

I clung to his neck as he limped behind Kroupa and Doug. "Will he be okay?" I asked.

"They've stopped the bleeding, so he should be."

"Should be?" More tears threatened to fall.

"I'm sorry, Ashley. It's the best I've got right now," AJ sounded as worried as I felt.

After AJ helped me into the back seat, Kroupa arranged Nathan so his head rested in my lap and his legs were elevated.

When Kroupa whistled, Havoc jumped in the back of Al's SUV.

"Please don't die," I begged as I stroked Nathan's hair.

The ride to the cabin had seemed rough, but it was nothing compared to the ride out with Kroupa driving as fast as he safely could.

"AJ, are you okay?" I asked after hearing him grunt for the third time.

"Yeah, some fucker shot my leg. It's not bad, but the turbulence isn't helping," he joked.

"Is Havoc okay?" I could hear him whimpering every time big bumps jostled us off our seats.

"He will be. The cut isn't deep, but he'll need stitches and lots of rest," Kroup answered.

"Can I pet him?"

"He'd like that," Kroupa said. He issued an order two seconds before a wet snout nudged my shoulder. "Now you can reach him."

"Thank you, Havoc." I sniffled. "I'm sorry you got hurt trying to save me."

"No one blames you, but if you need to hear it. He forgives you," Kroupa said.

I needed to hear it. Not just from Havoc, but from AJ, Jay, John, and Nathan. And from Jamie and Jack because their dad got stabbed. And from Cate because her fiancé got shot.

I needed to hear it from everyone because the guilt was piling up.

If only I'd been stronger and hadn't needed time to process the negative pregnancy result.

If only I'd stayed inside at the clinic.

If only I'd screamed, alerting Nathan that something was wrong.

If only I wasn't the reason my friends had gotten hurt.

"Ashley," AJ yelled my name.

"What?"

"Are you okay?" he asked.

"No, I'm not. This is all my fault." I finally admitted.

"No, it's not," AJ said.

"Not even a little," Kroup added. "Perpura was a sick bastard."

Havoc nudged my hand, which had stilled while I confessed, so I rubbed his head again. The other hand was alternating between rubbing Nathan's head and caressing his cheeks.

After a particularly jarring bump, I heard my name whispered with a gravelly voice and looked down to see Nathan's eyes fluttering.

"Nathan!"

Chapter 57

Nathan

My head felt woozy, and my leg hurt like hell from the tourniquet, but the pain meant I was alive. And more importantly, so was Ashley.

It wasn't easy, but I raised one hand to hold hers. "You okay?"

"I'm not the one who got shot," she answered, her grip crushing my hand.

"What about the baby?"

"What?" AJ asked, whipping around in the front seat.

Ignoring him, I waited for Ashley's answer.

"Fucknut nabbed me before I could tell you. The test was negative. I'm not pregnant." Her fingers tracing my scar went mostly unnoticed as relief flooded my system.

"You're not—"

"No." She laughed. "I'm sorry. I should've told you sooner."

"Don't apologize. You were a little preoccupied." My laugh turned to a cough, reminding me I'd taken a bullet in the side, too.

"I'm glad," I said, my eyelids getting heavier by the second.

"Me too."

Kroup started talking, but the world around me faded as I lost the battle to stay conscious.

Chapter 58

Ashley

I refused to leave Nathan when they put him on a gurney and transferred him to the ambulance. I held his free hand while they checked his vitals and inserted the IV needle.

Kroupa said he'd follow and drop AJ off at the emergency room before taking Havoc to the vet.

No one promised me Nathan would be okay. Which I appreciated as much as it pissed me off. I didn't want false hope, but I needed someone to tell me everyone would be okay.

There wasn't much more the paramedics could do. The tourniquet had stopped the bleeding. They said the doctor would remove it later. They replaced the bandage on his side, but then they did nothing. Or at least that's what it seemed like.

"Will he be okay?" I asked.

The paramedic looked at me, then at his notes. "He's stable for now."

I could've done without the *for now* part, but hearing Nathan was stable helped me breathe a little easier.

"Ma'am, are you injured?" the paramedic asked.

"No." I looked like hell warmed over, but I wasn't hurt. I was dirty and stinky but uninjured. "I'm fine."

He asked me for personal information about Nathan, but I didn't have any.

What kind of girlfriend was I that I didn't know his date of birth? Or anything else about him. *A bad one.* "I swear I'll learn everything about you if you'll just be okay."

The sirens cut out as the ambulance stopped.

"We're here." The paramedic helped me out before he and his partner wheeled Nathan out and into the emergency room.

I followed them until they told me I couldn't.

I was standing in the ER waiting room, staring at the doors Nathan had disappeared through, when AJ walked in.

"Have you seen a doctor yet?" he asked, pulling my attention away from the swinging metal doors.

I shook my head. "You need one more than I do." I pointed at his leg. The red stain on his bandage was spreading.

"Let's go to the counter." He wrapped his arm around me and steered me to the waiting nurse.

AJ took the forms, insisted on filling out mine before his, then brought them back to the nurse. The ER doors opened again before he sat back down. Paramedics rolled John in on a gurney, with Jay following close behind.

Jay said goodbye to his dad before plopping down in the seat next to me.

"You see a doctor yet?" he asked.

Why was everyone so concerned about me? I was the least injured person here.

"No, you need to see the doctor before I do."

"AJ first." He nodded at AJ's leg. "How bad is it?"

"Not sure. Hurts like a motherfucker."

Jamie and Jack walked in and beelined to us. "Any news?" Jamie asked.

"No, we just got here," Jay answered. He was probably right, but I felt like I'd been waiting forever.

"Andrew," the nurse called.

AJ shuttered. He still hated being called Andrew by anyone not Blake. "Keep me updated." He fist-bumped the guys and hugged me.

Tears stung my eyes as yet another person I cared about disappeared behind the doors.

Jamie took AJ's seat. "How are you holding up?"

I shook my head as more tears flowed. "Not good."

"Come here." Jamie wrapped his arm around my shoulders and held me. "Jay, you need to see a doctor, too."

"I'm fine."

"It wasn't a suggestion." Jamie sounded a lot like his father. *He'll be a great dad.*

"Sir, yes, sir," Jay said, standing up and saluting him.

Thinking of Jamie being a dad reminded me I needed to tell him about my negative test. "I'm not pregnant."

"That's good. Did you tell Nathan? He was insane with worry," Jamie asked.

"Yeah, I did." Though he might not remember since he'd passed out again after.

"Wait, what? How'd I not know?" Jack asked.

I'd just assumed Jamie and Nathan would tell the others. *Guess not.*

"Need to know," Jamie answered. "You didn't."

"Damn," Jack said without venom. He plopped down in Jay's seat. "You need me to get you anything?"

"Water would be nice."

When Jamie let go and walked away to find a phone, Jay stole his seat. It was like musical chairs in the waiting room. That wasn't entirely true. *The only seats that are never empty are the two on either side of me.*

"Where are Doug and Cate?" I asked, realizing they hadn't joined us.

"They stayed behind to deal with the local LEOs," Jack said.

"Kroupa at the vet with Havoc?" Jay asked, never taking his eyes off his form.

"Yeah, he said he'd be back as soon as he could," I answered.

"Ashley," a nurse called out.

Jack and Jay stood with me. Jack said, "We'll be right here."

In the room, the nurse took my pulse and blood pressure, and gave me a gown. "The doctor will be in soon."

I was actually happy to take off my stained pants, even if it meant my ass was hanging out.

Unable to sit still, I wandered around the room, reading everything on the walls to occupy my mind.

The door opened, and a young male doctor walked in. "Ashley?"

I nodded, backed my way to the bed, and sat back down.

He reviewed my chart. "Does it hurt anywhere?"

I shook my head. "No." I fidgeted with the bottom edge of my gown, drawing his attention to my hands and arms.

He washed his hands and put on blue medical gloves. "Let's have a look."

My only injuries were a bruise from Al's slap and scratches from the cuffs, ropes, and chain.

The doctor's hands were warm as he held my arms and checked my injuries. He confirmed I didn't need stitches, or even bandaids, as he cleaned the wounds.

"I'll have the nurse bring you some Gatorade and ibuprofen. Once you've finished, you're free to go. Any flavor preference?"

"Orange."

He made a note. "You can get dressed now."

"Is it possible for me to borrow some scrubs? I really don't want to put my pants back on." I'd have to overpay for them, but I could live with that.

"I'll see what I can do. For now, you're welcome to keep the gown."

I wonder if I can make a skirt out of it?

Only it was see-through thin, and my underwear needed to be burned.

"Thanks."

The nurse came in with a pair of green scrub pants tossed over her arm, a bottle of orange Gatorade, and a little paper cup with two pills.

I took the pills and chugged the Gatorade. Not only was I in a hurry to get back to the Sheppards and ask about Nathan, I was seriously thirsty.

"Doc said you asked for these." She handed me the scrubs.

"Thanks. Can I have a bag for my clothes?" I hated being so needy, but I wanted to seal off my gross clothes.

"I'll bring it with your discharge papers."

When I was finally free to go, I rushed back to the waiting room.

"Where's Jay?"

"He's with a doctor," Jamie said. "What'd the doctor say?"

"I'm fine, just need to hydrate." I set the tied-off bag under a chair and sat.

"Here." Jack handed me a water bottle. *He'll be a great dad, too.*

"Any news yet?" I asked.

"No. Not yet, but I'm sure we'll hear something soon."

Every second we had to wait lasted an eternity.

Cate and Doug arrived before Kroupa. When he finally did, he told us Havoc needed stitches but would be fine. "He's resting at the vet's for the night."

Jay also needed a few stitches and would be fine. His brothers teased him about having the same injury as Havoc, lightening the mood.

"It's not my fault you two let us do the heavy lifting," Jay teased right back.

The banter died down as we waited to hear about John, AJ, and Nathan.

"Mr. Sheppard." A doctor called out.

"Yes," John's sons answered as they stood and hurried to the doctor.

A few minutes later, Jack and Jay returned. "He'll be fine. The knife missed his lungs and other vital organs." Jack paused as a collective sigh of relief filled our area of the waiting room. "He needed surgery to repair his muscle." He closed his eyes and took a second. "But he'll be okay."

Cate hugged Jay. I hugged Jack.

Thank God. Now we had to wait for news about AJ and Nathan.

After using the phone at the nurse's station, Jack said, "The girls will be here soon."

Oh, my God. "What about Gran?" Why hadn't I thought of her sooner?

"Sammie's bringing her," Jack answered.

It was all too much. Too many things to think about. Too many people to worry about. I turned back into Jack's arms and cried.

"It's okay." He rubbed my back. "Everything will be okay."

Finally, someone cared enough to lie.

"Ashley!" Gran called out as soon as the automatic doors opened.

"Gran." I jumped up and ran to her. I thanked Sammie over Gran's shoulder as I hugged her. A fresh wave of tears, this time from relief, flooded my eyes.

Gran pulled back and glanced at my wounds, puffy face, and awkward appearance. She raised her eyebrows, questioning the scrubs.

"My clothes got ruined," I answered her unspoken question.

"You okay?"

"I will be. But Nathan's still in surgery, and I'm scared."

She hugged me again. "He's a strong boy. He'll be okay."

I prayed she was right.

Not long after, Mary, Beth, Meg, Emily, and Blake rushed in.

Beth handed out cell phones while Mary hugged everyone.

When it was my turn, Mary squeezed me tight. "I'm glad you're home safe."

"Thank you." I wiped my tears when I pulled away. So did she.

"Jackson, take me to my husband," Mary ordered.

He wrapped his arm around her shoulders, kissed the top of her head, and led her down the hall.

After hugging me, Emily handed me a bag. "Jamie said you needed clean clothes."

I snatched the bag, grateful to change out of the scrubs. "Thank you."

Jamie and Jack were in the waiting room when I came back, feeling refreshed. *And grateful Emily and I are about the same size.* I sat next to Blake. We weren't close, but I reached over and held her hand anyway. I needed the extra support and figured she did too.

"He'll be okay, right?" She asked, trying to hold back her tears and failing as she squeezed my hand.

"He said it was only a graze, and he'd be fine." I reassured her. But he'd been gone longer than I'd expected for a minor cut. *What if he lied?* It wouldn't be the first time one of them had lied about the severity of an injury.

Blake jumped when she heard the doctor call her name.

Jack stood beside her, offering emotional support.

When Blake left with the doctor to go see her fiancé, I was the only one left waiting to hear about the person I loved. Because yes, somewhere along the line I'd fallen in love with him. Hell, I'd probably loved him since Vegas.

He has to survive.

Meg and Emily sat on either side of me. They each wrapped one arm around me while holding my hand with the other. I didn't need to tell them I was terrified of losing him. They knew. They understood.

What if the bullet hit his spine, and he never walked again? I'd still love him, but would he be okay? Did his lungs collapse? Did they have to… *Oh God, I don't even know what they do for collapsed lungs.*

I gripped Emily's hand tighter.

"AJ's fine." Jack's voice pulled me out of my head. "Doc said they needed to take skin off his hairy ass because the tear from the bullet was too wide for stitches."

Subdued laughter filled the room.

"The doctor said hairy ass?" Jay asked after breaking eye contact with me.

"No, I paraphrased."

"How do you know AJ's ass is hairy?" Jay raised an eyebrow, then turned towards me and winked.

Is he doing this for my benefit? Trying to make me laugh?

It worked. Though my laugh was more of a strangled chuckle. At least I was no longer on the verge of panicking.

"Are you telling me you've never seen another man's ass?" Jack asked.

"For the love of all things holy, can we please stop talking about AJ's ass?" Cate asked.

"If AJ were here, he'd suggest talking about yours just to piss off Jay," I said, surprising everyone.

This time, the laughter wasn't subdued, and I joined in.

When a doctor asked who was here for Nathan, ten people stood up and turned.

I was the only one whose knees wobbled.

The clock stopped ticking until Jamie said, "Come on, Flirty, let's go." His hand on my shoulder helped remind me that I needed to breathe.

Please let him be okay.

Chapter 59

Nathan

My eyelids felt like sheets of lead. The rhythmic beeping hurt my head. A heavy weight pressed into my chest. *Ignore the pain and open your eyes.*

With great effort, I did. The bright white room confirmed my guess; I was in the hospital.

The weight on my chest was Ashley. *Thank God.*

I wrapped my non-IV arm around her. "Hey." My voice made sandpaper sound smooth.

"Nathan!"

I moaned when she pushed off my chest.

"Sorry," she said, pulling away.

"Don't apologize." I coughed.

Ashley extracted herself from my grip and grabbed a glass of water. "Here."

After finishing the cup, I asked Ashley if she was okay. And about the baby.

"I'm fine, I swear." She confirmed her test was negative, then asked if I remembered the car ride.

"It's a bit fuzzy, so I wanted to verify I wasn't dreaming."

"You weren't."

Is that sadness I hear in her voice? That didn't make any sense.

"Ashley." I pulled her chin until she faced me. "Are you sad you're not pregnant with Finn's baby?"

"No!" She shook her head. "It's just… it's nothing. I'm stupid."

"Hey, no one calls my girl stupid, not even you." I squeezed the back of her neck and pulled her down for a light kiss. "Now, tell me."

"I'm happy I'm not having his baby, but I kind of got used to the idea of Emily, Meg, and me raising our first babies together." She laughed at herself. "See, stupid."

"It's not stupid. You found a positive to focus on." I caressed her cheek. "If things were different, would you want to be pregnant?"

"I don't know, maybe." She shrugged.

I grinned. "If you want to, we can make a baby as soon as they release me."

Her eyes flew open, and her jaw dropped.

Thinking about baby-making caused me to look Ashley up and down to appreciate her gorgeous body. *She's wearing different clothes.* Before I could ask about them, she laughed.

It was loud and raw and real. And the most beautiful sound in the world.

"Slow down, Cowboy."

"Cowboy?" She'd called me that in the cabin, too, but I'd forgotten until she said it again.

"After what happened, I'll never call you Casper again."

Thank God. "Appreciate that."

"We can't make a baby." I raised my eyebrows, certain we could. She ignored my unspoken question. "We haven't even gone on a date."

"I'll take you on a date as soon as I get out of here." I thought about it. "Well, maybe I'll take a shower first." I joked.

"We're not married."

"Easy problem to remedy. Marry me." The only thing I could think about while feeling my life slipping away with every beat of my heart was Ashley. I'd probably been in love with her from the instant she hit on me with a devilish grin and cheesy pickup line.

"You can't be serious?"

"I am. Fuck dating, you're it for me. Marry me." I repeated the question, which sounded more like an order.

Of course, she argued. "Nathan, I'm jobless and homeless, and babyless, so it's not like you need to do the honorable thing." Her use of air quotes pissed me off.

"What? Were you not listening? I love you, Ashley. I don't need a first date to know you're it for me. I'm all in."

"You love me?"

"Yes."

"You left that part out."

This woman.

"Then let me say it again." I stared into her eyes and said, "I love you, Ashley."

"Well, I love you too." She smiled. "You really want to marry me and take on this hot mess?"

"For the love of God, woman, yes, I want to marry you. Now say yes, or say no, but please fucking answer me."

I hadn't intended to throw a proposal at her five minutes after regaining consciousness, but nothing with Ashley ever went as expected.

"You haven't actually asked me anything. All you've done is bark orders." Her laugh made me wish I wasn't in a hospital bed with stitches holding my artery together. And I definitely wasn't happy that the tear in my femoral artery meant I had to be extra careful for eight to ten weeks.

"Ashley Nicole York, will you please marry me?"

"Yes. But only because you said please." Her smile lit up her face as she leaned down and kissed me. My EKG monitor sped up, which meant a nurse would probably interrupt us any second.

"You should know what you're getting into."

I did, and I couldn't wait. Before she could say anything else, I grabbed her behind the neck, pulled her down, and kissed the fight out of her.

Chapter 60

Ashley

If it was wrong to get turned on when Nathan grabbed my neck and pulled me down for a kiss that short-circuited my brain, then I didn't want to be right.

When I finally broke the kiss, only after hearing him groan in pain, I touched my fingers to my lips.

"Now will you please stop talking trash about my fiancée?" he asked, using the term like it was the most natural thing in the world.

Nathan wasn't my first gorgeous alpha male, but there was no doubt he'd be my last. I smiled behind my fingers. "We're engaged."

"We are."

"Where will we live?" We couldn't live in his hotel room, and I didn't think he'd want to live with Gran.

"I'll build us a house."

"Just like that? You'll build us a house?"

"I'll have to hire an architect and builders, but yeah, just like that." His grin was hiding something.

But what?

Trusting he'd tell me eventually, I tackled my next concern. "But I don't have a job."

"Don't worry, I'll support you." He squeezed my hand.

"How? You'll be out of work while you heal."

He grinned. "Have you forgotten what I told you? I made good money in the SEALs and invested. I did well. Hawken's paid me a fuckton more, and I invested most of that, too."

Is he rich? "How much is a fuckton?"

"A lot." He shrugged.

"So when you asked me all those questions about what I'd do if money wasn't an issue?"

"I wanted to know if you'd be open to letting me support you."

"Because you have a fuckton of money. So, you're rich?" I didn't care about the money, but he was being so mysterious about it I couldn't help but ask.

"Yes."

"Like, Blake rich?" Blake was rich enough that she hadn't batted an eye when she made a very generous donation to the hospital, ensuring everyone from SSI would have a private room.

He tilted his head. "I don't know. How rich is Blake?"

"Almost a billionaire. She's the reason you won't have a roommate while you're here."

"Really?" His eyes opened wide.

Blake inherited her fortune, but you'd never know she was rich. She was down to earth and didn't flaunt her wealth. Even when she was making sizable donations to charities. *Or the hospital.*

"Yup. So?"

"I'm not a billionaire, but I have a couple dozen million in investments."

My jaw dropped, but a knock interrupted us before I could ask the rest of my questions.

"Come in," he called out.

"Hey, how are you feeling?" his friend asked.

"Alive and juiced up."

Kroupa laughed. "Enjoy it while you can. How bad is it?"

"I'll need a few weeks of light duty." Nathan winked at me. "But I'll make a full recovery."

My face warmed as color rushed to my cheeks.

"Ashley, can I have a minute with Nathan?"

"Of course." When I stood, Nathan pulled me back down for a kiss. Blushing, I said, I'll be right outside."

Chapter 61

Nathan

"So, I take it you two figured out your shit?" Kroup asked with a knowing smirk.

"I'm marrying that woman." My stupidly big smile pulled at my scar. I'd spent the last year dreaming about Ashley, missing a future we never got to explore. No way was I letting her out of my grasp a second time.

"Does she know?" Kroup laughed.

I laughed with him. "Yeah, she even agreed."

"Good for you."

"Thanks, man," I said, wishing I had a stronger word. "I couldn't have saved her without you. And the entire team."

"You finally done being a lone wolf?"

I nodded.

"Good, it never suited you. You're meant to lead a pack."

"Speaking of packs. How's Havoc?"

"He needed a few stitches, but luckily the injury looked worse than it was. He's soaking up all the love and attention the vet techs are giving him. I'll take him home in the morning."

"How's everyone else?"

"Ashley didn't tell you?"

"Other things got in the way." I'd smiled more in this stupid hospital bed, with stitches holding my artery together, than I had in the last year.

"It's good to see you happy. You deserve it."

"It feels good."

Kroup summarized. "John and Janerek are staying the night. Mary and Blake refuse to leave. The doc discharged the youngest Sheppard after stitching him up. He's pissed it's fucking up his ink." He laughed. Jay was like us; if an injury wasn't life-threatening, we considered it an annoyance.

"How bad is John's injury?"

"The knife missed his lung, but it tore him up. Doc stitched up his muscles, so he'll be on desk duty for a while, but he'll make a full recovery."

Thank God.

"Janerek understated the severity of his graze; the doc used skin from his ass to close the wound. Luckily, the damage to his muscle isn't too severe."

I listened, grateful no one had suffered life-altering injuries.

"You found yourself one hell of a team."

"Yeah." I nodded. "Thanks for that." He'd suggested I apply for the job.

"I'm glad it worked out."

"And thanks for saving my ass."

"Anytime, but maybe not anytime soon." He laughed.

"Amen to that, brother."

He shook my hand. "If you're good, I'm taking off. Call me when they release you."

"Will do. Can you send Ashley back in?" *I already miss her.*

"Dude, you've got it bad."

God help me, I did, and I couldn't wait to get out of the hospital so I could finally show her.

Chapter 62

Ashley

"Come here," Nathan said as soon as I sat in the driver's seat. He reached over, grabbed my neck and pulled me in for a kiss that was most definitely not suitable for a Sunday morning, or the hospital parking lot.

It wasn't suitable in the hospital bed either, but that hadn't stopped him from kissing me senseless any time we were alone over the last four days. Technically, three and a half, but who's counting?

My lips continued to tingle after I pulled away. "Hi."

"Hi." He smiled.

"Good thing I didn't bring Gran."

He chuckled. "She would've clapped."

I blushed. Just because he was right didn't mean I wanted her seeing us making out like horny teenagers. To say Gran was happy when we announced our engagement would be the understatement of the year. She would've done cartwheels and backflips if she could have. Instead, she squealed and clapped and hugged us repeatedly.

Gran had insisted on coming to visit John and Nathan every day. Every day, she snuck in homemade snacks, which they loved. Thankfully, Emily had volunteered to stay with Gran during the hours I spent at the hospital with Nathan.

But not today; today I'd dropped her off at SSI before I picked up my fiancé. The word still felt foreign on my tongue, but I liked the sound of it. Nathan was everything I'd wanted in a man, in a partner, but didn't think I'd ever find.

He was kind, supportive, and generous. Not to mention gorgeous, sexy as sin, and protective as fuck.

"Can we grab food on the way home?" I loved how he referred to Gran's as home.

We were staying there until we found a place of our own. Gran had argued, insisting we live with her rather than renting until we bought a house. But Nathan was just as stubborn and insisted we needed privacy.

They compromised. We'd rent an apartment, I'd spend my days with Gran while working from home, and we'd have dinner with her most nights.

"Sure," I agreed. "Are you okay if we stop by SSI first? I need to get something from Meg."

"That's fine." Nathan leaned against the headrest and sighed. "I can't believe I had to take medical leave two weeks into a new job." He laughed.

"Are you worried about getting fired?"

"No." He turned towards me. "Wait, should I be?"

"Of course not. You got hurt saving me." Not just Nathan but John, AJ, and Jay. Unlike Nathan and John, Jay returned to work the next day, and Blake took AJ home the day after his graft.

Poor AJ, he'd never live down the fact that he now had ass skin on his leg.

Nathan and John needed to stay longer, much to their displeasure. Mary and I bonded as we shared stories of our men complaining non-stop about being laid up in hospital beds. I'd laughed when she said she'd taken John's phone away, so he'd stop working and get some rest.

Nathan was obnoxiously vocal about wanting to leave. If he'd listened to the doctor and rested, he could have left sooner. But he'd moved around too much and ripped out his stitches. It scared the hell out of me when he'd started bleeding.

"Saving you made every second in the hospital worth it." He squeezed my hand.

"Didn't seem that way when you were whining."

"It's not my fault I don't like sitting around doing nothing."

I mimicked his doctor's deep voice. "Nathan, healing isn't doing nothing."

He held his side as he laughed. "That was awful."

In the parking lot, I said, "I'll be a few minutes. You should come in."

"That works. I can talk to Jamie about coming back on light duty next week."

"Seriously, you've been out of the hospital for less than an hour."

He raised an eyebrow.

"Fine." I put one hand on my hip and pointed the other at him. "But if you hurt yourself again, I'll kick your ass."

His gaze sent shivers down my spine as he looked me up and down. "Noted."

"Come on, Cowboy. Let's go."

Chapter 63

Nathan

"You knew about this, didn't you?" I asked Ashley. It was a stupid question. Gran was front and center welcoming me back.

"Who, me?" Ashley batted her long eyelashes, playing innocent while beaming at the crowd and the Welcome to the Family banner hanging in front of my office. A Welcome Home banner hung over John's door.

I didn't tear up often, and if anyone asked I'd lie about it, but damn if my eyes weren't a little blurry.

Family.

A bark cut Ashley off just as she opened her mouth.

"Havoc. Come here, boy." Havoc sat at my feet, sweeping the floor with his tail as I praised him.

"Good to see you back on your feet."

I stood and hugged Kroupa. "Thanks, man. I see Havoc is cone-free."

"I took it off for the party." He laughed. "He may not let me put it back on."

Havoc barked again before rushing off to play with the only kid in the office. I assumed he was Chase, Doug's son. Watching them play, I couldn't tell who was happier: the kid or Havoc.

"Thanks for letting Havoc play with Chase." Doug's voice sounded anything but thankful. "Of course, now he'll never stop asking for a puppy." Doug clapped Kroup on the shoulder.

"Sorry." Kroup laughed. "If you want help finding one, I know a guy," he answered.

"You don't look or sound sorry," Doug said. If his smile was any indication, he'd buy that kid the moon.

"I'll be around more often now that Blaze is settling in. I'd be happy to train your new puppy." Kroup suggested as if it were a given that Doug would have one sooner rather than later.

Doug ran his hand through his copper-red hair. "Beth would kill me."

We all laughed.

"Ma just texted. They're almost here." Meg updated the group.

A few minutes later, John and Mary walked in. They looked tired, but seemed happy. And genuinely surprised.

John scanned the room, nodding as he made eye contact with everyone. "Thank you," he finally said.

He walked slowly around the room, stopping to hug or shake hands with everyone. When he got to me, he pulled me into a hug, slapped my back and said, "Welcome to the family."

If anyone asked, I'd have to lie again about the extra moisture in my eyes.

"Thank you. How are you feeling?"

"Good. Mary's pissed I won't take more than ibuprofen, but I'm done sitting around. You?"

I glanced up to see Mary watching John like a hawk. If I had to guess, it'd be a long time before she let him out of her sight.

"You're lucky to have her." He looked over and smiled. His love radiating off of him.

"I am." John glanced at Ashley. "So are you."

"Don't I know it."

"Speaking of, you'll want to re-propose."

"Sir?"

"She's a hopeless romantic, and while a surprise proposal in a hospital might seem romantic to us, I've been informed it isn't."

"It's not?"

"No. Or so I was told by someone wiser than me." He looked back over at Mary.

"Noted." John's fatherly advice, offered with humor, helped me feel even more accepted.

"Let's go. The foods in the back," Jamie said.

As soon as the door opened, the rich scent of grilled meat hit my nose, making my stomach rumble. "Tell me you're grilling burgers."

"Steaks," AJ answered.

"Even better."

Two grills produced mouth-watering aromas. They'd set up folding tables, which were covered with food and dishes.

"You must be Nathan" A guy I hadn't met wiped his hand on his jeans before holding it out for me to shake. "I'm the other new guy, Matt Robinson."

"Nice to meet you. Thanks for cooking."

When he said, Hooyah, it set off a chorus of Hooahs and Oorahs.

"The Army guys and Marines will never let our Hooyah go unanswered." We laughed.

"I heard you started your career with a bang." He looked down at my leg. Not that he'd see anything—the bandage was under my pants.

"Two, actually."

"And a proposal?"

"Only one of those so far." When he raised an eyebrow, I explained that according to John's sources, I'd have to do it again. I called Ashley over and introduced her.

"We've met," Ashley said. "You're literally the only person he hasn't met." She patted my arm.

That made sense. He would've interviewed with the team, just like I had. And since he'd been here all day, he would've met the significant others too.

Lunch was delicious, loud, and chaotic, reminding me of outings with my SEAL brothers. I finally got to try Meg's famous bacon mac and cheese, and it didn't disappoint.

I excused myself and went inside to use the men's room. And to take a minute to process the overwhelming emotions flooding my system.

"You good?" Kroup asked as soon as I walked back out into the hall.

Ashley, the Sheppards, and everyone at SSI had given me the family I'd always wanted. Well, half of it. Ashley was on her own to give me the rest of my dream family.

"Yeah, just a little overwhelmed." *In the best way possible.*

Six weeks later...

Ashley

"Where are we going?" I asked, feigning impatience. Nathan had been dropping less-than-helpful hints about his surprise all morning. Not that I'd complain, I loved surprises.

Plus, he'd been spoiling me non-stop after making good on his promise to give me a first date I'd never forget. My cheeks felt a little warmer just thinking about it.

I kept telling him he didn't have to spoil me, even though I secretly loved it. He always said the same thing: I don't have to, but I want to.

I remembered him saying "It's sad that you think I'm spoiling you when all I'm doing is taking care of you". Apparently, I'd been dating the wrong guys my whole life.

The warm September air felt good on my skin as I let my hand hang out the window. A comfortable silence settled in the truck's cab after I stopped pestering Nathan with questions.

He parked in front of a rundown farmhouse just outside of town.

Did he buy this place? He'd talked about buying land more than once.

Our current situation was a little unconventional—we had a small studio apartment, furnished from my old apartment, smack dab in the middle of Main Street. We spent our nights there, but per our compromise with Gran, I worked at her place during the day and we had dinner with her most nights.

I hopped out and met Nathan in front of his truck. Appreciating his rugged good looks and the way his tight gray T-shirt showed off all his delicious muscles.

"Let's take a walk," he said, reaching for my hand.

He walked me around the neglected property, staring at me as he asked me question after question.

When he asked if I thought I could live there, I looked around and smiled. *I can absolutely see myself living here.*

But I wouldn't be me if I made it that easy. "It's kind of a mess."

"That's why it's so cheap, but the land is perfect and we can renovate or rebuild the house."

Still staring at the rundown farmhouse, I feigned nonchalance. "I think we can make it work."

When he didn't respond, I turned around to find Nathan on one knee.

"Will you marry me?" His lopsided grin made my heart flutter.

In his left hand was a red velvet ring box. Inside the box sat a large, gorgeous, solitaire diamond that sparkled in the sunlight.

"Aren't we already engaged?" I asked, reaching for the ring.

"We are. I wanted to do it the right way," he said, snatching the ring away.

"Hey!" I pouted.

"Hey what? You haven't answered me yet," he teased.

"Yes, Nathan. For the second time, yes, I'll marry you."

He slipped the ring on my finger, picked me up and swung me around. When I wrapped my legs around his waist, I leaned back so I could see his eyes.

Running a finger down his scar, I said, "I love you, Cowboy."

After he kissed every thought out of my head, he said, "I love you, Slick. What do you say? How about we buy some land and start a family?"

It was one of the best days of my life.

Six more weeks later…

"Morning," Nathan said as he pulled me close and put his hand on my belly.

"I wish we didn't have to work today." Nathan had only been back on full duty for three weeks, and while I was happy for him, I missed him when he had long days and overnight assignments.

"Will you feel better if I promise to pick up your favorite ice cream on my way home?"

"Maybe." I laughed as I straddled his hips. "I'd feel even better if we had some fun before you left."

He never said no. He couldn't always take his time, but a quickie was nothing to complain about.

"You, my gorgeous wife, are insatiable." He ran his hands down my sides, tickling me with his feather-light touch.

When I giggled, he sat up and kissed me until my giggles turned to moans.

Then, he flipped me onto my back. "I'll have to set my alarm an hour earlier if this is how you want to start your days."

I wasn't a get-up-at-the-crack-of-dawn kind of person, but for this… Yeah, I'd get up early for orgasmic bliss courtesy of Nathan.

Afterward, I lounged in bed while Nathan showered.

We didn't start every day like this, but the pregnancy hormones were making me crazy horny. It was probably too soon to blame them, but I didn't care.

Nathan and I started baby-making practice the day he left the hospital. It was an exercise in creativity, making sure we didn't rip open any of his stitches.

Which we only did once.

I'd stopped taking the pill because of my earlier scare and was waiting for my next cycle to restart, but after a discussion we decided I wouldn't take them anymore and he wouldn't wear a raincoat.

As a result, Baby Blaszek was conceived about the same time as Nathan's romance-novel-worthy second proposal.

We'd vowed to love, honor, and cherish each other in a small ceremony two weeks after said proposal. The late September weather was perfect, the fall colors made everything beautiful, and our friends and family made it a day we'd never forget as we celebrated in Gran's backyard.

No muss. No fuss. Just our friends, a Justice of the Peace, and Prince, because of course Gran insisted he attend. She even bought him a tie for the occasion. Prince wasn't the only nonhuman at our wedding. Kroupa brought Havoc.

When Gran insisted on introducing Prince to Havoc, I expected chaos. But Havoc was far better trained than Prince, and he sat perfectly still while Prince checked him out. When Kroupa released him, he nosed the tiny cat, making us all laugh when Prince fell over. They're best buds now, and whenever Kroup comes to visit, he brings his wife and his dog.

After the ceremony, we celebrated with a potluck party and lots of beer. *If anyone noticed that I wasn't drinking, they didn't say anything.* Who am I kidding? They noticed. Stupid PIs and their ridiculous observation skills.

The only person we'd actually told about the pregnancy was Gran. She was beside herself with joy, knowing she'd get to meet her great-grandbaby. More than once I heard her warning Prince he'd have to play nice with the baby.

I didn't have high hopes for her demon cat playing nice, but then again, I'd never had a cat. Technically, I still didn't. Prince was Gran's cat, though Nathan and I still helped take care of him. John had eventually solved that mystery, turns out a couple abandoned the little guy when they moved.

I couldn't imagine someone abandoning a cute, sweet, cuddly cat like Prince.

Yes, I thought he was both cute and cuddly, and a demon cat. Sue me.

Thanks to Nathan, Gran was using a cane at our wedding. He'd hired a nurse to help Gran during the nights, but we didn't need her for very long, thanks to Gran's upgraded therapy. It was a blessing and a curse. She was stronger and moved faster, but she wielded that damn cane like a weapon.

Nathan thought it was hysterical and taught her how to use it properly as a striking tool.

A choice he quickly regretted because she thwacked him regularly for not calling her Gran. Something he finally did after we exchanged our vows.

"Aren't you working today?" Nathan asked, interrupting my walk down memory lane.

"You know I am. We're meeting to make sure everything is perfect for the fundraiser tomorrow."

I loved my job at the Wyatt Foundation, and now that I didn't have to worry about Gran's medical care or paying rent, I was happy working part time.

It gave me time to work on my romance novel. Which I'd finally told the girls about during our last girls' night out. Though I still hadn't let anyone read it. When I told them I wanted to finish it first, I was only half-lying. My nerves were the other reason.

I let Nathan read it, and he thought it was funny. Which gave me hope, since I was writing a rom-com about three sisters and their small-town shenanigans. He especially liked the spicy scenes and said he'd be happy to help me make sure they were realistic.

I lost track of the number of times we did research in our studio, and the number of times I thanked God the offices below us were empty from five to nine.

"I thought maybe you'd cancelled and decided to stay in bed all day," he teased as he tugged the covers off me. The end of October was the perfect time of year in Texas. It was cool at night, making it perfect for cuddling under the comforter, or with a smoking hot husband.

"Hey!" I grabbed the blankets. "I don't have to be there for another three hours."

He laughed. "Come on, Slick, I'll make you breakfast."

I jumped up, making him laugh even harder as he left the room.

If you'd asked me six months ago if I thought I'd be happily married and pregnant before the fourth annual Wyatt Foundation Halloween fundraiser, I would have laughed in your face.

Not a delicate feminine laugh, but a full cackle complete with flying spit.

But here I am, walking around in one of my husband's well-worn SEAL T-shirts, his name in big black block letters on the back, barefoot and pregnant. And as if it wasn't enough that he was kind, generous, protective, and gorgeous, he also liked to cook.

Which made me extra happy now that I was eating for two.

The next afternoon, I walked into the hotel conference room wearing my favorite cowboy boots, a miniskirt, and a Baby on Board T-shirt. Nathan thought I was crazy for telling everyone this way. I thought it'd be fun.

The fundraiser had always been at Grannie's, but the response to the new marketing campaign had far exceeded our expectations. We rented a hotel conference room, so we'd have room for all the extra guests. It sucked having to pay for the space, but it'd be worth it when the donations came in.

Emily's squeal brought the room to a standstill. "I knew it. You're pregnant!" she squealed as she rushed over to wrap me in a hug. The others weren't far behind.

"I am." My smile felt too big for my face.

After a round of hugs for me, and manly handshakes and slaps on the back for Nathan, Jamie said, "Let's leave the girls to their celebrating."

Nathan leaned down and kissed my temple. "Love you, Slick."

"Love you more, Cowboy."

It'd been a long, painful journey, but Nathan and I had finally found our happily ever after.

It isn't always scary when the past comes back to haunt you…

Pick up BURNEDBook 7 in my SSI series. A fake dating romantic suspense with the only Sheppard sister, Madi, and the US Navy SEAL who works for her father and three obnoxiously overprotective brothers.

Love Christmas Stories? Pick up the standalone Sheppard Christmas Special and spend time with your favorite small-town family.

Acknowledgements

T hank you, Reader, for choosing to spend some time in my world. I hope you enjoyed it.

I want to thank my Proof Readers: Nina, Paige and Jocelyn. And my editor: Nina. Your feedback was invaluable in helping me polish my story. A big thanks to Maria Secoy, and the mentor team at All Write Well–this book wouldn't be in your hands if I hadn't found them!

I also want to thank my friends, who have surrounded me with love and support while listening to me chatter on endlessly about my characters and plot lines over many glasses of wine.

Thank you all!

Also by

Sheppard & Sons Investigations:

TAKEN: Jack and Meg's story
BEATEN: Jamie and Emily's story
MISSING: Doug and Beth's story
BETRAYED: AJ and Blake's story
CAGED: Jaden and Catelyn's story
TRAPPED: Ashley & Nathan's story
TBN Christmas Special : The Sheppards
BURNED: Madi & Matt's story

WebPage

About the Author

 Eveline Rose is an award winning author who fell in love with storytelling in a high school creative writing class. She currently lives in the Chicago area with her cat, Prince, where she pours her heart and soul into her characters for your reading pleasure. Eveline's a self-defense instructor and includes safety tips in every book. She spends her free time volunteering in her community, hanging out with her friends, and of course reading. One topic she can chat about for hours: Tudor history.

Eveline's promise to you: every romantic suspense novel will include a protective male hero who will save the woman he loves, not because she needs him to, but because she's important. Their HEA is guaranteed, but it won't be easy.

Eveline is a member of Chicago North Romance Writers Group.